I0547394

FALSE START

GODS OF THE GRIDIRON: BOOK 2

SHANNA SWENSON

FALSE START
Shanna Swenson

FALSE START is an original work of fiction. Names, characters, places, organizations and incidents either are the product of the author's imagination or are used fictitiously. Any resemblance to actual persons, living or dead, events, businesses, companies, or locales is entirely coincidental.

Copyright © 2020 by Shanna Swenson

Paperback ISBN: 978-1-7329626-6-8

All rights reserved.

No part of this book may be reproduced, distributed, or transmitted in any form or by any means, including photocopying, recording, information storage and retrieval systems or other electronic or mechanical means, without written permission from the author, except for the use of brief quotations in a book review.

Designations used by companies to distinguish their products are often claimed as trademarks. All brand names and product names, such as the NFL and its teams, used within this book are trade names, service marks, trademarks and registered trademarks of their respective owners. The publisher nor the book are associated with any products or vendors mentioned in this book. None of the companies referenced within have endorsed this book. The Atlanta Gladiators are a fictitious football team used for entertainment purposes only.

www.shannaswenson.com

For permission requests, write to the author at shannaswen@gmail.com

Edited by Jennifer Soucy

ebook design by: OliviaProDesign

Gods of the Gridiron logo designed by:
Books and Moods Designs

ZEUS- THE KING OF THE GODS

"O Zeus, much-honoured, Zeus supremely great, to thee our holy rites we consecrate, our prayers and expiations, king divine, for all things to produce with ease through mind is thine. Hence mother earth (*gaia*) and mountains swelling high proceed from thee, the deep and all within the sky. Kronion (Cronion) king, descending from above, magnanimous, commanding, sceptred Zeus; all-parent, principle and end of all, whose power almighty shakes this earthly ball; even nature trembles at thy mighty nod, loud-sounding, armed with lightning, thundering god. Source of abundance, purifying king, O various-formed, from whom all natures spring; propitious hear my prayer, give blameless health, with peace divine, and necessary wealth."

—*Orphic Hymn 15 to Zeus (trans. Taylor) (Greek hymns C3rd B.C. to 2nd A.D.)*

Zeus most glorious and most great, Thundercloud, throned in the heavens!

—Homer's *Iliad*

For my first cousins—Brandy, Jessica, Paige, April, Brooke, Diane, and Rachel

*I absolutely **loved** spending my childhood with you!*
May we never stop dreaming

FOREWORD

In case you weren't sure—the male MC in this book, Brett "Brickhouse" McFadden was inspired by none other than the legendary gunslinger himself #4 for the Green Bay Packers, Brett Lorenzo Favre.

Since I was thirteen-years-old, the man and his incredible talents have always captivated me.

So, without further ado, meet who I deemed Zeus, the king of the gods, on the following pages...

PROLOGUE

It was the coldest, most dreary day in February that Brett "Brickhouse" McFadden could ever remember. The wind was unrelenting and the rain merciless, coming down with such force that it stung his back through his thick, black leather jacket. He stood, frigid as stone, at the graveside service of his best friend and favorite wide receiver, Hunter Thomas. The torrential rain pounded along the tarp overhead, which whipped continuously in the wind. The storm drowned out the preacher's eulogy, adding to the already solemn mood of the day.

Brett looked over to Hunter's widow, Madison Hope Thomas, the woman who'd been his best friend since they first met as children at the ripe age of seven. She sat in front and to the right of him, not far from his reach or his gaze. His heart went out to her. She appeared broken and numb; he knew she was because he also felt the same way. He'd been in the car with Hunter the day he died. He was driving Hunter's car when they'd been hit. He'd been at the hospital when Hunter was pronounced dead.

It was a horrible nightmare he should soon awake from at any moment, yet he continued to be encapsulated unwillingly in it. He watched the tears stream down Madi's face in a continuous flow—or maybe it was the rain; he honestly couldn't tell. She'd given up the handkerchief long ago when it became as soaked as everything else was.

The preacher seemed to be done with his sermon and stepped toward Madi. She stood and wrapped her arms around his neck, sobbing into his shoulder. She'd known the old man most her life, Reverend James Young; he'd been her mentor, her preacher and her baptizer.

Brett's heart ached for her. She and Hunter had been married for a little over five years and they'd loved each other immensely. Hunter had been an easy going, fun-loving, class-clown type guy. He'd made everyone laugh, while Brett was the more serious one of the trio.

Madi was the girl next door: a smart, beautiful, classy, southern woman who was—and always had been—the epitome of perfect in Brett's eyes. He and Madi had been very close since childhood when Brett's father, Drew McFadden, was hired on as GM of the Atlanta Gladiators football team by Madi's father, Jerry Taylor, owner and president of the Gladiators— the team that Brett currently and Hunter, formerly, played for. Brett and Madi had been raised together, gone to every single school together, then met Hunter in college—quickly forming an everlasting bond with him. Hunter had immediately taken to Madi; they'd dated and were married not long after graduation. That day had been the worst day of Brett's life... well, at least, up until today.

Reverend Young had taken turns hugging everyone around the small group of gatherers at the graveside before suddenly and awkwardly hugging Brett. The old man's attempt was short-lived as his small frame couldn't embrace Brett's larger build. Instead, he pulled back, looped one arm around Brett's side, and patted his back.

"I'm so sorry for your loss, Brett."

"Thank you, sir," he replied despondently.

"I know how much y'all are hurting right now, but you must take great care of Madi."

Brett couldn't recall how *many* times he'd heard that in the last few days, as if he didn't intend to do exactly that. He'd known what he had to do the minute he saw Madi in the ER waiting room, the minute she'd seen the look of despair on his face, the minute he'd caught her in his arms.

THE LOOK MADI gave Brett when she entered the automatic doors of the ER tore his heart right open. She ran to him and looked into his face. He knew he was as white as a ghost—his friend had just died minutes before as he'd held his hand. Hunter had been in such pain, professing his past transgressions, and making Brett promise all sorts of things as he lay dying in a pool of his own blood.

Brett grabbed Madi as she fell to her knees before him. She breathed in and out rapidly as she bowed her head. "Oh, God! He's gone, isn't he?" She felt like putty in his arms, her voice ragged, on the verge of breaking.

"I'm so sorry, Madi. I...I don't even know what to say."

Hunter had wanted Brett to drive the brand-new McLaren he'd just bought. A ridiculous car, but Hunter was proud of it and wanted to show it off. Brett had obliged.

The next thing he remembered was a deafening roar and screeching as time seemed to stand still. He remembered not being able to hear right away then assessing the situation: seeing Hunter crushed into the dashboard and thinking he was dead, right then and there; seeing red—so much red blood —and realizing Hunter wasn't moving. The next thing he recalled was calling out for help, getting out of the car to find someone, the fear, trying to figure out what to do, praying, pleading, watching as the firefighters used the jaws of life to get Hunter out, the ambulance ride, the guilt, trying to save face as the EMTs worked on his friend...

Then—sitting next to him, telling him that everything was going to be ok even though Brett knew in his heart it wasn't going to be "ok"—the guilt. The conversation in the trauma bay after the doctor told Brett that nothing could be done to save him, that it was too late—regretting that it was too late—watching the light fade from Hunter's eyes... The guilt, the ultimate guilt.

"...so just turn to God in this time of need as He can hear your prayers and knows what you need before you even ask Him for it," Reverend Young stated, giving a weak smile as he patted Brett on the arm.

Brett came harshly back to reality and just nodded his head. The flashbacks were taking a toll on him. He inhaled deeply and moved behind Madi who spoke to Travis Redmond, Skyla Larson, Lincoln and Valeria Porter, TJ Rawlins, and Paxton Guthrie. Brett nodded solemnly to his teammates, the two women, then gently took Madi's elbow with one hand, covering her with the large umbrella he'd been holding the entire time with the other. He pulled her into his side, tightly holding her as they walked in the direction of the road.

No words were spoken as he and Madi's mother, father, and sister headed toward the car. Brett held the umbrella over her as she stepped robotically into her father's Buick then slid in beside her, closing the umbrella and placing it on the floorboard next to his leg. She fell into his chest as he wrapped his arms around her and sobbed into his shoulder as she'd done for the last three days. His heart broke once again. *Oh, how many times can a heart break?* he wondered again for the umpteenth time. It was as if the breaks simply got deeper and more painful as each piece re-broke over and over again.

He looked over to Brooke—Madi's sister, who was seated beside them—and frowned. Brooke just shook her head and looked away, propping her chin on her arm; she gazed out the window as a tear fell down her cheek. Madi's dad, Jerry, who sat in the driver's seat, caught his eye in the rear-view mirror, exhaled, and started the car. He simply stared ahead. Brett noticed the tears in the man's eyes as he turned his head to look at his wife. Amelia, Madi's mother, shifted her position in the passenger seat and reached out to take Madi's hand. She gently squeezed and Madi returned it. Amelia frowned, tearfully looking up to Brett. He just gave her a weak smile.

These people were his family, every single one of them. His parents were best friends with Madi's parents. They'd all been as close as two families could've been. He'd always treated Madi's mom and dad as his second mom and dad. And now, they'd lost one of their own.

The silence was deafening as they rode back to Madi's house. Only the pounding rain and wind seemed not to take the hint. Brett passed Madi a tissue from the center console and looked ahead as she sighed, blew her nose, and tried to calm herself. He simply sat, stroking her hair and arm in comfort.

It wasn't long before he closed his eyes, and all at once, they were pulling into Madi's garage. They all got out silently, Brett taking Madi gently from the car and cradling her against his side as they walked into the house. Stepping through the mud room, Madi placed her handbag on the side counter and kicked off her shoes, sniffling as she went. She broke away from Brett as they entered the kitchen then stopped at the counter, seeming to be at a loss for what to do and where to go from there, staring off into space. Brett slipped his jacket off and placed it on the back of one of the kitchen stools, watching her the whole time. The rest of the family ambled in and removed their wet jackets, cautiously watching and waiting.

Suddenly, Madi swung around and looked over to Brett with the most horrified expression on her face. As if she'd just realized something terrible, she brought her shoulders up into a shrug and her face crumpled. He moved to her swiftly and embraced her, holding her to his chest as she bawled like a baby. Amelia came up behind her and embraced her, stroking her hair. She shushed her daughter and tried to calm her, but to no avail. Madi was simply overcome with emotion, and no attempt at comfort would help at that moment. Healing was simply going to take time. Amelia pulled, and pulled, finally succeeding in separating Madi from Brett's embrace.

Madi was reluctant and protested, "No, Brett. I—"

"Shh, hush now. Let's go get you out of these wet clothes and into a warm bath, hmm?" Her mother stroked at her cheek and kissed the tear running down it. "C'mon," Amelia soothed her daughter, taking her hand and leading her away and up the stairs.

Madi continued to protest, "But, Brett...I—" She turned and reached for him, but her mother reassured her once more. "It's alright, Madison."

"It's ok, Sunflower, I'll be up shortly, alright?" He nodded and smiled in encouragement. She contemplated that for a moment then finally turned and went upstairs with her mother.

Jerry was the first one to break the silence. "Jesus, I don't know about you, but I could sure use a drink." With that, he walked toward the parlor. Brett turned to Brooke, who shook her head again. She grabbed a bottle of pills out of the pantry and mumbled, "I assume Madi's gonna need these." She headed up the stairs after Madi and her mother.

Brett followed Jerry into the first room adjacent to the front door, the formal parlor. It was where the Thomas' hosted a small group and formerly where Brett and Hunter would have some drinks at the end of the night, on occasion.

Jerry poured scotch into a highball glass, motioning with his eyes to Brett, who nodded that: yes, he *did* indeed want one. Brett lit the fireplace and threw some logs in while Jerry grabbed another glass, pouring a fair amount of scotch into it as well. He then grabbed both, handed Brett his glass, and they took a seat opposite one another as Jerry toasted Brett.

"What a week, huh?" He meant it as a rhetorical question and continued. "Damn...I don't even know...just DAMN." He cursed and slammed his fist on the arm of the large, overstuffed Queen Anne chair he sat in. "Sorry," he apologized, "but I hate to see my daughter like this. I know you do, too." Brett just nodded and swallowed hard. "I'm gonna miss that son of a bitch, ya know?" He laughed tearfully, then sighed heavily and sat silent for several long moments.

Brett listened to the rain and the crackle of the fire, struggling to relax his heavy heart and mind. "The next few weeks are gonna be real hard on my Madi. I just appreciate you being here for her, Brett." Jerry reached forward and patted Brett on the knee. "You're a good man. I've always known that, but the way you've been with Madi is truly commendable. She needs you. I guess you see that." Jerry raised his eyebrows and scoffed. Then he fell into silence and sipped his scotch slowly.

Suddenly, the front door burst open and in stumbled Frank Thomas, Hunter's father. He struggled to get his sopping wet umbrella closed, mumbling curses all the while.

"Well, c'mon in, Frank," Jerry stated. "Would you care for a libation?"

"Damn this weather today," Frank said, slamming his umbrella into the slender stand near the door. "Nah, thanks though, Jer. I'm just gonna grab that casserole for Rita and I, and we'll head on home. She's not doing so well right now." Brett took that as his cue; he stood to go fetch the dish, motioning for Frank to take his seat. Frank shook his offered hand. "Too bad you couldn't hear the damn preacher over this stupid rain. The flowers were awful beautiful though, huh? How's our girl holding up?"

Brett just shook his head sadly. "Not well, sir, not so well. How about you?"

Frank sadly shook his head in return. "I'm trying to be as strong as I can for my wife, but I never expected to have to bury my only child today." He ambled over to the sofa Brett had been sitting on as Brett turned to exit the room; guilt, once more, riddling his soul in ripping torment.

"I'll go grab that casserole for you." Brett excused himself and went to the kitchen. He opened the well-stocked fridge, took the medium-sized chicken casserole from the second shelf, and brought it out to Frank.

"Thanks, Brett. I doubt we eat it today but...well, maybe tomorrow."

"No worries," Brett said. "There's so much food in there I don't know if it will ever get eaten. Want to take some more stuff home?" Frank shook his head in reply. "I can't hardly get Madi to eat anything. Come to think of it, I guess none of us has had much of an appetite..." Brett trailed off as he propped his hip against the door jamb and wrung his hands.

Frank sighed. "I guess your folks stayed home today?"

"Yes, sir. Momma's sick with a sinus infection, but Dad said to give him a call if any of us needed anything. So, please don't be afraid to ask."

"That's mighty kind of Drew. I tell ya, everyone has been so gracious amid all of this." Frank teared up a little. Jerry reached over and patted his shoulder, then walked over to the bar to make another drink—this one for Frank, who took it obligingly. The men sat in companionable silence once again. Finally, right before Frank was about to get up, Brooke came to the landing of the stairs.

"Brett, I'm sorry to interrupt, but... Madi, she's refusing to take the Valium. Again." she yelled down at him.

Jerry sighed, and Frank looked over to Brett who nodded, "Ok, I'll be right up," he hollered back.

Brett grabbed his drink, slung it back and downed it, said his goodbyes to Frank, and headed up the stairs.

He wasn't entirely out of earshot when he heard Frank say, "So... how long's Brett been in love with my daughter-in-law?"

He heard Jerry laugh humorlessly and reply with, "Hell, I reckon for as long as he's known her."

CHAPTER ONE

"No, Momma, I already told you I don't want it! Please don't argue with me," Madi whined as Brett came through the door. He watched as she pushed the pill and water glass away.

"Madi, *you* are the one arguing with *me.*"

"Brett!" Madi stated, relieved. She turned her back on her mother as she crawled under the covers.

Amelia huffed in annoyance and walked away from the bed. She pulled Brett back out of the room and closed the doors, making sure Madi was out of earshot.

"She *has* to sleep! She hasn't slept in three days," Amelia whispered and put her arms up in defeat.

"I know, Millie, I'll handle it. Don't worry."

Amelia handed over the pill and glass, shaking her head. "I don't understand why she's acting like this. I mean, I guess I really *can't* understand, can I?"

"It's alright. Y'all go on home and get some rest. I got Madi."

She looked relieved. "Thank you, Brett. I can't thank you enough. I don't know what we would've done without you." She reached up on her tip-toes and kissed his cheek.

"You know I wouldn't be anywhere else," he confirmed.

"Well, we love you. Let us know if you need anything, alright?"

"Yes, ma'am. I sure will." He nodded as Amelia fetched Brooke, who was cuddled up against Madi whispering something into her ear. She kissed the back of her sister's head and rubbed her back, then hopped up to join her mother.

"Bye, Brett," Brooke said, kissing his cheek as her mother had. "I know you'll take good care of her." She winked, and Brett rolled his eyes playfully.

"Shut up, Brooke," Madi yelled from the bed. "You're such a perv."

"Me?" Brooke feigned ignorance. "I didn't *say* anything!" She smiled like the cat that ate the canary.

"Yeah, sure. I know what you meant…jerk." Madi turned over and slanted her eyes at her younger sister. "I love you, Momma."

"I love you too, baby. Please get some rest." She came back over to kiss her daughter.

It was another few minutes before everyone got their things, said their goodbyes, and headed out.

Finally, Brett was in the house, alone with Madi.

"God, can you believe my mother is trying to shove pills down my throat?" Madison sat up in protest, crossing her arms over her chest. "I wish she would stop treating me like I'm a child! And, before you say anything, I *know*; she just means well. But you know how I feel about that crap."

"Yes, I know. I'm not going to argue with you about it. I'm just going to crumble it up in your food and not tell you."

She opened her mouth in shock. "You wouldn't dare!"

"Wanna bet?" He arched his eyebrow. They had a hard stare-off for what seemed like an eternity. Finally she narrowed her eyes.

"Fine." She reached her hand out. "Give me the stupid pill! But I'm only taking it this one time so don't even think of asking me again." He didn't mention the fact that he didn't even ask the first time. He just let it slide and handed it over, watching her swallow the pill. "What? Yes, it's gone, I took it." She opened her mouth to show him. He wanted so badly to laugh, but he didn't have the energy to do so. She flipped back over on her side, her back to him, and pulled the covers up to her chin.

"Are you hungry?" he asked.

"Nope."

"Madi," he groaned.

"What? I'm not hungry."

"What if you just tried to eat a little something?"

"Like what?"

"Hell, I don't know; the fridge is full of all kinds of foods: good food, *church* food—the stuff that you and I don't get to eat often. Chicken casserole, mashed potatoes, mac and cheese—"

"Stop. You had me at church food."

"Ok, so you'll eat?"

"Yes."

"Thank you. Now was that so hard?" He came over on the other side of the bed and kissed her cheek. "I'll be back up in a few minutes." She had a pout on her face as he walked away, but he still didn't feel as if he'd won. He might heat up the food, but that didn't mean she would actually eat it.

Brett headed down the stairs, noticing how empty and barren the large foyer felt; its cathedral ceiling echoed the lonely sound of his footfalls. He entered the vast kitchen and turned all the lights on, as much to fill the bleak space as for the necessity of the light itself.

He pulled several dishes out of the fridge, plated the feast, and started the microwave. The smell of hearty food warming up hit his nostrils, and suddenly, he was hungry too. He couldn't remember the last time he'd eaten.

The last several days were kind of a blur. He remembered getting Madi home from the ER, then everyone and their brother being there in the house. So many people, so many tears—so much food being brought in. That was the southern way. Someone died and they brought you fried chicken, casseroles, and pies.

Then there was the funeral home and even more food. Brett sure wasn't going to complain.

Once dinner was to temperature, he grabbed the plates and headed upstairs. When he entered the room, Madi was sitting up in bed with a photograph in her hand. He stopped, taken aback by the look on her face.

"I can't believe he's really gone." She gazed at the photo, a single tear streaming down her cheek. "It's all like a bad dream. I keep waiting for him to just walk through the door at any minute."

He sighed and set the plates down on a small table centered between two arm chairs angled in front of her bay window. He grabbed the photo from her hand and replaced it on the nightstand.

"Dammit, Madison, we're going to *eat*," he growled, more annoyed than angry.

She looked at him, aghast. He grabbed her face in his hands and sat next to her on the bed.

"I'm sorry. I didn't mean to sound so harsh, I just..." He looked down. "Madi, it should have been *me*."

"What?" Her shocked intake of breath drew his eyes up. "How can you say that?"

"He was a husband, *your* husband. And me, I'm—" Brett shrugged, at a loss for words.

"Look at me," Madi stated sternly. Brett's eyes were blurry from tears as he looked up into the beautiful greenish-blue eyes of the woman he'd secretly been in love with for over twenty years. "Do you honestly think it would have been easier for me if it'd been *you* instead?" Brett nodded, feeling a tear fall from his eye. She shook her head, her face crumpling. "No. It wouldn't have! You're my best friend, Brett. I love you! And I'm just so thankful that I didn't have to lose *both* of you."

With that, they fell sobbing into each other's arms where they stayed for a time. He finally pulled his face from her shoulder and noticed which picture she'd been holding. It was a photo of the three of them, taken at Madi and Hunter's wedding. He looked back at Madi. She wiped at the tears, her face blotchy from crying.

"I'm so sorry," he said earnestly.

"Please don't be. It wasn't your fault. I know you think it was, but it wasn't. Just please, don't ever say that to me again. *Please?*" He nodded in agreement then pulled some tissues from the box on the nightstand.

After they'd attended to their wet faces, Madi said, "Wow, that smells so good." They had forgotten about the food, but now that she mentioned it, it *did* smell good. Brett's tummy growled in response. He moved to grab the trays, setting Madi's plate before her.

"Man, this medicine makes me feel like I'm drunk...only worse."

"Good, let's eat so you can get some much-needed sleep." *That goes for both of us*, he thought.

Brett placed his own plate on a tray and dug in. He'd loaded them down with chicken casserole, mashed potatoes, green beans, mac and cheese, and coleslaw. Each bite was even better than the last, and they laughed about how sick they would be in a few hours. Truth was, that was definitely bound to happen. Despite that football season was over, Brett still trained daily and tried to eat his usual diet that didn't include any of these "cheat" foods.

Brett was surprised to see that he'd quickly finished his plate, and Madi had made a good dent in hers.

"Thanks, Brett. That was so good. I'm full now."

He smiled, grateful she had finally eaten something. "I'm glad you enjoyed it; it *was* good. I'm gonna go shower now and get out of these damp clothes. You get some rest. That's an order, Sunflower."

She nodded, and he took the plates away.

BRETT FELT REFRESHED after taking a hot shower and getting into some warm, dry lounge clothes. The shower washed away some of the stress he'd been feeling and relaxed him; but as he dressed, brushed his teeth, and dried his hair, he felt the weight of the day's events taking their toll. He was suddenly so very grateful for the luxury of leisureliness. It was just him and Madison in the house now. It was nice not to have to cater to everyone else, run to fetch something, entertain, and plaster on a smile in the midst of all the crushing sadness. He could take his time to grieve for his best friend Hunter now—not that he hadn't grieved, but funeral homes and funerals were overwhelming. Now was the real tough part, especially for Madi. Getting back to life...without Hunter.

He exited the bathroom of the guest room, the room he always used when he stayed over, then headed back to Madi and Hunter's room to check on her. He ever so slowly opened the door and saw her curled up on her side facing him, snoozing away. *Good, the medicine worked*, he thought. Just as he was closing the door, he heard a sleepy groan and her eyes shot open.

"Don't leave me." She pouted sincerely.

"I wasn't going to," Brett lied. "I was gonna go put the dishes in the dishwasher."

"It's ok. Maria will be here tomorrow." She patted the bed beside her.

He sighed internally and cut the hall light before coming back to join her under the covers. He crawled in, facing her. This marked the fourth night in a row they'd fallen to sleep together—the few hours they'd gotten over the course of the last several days. The first night, Madi had been completely inconsolable; he'd held her all night on the couch as she came in and out of her grief. The second night, her family had gone home to rest and she'd finally gone to her bed but hadn't stayed as she couldn't stand being alone. She'd crawled into the guest bed with him, where she cried again most of the night and couldn't sleep so they'd watched TV instead. The third night, Amelia had finally gotten Madi into her own bed, only for her to come get Brett in the middle of the night when Madi had a breakdown.

Saying that it'd been awkward for him to sleep with Madi would've been an outright lie. It *should* have been awkward for him, but it wasn't—not in the slightest—which made him feel even worse about it. He was sleeping with his best friend's wife, who was also his best friend, but he was ok with it. *Damn, I'm gonna burn in Hell*, he thought.

As childhood friends, they'd shared the same room—and a few times, the same bed—when they were younger. Brett remembered them coming to sleep in each other's beds when their parents went to sleep. They'd wake up together and were scolded for doing so. But they kept doing the same thing on into high school and college, too, when they'd stayed up too late at parties or were just hanging out and simply never parted ways. They were best friends; it was bound to happen on occasion.

This was all a comfort thing for Madi so she wasn't alone. It didn't have to do with anything sexual...at least for her, anyway...at least that's what he thought...at least that's what he told himself... *I'm truly going to burn in Hell.*

"Brett?"

"Yeah?"

"What are you thinking about?"

The fact that I'll wake up with a raging boner spooning you. "Umm, I was just thinking about Hunter." *Rhetorical Liar!*

"Me too. Thank you for staying with me." She reached her hand out and stroked his arm. He smiled to himself and took her hand in his, stroking the backside of it with his thumb.

"Of course, Madi. Where else would I be?"

"I mean sleeping with me. I don't want to be alone. I can't stand the thought of it. I know eventually I'll have to but...I'm sure it may seem a little weird for you. I don't mean for it to."

Is she reading my mind?

"I mean, I'm sure you probably want to sleep in a bed by yourself. I'm sure you're used to sleeping alone. I bet this is difficult for you."

Yeah...not!

"You can tell me the truth; I won't be mad if you don't want to sleep with me."

All I have ever wanted was to sleep with you. And be with you. And love you...

"Brett?"

"Madi, it's really ok. I promise." To reassure her, he cupped her cheek and kissed her forehead. "Now, please get some sleep, ok?"

Madison nodded against his hand, and he adjusted himself in the bed, pulling the covers up to his chest. Brett could see her face bathed softly in the glow of the dwindling daylight. The sound of the rain outside was soothing—no longer torrential as before, just soft and steady. He watched Madi's eyes as she gazed back at him, taking in her soft red-glazed, blue-green eyes and the dark circles beneath them. She'd never looked more exhausted than she did now. She licked her plump lips and gnawed softly at them, deep in thought. He followed the line of her straight, pert little nose, admired the definition of her brows, the set of her cheekbones and the subtle jut of her chin.

Brett studied her, the woman he'd been head over heels in love with for as long as he could remember. The woman he'd loved since he was just a child, before he'd ever even known what love was, before he'd had a chance to know a woman's heart or her touch, he'd felt an immediate connection and spark with this amazing woman laying next to him. Everything in her being sang to every cell in his body, his mind, and his soul, and—upon first touching her and seeing her—he'd known it. He remembered telling his father that he'd met the girl of his dreams and his father just laughing and ruffling his scraggly hair at the notion. He'd been dead serious though. From that moment on, he'd never loved anyone else. He'd truly tried to let her go and move on once she had married Hunter, but he'd never succeeded in doing so.

"What is it, sweetheart?" he asked finally, before she chewed her lips off.

"I'm just so lost. What am I supposed to do now?" Madison whispered. He just shook his head, indicating that he didn't have the answers. "This house is so big…and quiet without anyone else in it. I can't stand the thought of being here alone."

"You won't be alone, Madi." He brought the hand he was still stroking to his lips and kissed her knuckles ever so softly. "I'm here. For as long as you want me to be."

She gulped, taking in the meaning of his words. "But, Brett, you have a home of your own…a life of your own."

"Madi, you've always been my life. You're my family, and you always will be. As far as my house goes, I can sell it. It's just a house."

"I can't ask you to do that." She sighed.

"Then we'll sell this one," Brett offered, and Madi smiled weakly in return. "Let's just take it one day at a time. Nothing is set in stone. There's no rush. You've had a very rough week, and you need to get some rest now and take care of *you*. Everything else can hold off until you've had some time to grieve." He pulled her gently into his chest, tucking his chin against her scalp and wrapping his bulky arms around her, completely enveloping her tall, curvy frame. His lips grazed her hair line, kissing her there. Ever so gently, he began stroking her back with his hands. "I'm not going anywhere, Sunflower, you know that. Please don't worry about being alone."

Brett could feel her silent tears falling onto his skin as he continued to stroke her back. He tried to absorb her grief and at the same time dissolve his guilt, even though he knew there was nothing he could do to change what had happened. He felt if Hunter had been the one driving his own vehicle, he would still be alive to be here with his wife. Hunt would be the one here comforting her and holding her, and taking in the sweet, floral scent of her hair, those golden swirls of curls that fell over Brett's arm, tickling him. He couldn't help but bury his nose into that heavenly aroma and breathe her in. She was like a drug to him, and he closed his eyes and sighed, savoring her fragrance across his nostrils and his tongue. His groin responded to the stimulation, and Brett cursed to himself. Now he had something else to feel guilty about. He truly was going *straight* to Hell…

It seemed like hours had passed before he finally felt her breathing slow and her body still, succumbing to sleep. He peeled her from his numb arms and settled her just a little farther away from him so that his nocturnal movements wouldn't wake her. She stirred ever so slightly as he rearranged her head on her pillow, her cheek hot and red from its contact with his chest. Her hand innately sought him out. He moved a little closer and tucked her hand into his as he kissed her cheek and bade her a whispered good night. She just moaned in response. Success! He'd finally gotten her to sleep. Now, hopefully it would last longer than it had the last few nights.

Brett watched her sleep. How could she have gotten even more beautiful than she'd been before? Madi looked like an angel, her long, blonde lashes touching her cheeks. He smiled to himself and closed his eyes, letting sleep take him too.

BRETT AWOKE to his own screams as he threw himself upright on the bed. He was drenched in sweat, and his heart felt like it was coming out of his ribcage. He tried to calm himself as he turned to Madi who just looked up at him, her hand to her chest.

"Are you alright?" he asked. She just nodded, shaken. "I'm sorry. I had a bad dream."

He tried to reorient himself with his surroundings. He'd been back in the McLaren as the big truck had collided with it. He could feel the twisting metal, the momentum swinging them around, and heard the crushing sound of the car... Viscous, crimson red liquid covered him in a blanket of sticky warmth. Everything had been in slow motion.

"It's ok, I did too. I wasn't sure at first which one of us was screaming." Madi looked around, sniffing as Brett slowed his breathing and took her hands. "I don't want to stay here, Brett." Her eyes were deep pits of emotion.

He simply nodded and jumped up off the bed. "Ok, grab what

you need and get dressed. We'll go to my place."

MADI YAWNED as they headed down the road. Brett's house was an old, colonial-style house about 20 minutes from Madi's. It was a beautiful, three-story white beast with at least a dozen bedrooms and half a dozen bathrooms on a solid twenty acres of land. Brett had always wanted acreage and horses and privacy, and when he'd found it, he knew he was home. It was traditional with a few modern niceties—new stainless-steel kitchen appliances and countertops as well as a new stove hood and backsplash. The architecture was what he'd fallen in love with so he'd tried to keep to the original wallpaper and furnishings as much as possible—the hand-carved wooden bannisters and rustic fireplace, the original wooden floors, the crown molding and huge back porch. Madi had also loved the house. She was a sucker for old houses, and his had been built in 1891. He'd had a lot of work on his hands to begin with, but he'd hired a terrific contractor; within eight months, he was moving in.

When they pulled up into the gated drive, he punched the code into the keypad and glanced over at Madi as the gates slowly swung open. Her head leaned against the window, her knees drawn into her chest. He smiled to himself and drove down the long driveway to his large, farm house. He sighed, feeling grateful to be home for the first time in days. Once he was parked in the garage, he came around to Madi's side and scooped her up. She stirred as her head hit his shoulder and was out again.

Brett opened the door and shuffled inside, turning off the alarm and pushing the door shut with his leg. He carried her up the staircase and to his bed, pulled off her shoes, and tucked her in.

He walked back over to the monitor and reset the house alarm. Then he took the big recliner across from the bed and pulled the lever, readjusting himself as his feet went up. He just sat watching Madi for the longest time until he finally closed his eyes.

CHAPTER TWO

Madi awoke to the light of the sun in her eyes and Brett watching her from the recliner. She blinked several times then stretched and sat up, pulling the comforter from her legs. Brett stood and walked over to her.

"You ok?" he asked.

She nodded. Her eyes felt itchy and sore from crying and a lack of adequate sleep; she was sure there were dark circles beneath them. "Just numb."

He sat down on the bed next to her and rubbed her knee through her flannel PJs. "I know. It's gonna be like that for a while though. Just remember, one day at a time." She nodded. "Want some coffee?" Again, she nodded. "Ok, let's go."

Brett took her hand as he led them downstairs and into his bright, yellow kitchen. He began making coffee as Madi turned the house alarm off and grabbed a fleece blanket from the living room, stepping out onto the covered back porch. She wrapped it around her shoulders and picked her usual spot, in a wooden rocking chair in the middle of the expansive wrap-around porch, looking out on the dense fog rolling along the dewy green pasture.

Once the coffee was made, Brett brought two mugs out and joined her in the rocking chair next to hers. They sipped their hot coffee in silence as they watched the sun peak over the distant crest of the Blue Ridge mountains, their breath and mugs steaming in the cold chill of the morning. Brett's horses, Bandit and Senora, grazed near the fence closest to the porch, the haze of morning fog floating behind them. It was a beautiful, peaceful morning with various birds chirping to them from nearby oak trees overhanging the property.

At any other time, Madi would smile and feel rejuvenated to be here on one of her favorite pieces of land—Brett's 20-acre estate. She might even look over to her best friend and recommend they go riding, take a picnic lunch, and just enjoy the day—especially after the torrential downpour yesterday. But that wouldn't be the case. Her heart felt hollow, her mind numb, and her soul ripped apart by the sudden death of her husband.

She and Hunter had been happy together. They'd had an instant attraction when Brett introduced them after practice one day. Hunt had been funny, cocky, and handsome. Following Brett's rejection that night after the frat party in college, she'd needed the confidence boost Hunter had given her. He'd asked her out almost immediately, and she'd been helpless to his spell. Barely a year later, he asked her to marry him; not long after they'd finished college and he'd been drafted to the Broncos, they'd gotten a dream wedding in Ireland. Within six months, he'd been traded to her father's team. Jerry Taylor had pulled lots of strings and given up two key players in order to get Hunt.

Tears streamed Madison's face as she recalled all the wonderful memories, the joy of Hunter's induction into the Gladiators, and how well Hunter had fit into the family. Then her stomach burned with anxiety at the thought of going back to the complex without him; it literally jumped up into her ribcage.

"I'm gonna be sick," she murmured and thrust her coffee at Brett. He took it as she threw the blanket off her shoulders, ran to the porch railing, and hurled the contents of her stomach over the side.

She felt a hand come to her back; Brett's palm comforted her, rubbing up and down. His deep voice penetrated her panic-stricken brain. "Shh, calm your breathing. You're ok. Just breathe, Madi. Breathe."

Was she breathing? She wasn't sure. She attempted to pull air into her lungs, but they burned. Her heart hammered and her mind reeled. She feared she would pass out. The grief was all-consuming as she attempted to block out the fear, but it was no use. Her ears began to ring; collapse was inevitable as darkness rimmed her vision.

"Brett..." she whimpered even as his big hands came to her face and cupped it.

He would be the last thing she saw—the man she'd always loved —as the blackness took her and she fell.

TWO WEEKS LATER

"MADI, I SAID TO GET UP!" Brett thundered, snapping the lights on. "Now, dammit! This has gone on long enough."

"Piss off, Brett," Madi whined and turned over in her king-sized sleigh bed.

"Oh, that's rich coming from *you*, little girl," he muttered sarcastically.

"Why? Why do you come in here and bother me? I'm sleeping. Can't you—?" she stopped talking as he literally ripped the covers from her frame.

"Up! I'm not saying it again, or I'm stripping your ass naked. You're taking a damn shower. You stink, Madi." He planted his hands on his hips, glaring down at her.

"I'm grieving," she screamed up at him. Her golden-blonde hair was a tangled mess, her PJs were rumpled, and her eyes were puffy.

"Yeah, well, I'll be damned if I let you follow him to the grave. Now get up, and get in the shower!" he roared.

She'd been practically bed-ridden for close to a week now, and he wasn't gonna allow her to wallow in pity any longer. They were going to Cancun; he was taking her to Linc's beach house for some much-needed sun.

She sat up, crossing her arms over her chest. "Make me."

Ha! Brett grabbed her even as she screamed and fought him. He lifted her and threw her over his shoulder as if she weighed nothing more than a bag of potatoes. She continued to wail like he was murdering her as he moved into the master bathroom and stepped into the oversized, stone-tiled shower. He sat her down and gripped her wrists as he turned the water onto hot, stepping just out of reach of the three showerheads.

Madi screamed again as the downpour hit her still-clothed body. The water splashed onto Brett too, but he didn't care; his sweat-soaked gym clothes were about to go into the washing machine anyway.

He'd been patient, allowing Madi time to grieve the loss of Hunter, but she was bordering on clinical depression now. Soon, she'd need medication, therapy, or both, and he couldn't continue to watch her health decline. She'd thrown the medications back at him, refusing help when he offered to take her to see a psychiatrist, and had shut herself in her room. She wouldn't eat, lost weight, and slept for much longer than was humanly necessary. Now it was time to act.

She began to scratch at the hand holding her wrist and lunged for the door, but Brett was far stronger and much, much bigger. She wouldn't be escaping him, even if he had to hold her down and bathe her himself. She shoved at him even as he stepped closer, soaking his clothes in the process.

"Stop it, Madi," he murmured, pulling her into his chest as her fists pummeled his pecs.

She sobbed in pain, anguish, and grief as he stroked her now-wet hair and cooed to her. He comforted her as best he could, all the while drenching his clothes in the shower. After a time, she finally looked up, and he gave her a soft smile.

"You have to take care of yourself, baby. Eat, shower, and come out of the damn house. You can't just die along with him. I can't lose you, too." He fought the emotions rising in him.

"I miss him so much, Brett." Her voice broke, and he cradled her head back to his chest, stroking her hair and back once more.

"I do too, Madi. So much." It was true, even if Hunter had been married to the woman Brett had been in love with for as long as he could remember. "But we have to go on without him. Both of us do. We simply have to find a way to keep going. Starving yourself and wallowing in depression isn't going to cut it, Madi. You need help, honey. Let me help you."

She looked up at him, fear darkening her Caribbean blue-green eyes, and he gulped. She looked down at herself, her trim frame pounds lighter and small enough to cause concern. She lifted her shirt, looking down at her thin belly, and Brett could have sworn aloud. She wasn't emaciated by any means, but her healthy body looked hungry. He blamed himself.

Amelia had come by two days ago and threatened to have Madi committed into psychiatric care if she didn't get out of bed. Brett told her to give him by the weekend. Madi was still eating and drinking, and he swore he'd get her up and showered...and out of the house. He hadn't told Amelia his plans to take her to Mexico. But he believed it was for the best. This house was making things worse for Madison.

"Do you need me to bathe you?" he asked in all seriousness. He knew it wouldn't be easy for him to see her fully naked and be able to control his arousal, but he would do whatever needed to be done to get the woman he loved back to reality.

Again, those eyes bore into his, and she finally shook her head. "No. I...I'll bathe. I—"

"Alright. I'll step out and give you some privacy, then." He nodded and released her, closing the shower door behind him as he stepped out. "Take your pajamas off and hand them over. I'm gonna go start a load of clothes."

He turned his back to the glass shower door and lowered his eyes, for there was a large mirror in front of him behind the vanity. He wouldn't have been able to see her despite that since he towered over her by almost a foot, but still, Brett McFadden was a gentleman and would never disrespect Madison, no matter what.

She did as he asked, and when she opened the shower door, he grabbed her soaking wet clothes and moved to the sink to wring them out.

"I'll give you a little time to collect yourself. I'll be downstairs when you're ready."

"Wh-where are we going?" Madi asked, apprehension filling her voice.

"I'm getting you out of this house. And well fed today. So dress warm. No arguments. Or I'm taking you to your mom's, and you know what she'll do." Brett couldn't fight the gruffness of his voice.

He didn't want to admit how worried he was, or that he'd allowed this to get as out of hand as it had, but he'd never dealt with death before. Not a death like this, anyway; so unexpected and someone so young, a man in the prime of his life. Brett knew grieving took time, but he also hadn't realized how little Madi was eating or how much she'd shut him and her family out, even though he hadn't left her side for more than a few hours these last two weeks.

He'd wanted to give her privacy to grieve, and he'd needed his own. They'd spent last week watching TV, reading, or walking the property when they weren't sitting around attempting to rein in their heartache. He'd spent the night with her every night last week until leaving her bed last Saturday night; he hadn't offered to return.

It had been difficult to do, seeing as he'd gotten used to being in her bed, smelling her hair as he buried his nose into it, feeling her curvy body pressed into his own. He'd awoken every morning to the familiar stiffness between his legs and fought hard to hide it from her, even knowing she had to feel it digging into her hip more often than not. Having her so close made his desire for her worse than it had ever been, and he'd had to relieve himself in the shower on multiple occasions.

But he'd left her bed as much for his own reprieve as to give her time to get used to life without Hunter. Brett had feared Sunday night would bring a panic-stricken Madi to his own bed; he'd left the door open, but much to his surprise, she hadn't shown up. The selfish side of him wanted to be disappointed, but he knew it was what was best. If they continued to sleep in the same bed together, he'd end up taking her, and right now, their grief consumed them and would destroy any future plans he might have for a relationship with her. No, Madison needed time to heal from the death of her husband. Having sex with Brett would only complicate her feelings —and might drive her away from him. Brett had to be patient, and he would be….as he always had been. It was his greedy cock that couldn't wait.

He walked down the wooden steps of Madi and Hunter's immaculate eight-bedroom home, careful to hold Madi's soaking clothes against his body to prevent dripping. He entered the laundry room that could've fit a decent number of his teammates inside. He peeled his own clothes off and turned the dial to the washing machine, poured in some detergent, and started a load. He was naked and walking back up the stairs, noticing that despite the design—soft earthy tones and pictures of Madi and Hunter, her family, Brett, his teammates, and their other friends—how sterile and stark the house felt. Perhaps it was because it was devoid of Hunter's constant laughter, the noise of their get-togethers, and the happiness that familiarity always invoked. It could simply be that the house was quieter than it had ever been or because there was more sadness filling up the space than it'd ever known.

Brett hopped into the guest room shower and did so quickly. He brushed his teeth, dressed in a blue Henley and jeans, threw some gel in his hair, and sprayed a fair amount of his cologne on. He was always amazed at the amount of clothes he'd always had here. When he wasn't at his own home or on the field, he was here, at Madi and Hunter's...well, just Madi's now. It was so strange, and he didn't know if he'd ever get used to it. Despite his love for Madison Hope Thomas, he missed his other best friend more than he ever imagined he possibly could.

Brett and Hunter met their sophomore year in college, at UGA, where they played football together. One day he was chumming it up with the charismatic wide receiver, the next the bastard was dating the woman of Brett's dreams. And Brett could say nothing, for he'd never had the guts to tell Madi how he felt and by the time he'd finally gotten up the nerve to do so, it'd been too late.

Madi had been drawn to Hunter, like everyone else—hell, like Brett had been too. Hunter was like a flashlight in the darkest night; there was something about him that people just flocked to. His humor had been genuine, his smile bright, his aura all-consuming. He'd been one of those people that no one could dislike, it simply wasn't possible. And Brett soon found himself being the third wheel, constantly. Although Madi and Hunter had never made him feel that way, it was still what he'd been. The forgotten best friend, the unrequited lover, the man who suffered in silence while the woman he loved gave her heart away to another.

Now Brett was the man left to pick up the pieces of that woman's heart. And he was to blame for Hunter's death. Brett wondered again if he would ever stop having nightmares of that day, ever stop reliving the fear, pain, and loss he felt as his best friend died in the bed next to him.

The flashback hit him again, a memory as sharp as the day it happened:

. . .

"YOU HAVE *to swear to me, Brett. Swear,*" *Hunter rasped, his voice strained, as it became increasingly difficult for him to breathe. Brett could hardly hear him over the incessant beeping of the machines around him. Hunt's bloody, battered body lay atop a gurney in the trauma room of the ER. Brett sat next to him in a chair that was much too small for his big frame, Hunt holding his hand like it was his lifeline instead of the IV tubing running into his arm.*

"*Swear what, Hunt?*"

"*That you'll take care of the woman we both love.*"

Brett's eyes came up to his best friend's, a mixture of regret, uncertainty, and hesitation.

"*I know, Brett. I've always known.*" *When Brett didn't respond, Hunter continued,* "*And yet, I didn't care. I was gonna have her no matter what... Now look what it's cost me.*"

Brett gulped. How had he known? Brett had never told anyone. *Not even his parents knew...well, maybe they'd known, but it hadn't been because he'd told them.*

"*But it's* your *turn now. You have a second chance, buddy. To do what I couldn't. Love her like you were always meant to. The way I failed.*"

"*No, Hermes, you—*"

"*Hermes! Ha!*"

Travis "Ares" Redmond, had pegged Hunter "Hermes" when he'd joined their team back in late September. Brett had gotten the name Zeus for the "thunderbolts" he'd been throwing.

"*I'm a sorry excuse where my wife is concerned, and you damn well know it!*"

Brett almost crumpled at the sorrow on Hunter's face and the tears in his brown eyes.

"*Dammit, Brett, you know that what I did was all a huge mistake, right?*"

"*I know, brother, I know. It's—*"

"*Don't let her find out, please? It will crush her.*"

"I'll do my very best."

"Swear?"

"I swear, Hunt."

"It was the dumbest thing I've ever done, and I regret it like hell now. I'd do anything to take it back. She—" Hunter was sniveling now, the pain of his regret palpable. *"She didn't deserve it, Brett. You were right. Madi's been the perfect wife. I was a fool. I—"*

"Shh, hey, I know, man, I know. It's ok. Let's not worry about the things we can't change, huh?"

The last thing Brett wanted was for his best friend's dying words to have to be groveling. He gave him a big smile and gripped his hand tighter.

"I promise I'll take care of Madi," Brett assured.

At that, Hunter grinned big. "It was always supposed to be you, Brett." Hunter squeezed his eyes shut for a moment and a tear ran down his bloody cheek. "Give her children. She wants a boy, you know?"

Brett sucked a deep breath in, remembering that Hunter and Madi had been unsuccessfully trying to have a baby for the last six months. They'd both been tested to find out what the problem was but no answers had come. Hunter had been excited to tell his teammates about it, making jokes in his typical "Hermes" fashion, but Madi was under the illusion that it was a secret. Hunt really sucked at keeping secrets.

Brett's reverie was interrupted as Madison came down the stairs, dressed in a blue sweater dress and leggings with leather riding boots. She'd donned makeup, coral lipstick, and left her hair down in waves that framed her face. She looked downright edible, and Brett cleared his throat.

"You ready, Sunflower?" he asked, calling her the nickname he gave her when they were just children. She'd always loved sunflowers. She nodded and he moved in front of her, taking her face in his hands. "I'm sorry if I was harsh."

She shook her head. "I needed harsh, I think." He gave her a smile and released her, pulled her arm through his as he moved to the garage door, set the alarm, and guided them to his GMC Sierra 1500 Denali.

Madi moved to the passenger side and he took the driver seat, turning the radio onto a soft jazz station. They rode in companionable silence before he turned down Main Street and onto the road to one of the best restaurants for country food in town—Sanders House.

"We can't eat here," Madi stated in shock as he pulled into the parking lot.

"Don't worry."

They'd learned the hard way long ago that they couldn't just waltz into a place without unwanted attention, despite growing up in a small-town mountain city.

Brett pulled his SUV to a stop at the back of the restaurant.

"Brett, we—I can't—" Madi began.

"It's ok. Wait here. I'll be right back."

He gave her a reassuring smile and squeezed her hand before stepping out of the truck. He moved to the back door, gave three knocks and a big bellied woman with rosy cheeks and curly hair threw the rickety, old thing open and greeted him with a bright smile.

"Brett McFadden. How are you, sugar?"

"I'm well, Rosie. Thank you for doing this."

"Absolutely. It's my pleasure. You take care of that sweet girl of Jerry's now. Bless y'alls hearts." Rosie's eyes teared up.

"Will do, Rose. Have a good day."

"You too, hon." She leaned in and kissed his cheek, handing him a large basket of food.

He walked back to the truck and got a confused look out of Madi when she saw the overfilled basket.

"You got it to-go?"

"Yes, ma'am. I did." He beamed, and she relaxed some as he

turned and placed it in the floorboard behind her. "Let's roll the windows down. It's sunny out today."

He rolled all four of the windows down halfway and turned the radio on to his favorite country station, hearing Tim McGraw sing, "Where The Green Grass Grows." He sang along to the lyrics and nudged Madi to join in. She smiled but didn't sing along. Brett didn't press it. She was out of the house and that was a start.

It was a gorgeous March day driving through the valley, the birds were singing, the dogwood and cherry blossom trees were starting to bloom, and the sun was warm. Spring had sprung.

Madi continued to sit quietly as if in a fog as Brett turned back onto his land and headed down a dirt trail behind the barn. Maybe, if she felt up to it, they'd take the horses for a ride today.

He pulled up to his favorite clearing and cut the ignition. He got out of the truck, grabbing a big blanket from the backseat. He then came back and got the basket, motioning for Madi to sit as he began to do so himself. She glanced over at the creek that bubbled not far from where they sat and drained into a lake just fifty yards downstream, at the old oak tree with a swing he'd fashioned years ago, then she looked down.

Brett set to the task of pulling the goodies out of the basket—sweet teas in mason jars and the many containers of food: fried chicken, squash casserole, lima beans, creamed corn, sweet potatoes, and yeast rolls. He grabbed the plates and utensils Rosie had provided and began divvying up the feast.

"Am I ever gonna stop seeing him in everything I hear, see, and do?" Madi stated as if in a reverie.

"The point is not to stop, just to not breakdown when you do," Brett replied.

"My lord, we don't eat like this."

"That's kinda the point, Madi."

"Mmm," she moaned as he handed her the heaping plate he knew she'd eat three bites of and be done with. "This smells incredible."

"Yeah, said by someone who's been trying to starve herself."

"I wasn't. I just…" she trailed off as Brett dug into the food and she followed. She moaned again as she bit into the chicken. "This is so good."

"The soul needs comfort food." Brett grinned big and Madi returned it, after she'd swallowed her bite. "We're going to your mom and dad's for dinner tonight at six."

Madi's face fell and she looked away suddenly.

"I thought you'd want to see them, Sunflower. It's been almost a week."

"I do, I just…"

"Your mom wanted to have you committed, Madi. She thinks you locking yourself up was concerning to say the least."

"I just didn't realize how many days had passed. I wasn't tryin' to—"

"Hey, we all have to grieve. Some people grieve differently than others, ok? None of us have experienced what you have."

"*You* have," Madi whispered and looked up into his eyes, her seafoam green orbs lighting up in the sunlight, making her even more beautiful than she already was to him. "I haven't even checked on you. I bet no one has. They've been so worried about me. How are you holding up, Brett?" She'd set her plate down and was touching his forearm, bringing her hand down to his. He squeezed her soft, small palm in his larger one, admiring the feel and texture and touch of the woman he'd been hopelessly in love with all his life.

He'd been holding up as best he could for a man riddled with guilt at losing his best friend. The man who'd been more like his brother than not. They'd fought as much as they got along; he loved the goofy asshole despite his flaws, his arrogant ways, and how he'd treated his wife. Hunter had been funny, light-hearted, and one of a kind. And Brett had lived instead.

Brett found himself opening up for the first time since the accident to Madison—for if he couldn't open up to the woman who'd been his best friend since they were seven who the hell else could he talk to? "It was supposed to be me…."

33

He heard Madi pull in a shuddered breath. She'd told him not to say that again, but he wasn't saying it because he felt it to be true. He said it because it *was* true. It was Hunter's car. And Brett had been driving it. If Brett had been in the passenger seat, he would've been the one to take the brunt of the hit. He told Madi all this, and for once, she wasn't crying; she just looked at him, absorbing his feelings and emotions.

"Guilt eats at me every day, and I have to just swallow it down. God chose me."

Madi's smile was earnest as she fought the tears stinging her eyes. "He did. And I know we aren't supposed to question Him, but I've been really mad."

"Anger is part of the process. There's nothing wrong with that, Madi. I've been mad, too."

"You have?"

Brett nodded. "I've hit the gym every single day, started doing some kick-boxing to help get my emotions out."

"Has it helped?"

Brett nodded again. "Now you need an outlet, aside from sleeping all day."

Madi pulled her lips in and nodded, herself.

Brett pulled his phone from his back pocket, turning Spotify on to their favorite country albums. They ate in comfortable silence, enjoying the sunshine, and Madi laughed when Brett patted his tummy dramatically. It was good to hear that beautiful sound again; Brett smiled brightly, happy for the first time in a very long time.

When they finished eating and had set their plates aside, "I Hope You Dance" by Lee Ann Womack came on. Brett popped up, seeing the sorrow on Madi's face simply too much for him. He *had* to extinguish it. He extended his hand to her.

"C'mon, we got to. It's our song from senior prom, remember?"

Madi gave him a slow smile and took his hand, letting him pull her up and into his arms for a dance. He held one hand in his own, the other wrapped around her waist while hers went to his back. She smiled up at him again, and his heart literally flipped over in his chest. God, she was the most beautiful thing he'd ever seen. She was perfect, every bit of her five-foot, eight inch, one hundred fifty-pound frame. Her tan skin, light green eyes, cupid's bow lips, and golden-blonde hair. She'd invaded his heart, mind, and soul ever since she'd come into his life; he'd never been the same since. One day he was going to confess it to her.

Every single day since Hunt had passed, his words echoed through Brett's mind, "This is your second chance." It'd been like a mantra inside his head, and although the selfish part of him wanted it more than anything, the Christian side of him was hesitant. He knew if he did move in and take what he'd always wanted, it needed to be slow and sure. He couldn't rush this, couldn't rush Madi's grief...or his own, for that matter. He'd always been patient, and he would have to continue to be.

Madi's head now rested on his chest, his other hand wrapped around her as their feet continued to move to the song. They embraced each other tightly, and Brett reveled in the feel of her against him. Their hearts beat in cadence together, in perfect sync, and her smell was intoxicating him as it always had. As many times as he'd held her over the years, this was the first time it felt so bitter-sweet. This was his best friend's wife and Brett was here instead of Hunter, here to hold her and touch her and kiss her.

Now, Hunter's dead because you *were the one driving.*

Once more, Brett wondered if he'd ever get rid of the all-consuming guilt that never seemed to leave him. He felt Madi shudder and moved a hand to stroke her hair, kissing her temple as he leaned his head down.

"Shh, it's ok, Sunflower."

She pulled him tighter to her, fisting his shirt, her frame fitting perfectly against his much bigger one. At six foot five inches tall and almost two-fifty he towered over her like the damn Hulk. He was one of the biggest QBs in the league, which had garnered him the nickname "Brickhouse." Then Trav had come along and dubbed him Zeus.

Madi's tears were starting to trouble him, the need to comfort and protect her stronger than any emotion he'd ever had.

"Baby, what's the matter?" he murmured against her ear even as he laid his head onto hers.

After a few minutes of composing herself, she wiped her face and looked up at him, her cheeks rosy. "You're the best friend I've ever had, and I've been awful to you lately."

Brett couldn't stop the smile that pulled at the corner of his mouth. "Nah."

Her insistent nod said otherwise, and he put his finger to her lips before she could speak again. He settled her head back to his collarbone and rested his chin against her shoulder, leaning into her as they continued to shuffle their feet to the music.

"I haven't done anything you wouldn't have done for me. It's what best friends do. We take care of each other, kick the other's tail into shape when needed, and help bury bodies of our enemies."

He heard Madi smirk into his shirt and sniffle.

When the song was over, she pulled back and took his face in her hands. "I mean it. You're my best friend. And you'll never know what you being here means to me. I love you."

His heart sputtered. They'd said these words to each other so many times, even though she was clueless as to how much he meant them and how. "I love you too, Sunflower. Always and forever." He pulled her back to him for a hug, and she gripped him tightly.

Oh, Madi, will I ever get to show you just what you mean to me? In time... I will, in time.

CHAPTER THREE

"Mad, Jesus... I thought Brett had locked you up in a tower. You didn't answer your phone or..." Brooke trailed off as Madi pulled her to her for a hug. Her sister. Her clueless, crazy sister.

"I missed you," Madi stated and kissed her baby sister's nose.

Brooke's eyes misted over, and she grinned. "It's good to have you back, sis."

"Ah, there's our girl," Madi heard her dad call over Brooke's head. She moved from her sister's embrace to her father's, squeezing him tightly as his big frame comforted her. "You look great, honey." He took her cheeks in his hands and kissed her forehead before releasing her.

"You look awful," Madi's mother replied with a hand on her hip and a scowl back at Brett.

"Mom, I'm fine. I—"

"You are *not* fine. You've lost too much weight." Her mother approached and grabbed at Madi's dress.

Madi counted to ten before responding. Her mother never had anything go wrong in her life, let alone a death that caused the world to stop spinning. Brett had been right, no one understood what she'd gone through. She gave her mother a bright smile, despite wanting to slap her and tell her to chill the hell out.

Madi hadn't wanted to eat, she hadn't wanted to live, she hadn't wanted to do anything...except die, herself. How could she possibly express that to anyone? It was embarrassing. It made her feel insane. And yet it made every bit of sense. She imagined how her mother would feel if the same thing were to happen to her father; no, Amelia Taylor would continue to be stoic, unshakeable, oblivious to anything that rattled her tough outer exterior. And Madi felt shame, on top of all the other emotions that her soul had been consumed with since Brett told her of Hunter's demise almost three weeks ago. Had it really been three weeks already?

Amelia drew her in for a hug, tight and emotional. She pulled back and her hard, green eyes pierced Madi's soul as her mother whispered softly but intensely, "You've *got* to snap out of this, you hear me? It was a horrible accident. I'm sorry it happened, but life must go on now. Alright?"

Madi swallowed and nodded. Her mother had always given her girls tough love and death was no exception. She'd always wanted them to be strong, self-sufficient, not needing any man to "save" them. *There's no such thing as a knight on a white horse. You want a hero, become your own.* Her mother's principles stemmed from a mother who'd had husband after husband—yes, Madi's grandmother had had six—and seeing the damage of heartbreak tear Grandma Kate in two.

Madi's mother had always been a woman of doing, her accomplishments exceeding beyond what her husband had made possible for her. She was a woman of class, a woman of God, a woman of great undertakings. Amelia took on the world with speeches, books, and inspired others across the globe. It was her thing.

Madi knew this and tried not to let her mother's words hurt her.

"Brett, a word," her mother stated as she took Brett's hand and led him into the kitchen and out of earshot.

Madi's father smiled at her sudden unease and pulled her back to him, kissing her forehead. "She's just worried about you. You know your mother; the show must go on. I swear she should've been a drill-sergeant. She'd have made a hell of a fine one."

Madi and Brooke laughed at him as he moved them into the den for some cocktails. Madi nodded when Brooke asked if she wanted a cosmo.

"How are you holding up, Sunshine?" her dad asked as he took her hand and sat her down in the arm chair next to his.

"I'm doing better than I was." She wouldn't mention that she hadn't bathed until just this morning when Brett had literally dragged her ass from the bed and into the shower, screaming in protest.

"It's gonna take time, don't listen to your mother. She's like a damn fortress, nothing shakes her. But this is all normal stuff, ok? You'll get through this." His soothing voice reassured her, and Madi wondered how on earth the two of them—her mother and father— had ever fallen in love. Her dad was the most easy-going person on the planet, and her mom was ruthless, even though she did have a generous heart hidden in that "fortress" her dad mentioned.

"We gotta go get mani/pedis soon; your nails look awful," Brooke scolded and looked to the fingernails Madi had bit into the quick. Brett had already hounded her about stopping the chewing, threatening to tie her hands behind her back. They were red but not infected, thanks to Brett. God, he'd really been an angel. What had she ever done to deserve him?

Madi frowned back at her sister, who simply replied with, "Whenever you're ready of course."

The thoughts of being surrounded by people, aside from her family, gave her nausea. She didn't wanna be hounded, harassed, or have any reason to talk about how she felt to anyone. She didn't wanna have to answer untruthfully when people asked how she was doing, said they were sorry, or spoke of Hunter's life. She wasn't ready for all that.

Brooke quickly shelved it and moved to her side, telling her the latest on the gossip train. A friend of hers was having an affair, the other was being cheated on, and another was pregnant.

That news hit her harder than anything else, and Madi prayed that the last time she and Hunter had made love that it had taken. They'd been trying to get pregnant for so long and to have one last sliver of him left in her life filled her with hope. She begged God to give her one final piece of him since he'd been taken so fast and so violently from her.

Amelia and Brett returned to the den, and it was as if nothing had ever transpired; they were both smiling. Madi's mother came over and took her hand, squeezing it gently. Relief flooded through Madi; her mother wasn't mad at her.

"Ready to eat, baby? I made your favorite."

Madi nodded and she and her mother moved into the dining room, arm in arm.

Brett sat down next to Madi and Brooke across from her, while her parents took either end of the table. Grace was said and Madi smiled as her mother passed around a heaping plate of beef tips. Her mom always made the best, slow simmered all day in homemade beef stock, shallots, thyme, and some other herb she'd never shared with them. Madi topped her rice with a decent scoop and added some roasted vegetables to her plate. As she dug in, her taste buds hummed for the second time that day; suddenly, she was a young girl again, back home without a care in the world. She smiled over at her mother and thanked her. It truly touched her that her mom had been so thoughtful.

Madi nodded when her father told her mother, "This might be your best batch yet, love," getting a laugh and agreement from the entire table. She was taking a sip of her drink when her mom asked, "So, what time are y'all leaving for Cancun?" Madi nearly spewed but quickly brought her napkin to her mouth to keep herself from doing so.

"What?" she asked with a frown and didn't miss the self-satisfied grin on her mom's face.

"Uh, tonight, after we leave here."

Madi frowned over at Brett; what the hell was he talking about?

"Oh, you didn't tell her? You know how I always like to be prepared for trips." Amelia's eyebrow arched. "I can't imagine Madison would be any different."

"Brett?" Madi asked, her brows drawing.

"Surprise," he mumbled and took a sip of his scotch in front of him.

"How fun," Madi's father chuckled, trying to ease the tension.

Brett took a deep breath in and took Madi's hand. "Linc and Val wanted to do something nice and unplanned, so they gave me the key to their house in Cancun. We can stay as long as we want."

Madi gulped. A vacation. So soon? She couldn't leave right now. She had things to do. Closets to clean out. Hunter's locker to empty.

Oh, God, she was gonna be sick. She quickly excused herself from the table and ran to the hall bathroom. She pushed the door shut and hit her knees in front of the commode, feeling like she was going to faint. She shoved her head into the toilet and took deep breaths in, attempting to calm herself.

She felt a wet rag come to her neck and her mother's hand running up and down her back. "It's ok, baby. It's ok."

The chant didn't help. Madi began to panic. "B-Brett," was all she could get out.

She heard his heavy footfalls; when she felt his hand hit her back, she turned into him and held on tight as the dam of emotions exploded once again. How did she have any tears left to cry? What the hell? Maybe her mother was right, maybe she needed to be committed.

His stroking of her hair and his words soothed her and soon, she was looking up into his handsome face. "I-I'm sorry."

"Nothing to apologize for, Sunflower. I shouldn't have sprung it on you like that. We should've discussed it first. It was rather impromptu, and when Linc volunteered, I thought it was a good idea." He held her face in his big palms, his gorgeous green eyes burning into her own. "Madi, that house hasn't been good for you. We need to get away for a little while."

"But...what about his things, his locker, I—" she felt herself pouting again.

"Baby, there's no rush here. No one will touch his locker until you're ready." Madi looked up to her father, who stood in the door frame with his arms crossed over his chest. He nodded, solidifying his words.

"And Madi you aren't ready. You need this trip. *We* need this trip." Brett's pleading voice beckoned to her. She couldn't remember the last vacation she'd gone on since her wedding and honeymoon in Ireland five years prior. Their lives had been so swept up in the moment—in football, in the team—that nothing else existed. Madi had gone back to get her master's degree and worked hard to get to CEO status; achieving that goal had been her sole focus.

Brett was right; they both needed this trip.

"I HOPE you aren't mad at me," Brett said when they got in the car to head out. "I had Maria pack your bag. It's already on the jet. I figured if you need anything else we can either buy it or have it sent."

Madi just nodded, gazing out the window. She was used to people doing things for her, just as he was used to the same.

"Madi, I wasn't keeping it a secret from you; you need to know that. I just wanted it to be a surprise."

"I know, Brett. I'm glad you made the decision for us to go. It means a lot. You're so thoughtful."

"You just now figuring this out?" He winked, trying to ease some of the tension he'd felt all evening.

He knew Amelia wasn't thrilled at how he'd been handling things, but, contrary to what she believed, Madi didn't need pills or a shrink—or to end up wasting away in a damn psych unit somewhere for God knew how long before she was deemed "sane" again. She didn't need rehab, she didn't need therapy, she simply needed time to grieve. Tragic deaths took their toll, and if Madi was feeling even a quarter of the emotions Brett was—and he knew she was—she was in desperate need of release. She'd never been thrust into a situation like this, never had tragedy hit her so hard, never had her life altered in such a drastic way. That's all this was. He was planning to give her a couple months to adjust to her new life. He'd been reading books on grieving and talking to his own psychiatrist about it. Brett came to the conclusion that Madi wasn't depressed, she wasn't suicidal, and she wasn't crazy; she was simply mourning the loss of her husband. Plain and simple.

Of course he'd volunteered to drive her to a doctor, he'd offered to have his own come and visit her, but she'd refused. At first, he'd been gravely concerned, then he remembered how she felt about psychiatrists and shut his mouth. He knew all the warning signs; if she gave him any reason to question her mental stability, he would overrule her and get the help she needed. That was what he'd told Amelia earlier.

"Do you trust me?"

"Of course, but this is—"

"She's just devastated, Millie. That's all. She lost her husband, suddenly and in a horrible way. She needs to grieve him. It's gonna take time."

"She's gotta get out of that house, Brett. She—"

"I know. I'm taking care of that...tonight."

He'd proceeded to inform her of his intentions to fly to Cancun and vacation there, extending the invitation to them as well. She seemed relieved and relaxed for the first time since Hunter's death, and he was grateful that his second mom had approved of his plans.

He hadn't been expecting for Amelia to oust him before he had a chance to tell Madi himself but, then again, he wasn't surprised. Amelia was anything if not blunt.

"I've never been to Cancun," Madi said softly, still gazing out at the clear night, drawing Brett from his thoughts.

"Me either, believe it or not."

"How long will it take for us to get there?"

"A little over an hour and forty-five minutes; Linc's property isn't far from the airstrip there."

"Oh wow. That's fast."

"Yup. We'll be there to hear the ocean as we sleep tonight." Brett smiled big, drawing one out of her. She'd always loved the beach. He remembered the many trips they'd taken together to one of their favorite vacation destinations—Panama City Beach, Florida. They'd been at least once, sometimes twice, a year almost every year until she'd gotten married and the traditions stopped. He'd been happy for the girl he loved, but he'd also been insanely jealous and melancholy while she'd promised herself to another man right in front of him. It had been the second worst day of his life. Being the best man in Hunter's wedding and watching the woman he was in love with marry another man had put a giant stake through his heart. But he couldn't take her happiness from her. It had been what she wanted, and who was he to stand in her way? He'd drank himself literally under a table where he'd stayed the remainder of the trip.

Afterward, he came home and told himself that was it. It was time to finally move on and find a woman whom he could love in Madi's shadow. But, as much as he tried, his heart had never been able to heal. He was doomed to love no other. Each time he tried, he wound up hurting someone else as much as he was hurting himself. A year ago, he simply stopped trying.

Now, here he was, grateful—despite his blame—that God had given him another shot at being with Madison Hope Taylor. He just had to bide his time. He sure as hell didn't wanna be her rebound guy, so he had to play his cards right and be patient. Good thing Brett McFadden knew everything there was to know about the term.

They pulled up to the airstrip, not far from his house, where Max greeted them with a tip of the hat.

"Mr. McFadden." He smiled and settled behind the wheel as Brett moved to Madi's side of the car and helped her out. "Enjoy your trip."

"Thanks, Max," Brett said and closed the door.

Brett moved toward the plane with Madi's arm looped through his as Max pulled off in the truck. "You ready?" he asked and got a nod out of her.

They moved up the airstair of the Cessna luxury jet Brett had purchased years ago. The pilot and co-pilot greeted them, and Brett gave them a salute and thanked them. He always made sure to be appreciative of the people who made his life a little easier.

Madi moved to the couch opposite his and pulled a blanket across her legs as the stewardess came by and asked if they wanted anything. Brett requested a scotch; he hated flying even if this was going to be a short trip.

Within about ten minutes, they were in the air, and Brett pulled his phone out, checking his emails while Madi turned the television on to watch a movie.

He had some texts from Linc, Trav, Pax, and Coach Cavanaugh; he answered them all, thanking Linc again for the house. He didn't have any commitments aside from some endorsements and events he needed to be in attendance for in Atlanta come May. Brett always tried to keep busy during off season, staying healthy and in shape. He didn't understand the guys who let themselves go only to get killed come time to get back in. They'd blink and football season would be back; it always went by so fast. He'd be needed, starting in June, for meetings and practice, although those weren't mandatory til July. He also used this time to catch up on sleep, hobbies, and the few shows he watched. After all, *some* downtime was as essential as working out was. And right now, following Hunt's death, he was seeing that people had to focus on the simple things in life and enjoy the good while it lasted.

He looked over at Madi after tossing his phone beside him and sipped his scotch. She was almost asleep, and he grinned; she'd never been able to sit still for long. She was like him; they were both athletes. If they weren't working—and working hard—they were sleeping.

Madi had been a football cheerleader and tennis player back in both middle and high school. She'd trained her whole life. Workouts were as important to her as breathing, although these past few weeks she'd neglected everything including those, he knew. Perhaps in Mexico they could run in the mornings on the beach and get her back to her routine. She was like him, she thrived on her routine.

Brett let his own eyelids drift closed as the soft whirring of the jet flying through the air lulled him to sleep.

He awoke to the ding of the captain telling them they'd be landing soon and smiled as Madi sat up, eyelids heavy.

"Welcome to the Caribbean, Sleeping Beauty," he cooed and got a blush out of her.

Soon, they were landing and leaving the plane to be transported to their destination via car.

A black Lincoln Navigator took them to Lincoln's house, via a driver with a fun sense of style and a Latin American accent. His name was Patro; Linc had sent him.

In ten minutes, they were pulling through the gates of Linc's mansion in Paradise, a gorgeous two-story cream stucco home with a terra cotta roof and a beautifully manicured lawn.

"Oh, wow," Madi stated enthusiastically as the car stopped out front of the steps.

Brett seconded that as he came to her side, the driver grabbing their bags from the back.

They stopped in front of two massive mahogany wood doors as Brett used the key. When they came inside, Brett smiled at Madi's obvious approval. This home was perfect; he saw right away why Linc and Val had fallen in love with it. It was open, lavish, and felt like home. He'd have to send them a gift to thank them, maybe some tickets to an event or a fancy dinner—something nice.

When Patro dropped their luggage, Brett shook his hand,

planting a large tip into his palm as he did so. Patro tipped his fedora to them and left, telling them to call if they needed him. Brett had his business card in his pocket.

Madi smiled again and looked at him as if he'd given her the world. He'd do it a thousand times over to get her to gaze at him as she was doing so at that moment. She moved toward him then and wrapped her arms around his neck. Much to his absolute shock, she planted her lips softly on his. The contact jarred him. This wasn't the first time Madison had kissed him on the lips, not the first time she'd pecked them. Hell, she'd freaking made out with him prior to now, years ago when they were teenagers; but this time felt different. Perhaps it was wishful thinking on his part or perhaps he just felt more hopeful now that Hunter was gone—as horrifying as that might be. But either way, the touch of her soft, sweet lips on his had him yearning. When she pulled back, he fought everything within himself not to grab her and kiss her like he really wanted to.

"Thank you. I don't deserve you." She studied the lips she'd just kissed, and Brett stifled a moan.

Damn, this was gonna be tough. And tomorrow was gonna be tougher; he knew how good his best friend looked in a bikini and he'd end up with a raging boner the entire time. He was gonna need tape. And alcohol. And to take an ice-cold shower he realized as she walked into the foyer and squealed in delight, leaving him to push down the discomfort in his pants.

CHAPTER FOUR

Brett awoke the next morning with a start. It was bright as hell in his room. After rubbing his eyes, he grinned as he heard the sound of the waves lapping against the shore. Seagulls and pelicans called overhead, and a dolphin leaped in the waters as he stood and walked toward the open balcony. It was a beautiful day on the Yucatan Peninsula, sunny and warm. A beautiful day for a run, chilling on the beach, and snorkeling. Maybe they could go swim with the dolphins or stingrays or something. There were some ship-wrecks and reefs not far from here; maybe he could call and make a reservation for them to scuba-dive. They both had their licenses. There was also a hot nightclub he'd heard about, but then again Madi's melancholy might need to wait for that.

He stretched and checked his watch. Nine AM, he needed to get downstairs and work out. He brushed his teeth, dressed quickly, and moved downstairs, observing that the coffee pot was already going, either from Madi or it was automatic, he wasn't sure. He poured himself some into a mug then moved to the fridge and smiled as he saw it was stocked with everything a person could possibly need. He grabbed out the almond milk and rummaged through the pantry, finding a giant container of protein powder, and began mixing his shake. He took in the turquoise waters, so clear and enchanting, through the wall of glass in front of him. How could Linc and Val ever leave this place? It was breathtaking.

Once his shake was mixed, he swigged some as he moved to the back of the house where the workout area was and was surprised to see Madi running on one of the treadmills already; he'd assumed she was still sleeping. He felt his heart ache as he watched her red face crumpling. Dammit, she was crying, tears streaming her face as her pace accelerated. He took another swig of his shake and opened the glass door, letting it close behind him as he entered. Madi's sniffling and sobs drowned out the music she'd turned on but she didn't slow her pace. Brett became concerned, afraid her emotions were going to cause her to lose her concentration and fall.

"Madi, I think—" he stopped, coming to her side even as she ignored him, looking ahead as if he wasn't even there. His hand covered hers and he looked up into her face. "Mad. You should stop."

She shook her head, vehemently.

"Yeah, how about we—" Again, he stopped and sat his shake down in the cup holder. And he was grateful he did because her foot shifted and she started to teeter. Brett shuffled quickly behind her and grabbed her as she fell and bounced up and into his arms. They both fell backwards onto the floor, Brett hitting his ass hard. He winced even as Madi cried out, grabbing her bare thigh which was burned from the skid on the treadmill and bleeding. Brett stood with her cradled in his arms and moved over to the treadmill, slamming down the stop button, before he turned and carried her out the door. She was sobbing into his collarbone as her arms wrapped around his neck, probably a combination of her emotions and the embarrassment she felt.

Brett sat her down on the couch, mindful of her leg as he moved into the pantry and grabbed the bottle of peroxide and gauze he'd seen there while searching for protein powder. One thing about athletes, they always had medical kits for injuries handy.

Madi was holding the sides of her face when he came back to her side. She observed him as he took the bottle, inverted it onto a clean gauze pad, and gently placed it onto the big, oblong burn mark on her upper thigh. She cried out in equal parts pain and anguish, her hand covering his as her head flew back.

"Oww, oww, oww," she cried and whimpered, looking down at her wound.

After several moments, the pain subsided and her cries turned to sniffles. Her red eyes looked him over and he frowned. "What the hell were you thinking, Madi? This could have been much worse. You were too emotional to be running on a treadmill like that."

"I know. I'm sorry. I...I started my period."

Brett's brows rose. He knew what it meant for her, but he wanted the explanation out loud. He wanted confirmation that he was still her best friend, the one she trusted with her secrets, the one she told everything to. He waited, his eyes coaxing it out of her.

She huffed and looked away, her lips quivering. It took her another few minutes for her to confess, but she couldn't look him in the eyes as she did so, which hurt him. "Hunter and I were trying to get pregnant."

There it was. She wasn't pregnant with Hunter's baby. The period marked her final failure at conception. As sad as that made Brett feel for her, he also felt a huge sense of relief that she wasn't with child, wasn't with Hunter's child. *God, I'm such an asshole.*

"I was praying so hard that I got to keep something of him, some small part of him here on earth. But God is punishing me. I'm a failure as a wife, a woman. I couldn't even do *that* right."

"Jesus, Madi, is that what you think? C'mere." He pulled her roughly into his chest and let her cry. He let her sob and snivel and weep until his shirt was soaked in her tears and snot. She was a mess, but he understood. First, she'd had her husband's death to grieve for, now she had the child she'd never conceived to mourn, too. He was glad they were here alone in Mexico. This would've been another factor for her mother to add fuel to her fire; another indicator that Madi was "losing her mind."

"I'm sorry I didn't tell you," Madi murmured as she stroked his bicep, making him shiver.

He remembered the hit his gut had taken when Hunter had declared it to the team one day at practice months and months ago:

"GUYS, *you're looking at a future father right here," Hunter stated proudly in the locker room once they'd left the showers.*

Brett recalled feeling like he would hurl. The thought of Madi being pregnant with any man's child that wasn't his own made Brett physically sick. His stomach tightened as his center, Josh Robicheaux, asked what he couldn't. "Dude! Is Madi pregnant?" Josh clapped Hunt's back in celebration.

"Not yet, but we are certainly trying. Check this out." Hunter then took a racy picture out of his bag and began to tape it up to his locker. It was Madi, in a sexy white negligee lying flat on their bed; she was the very image of every fantasy Brett had ever had of her, hair splayed on the pillow, leg up, biting into her bottom lip as if she couldn't wait to be ravished. Brett gulped and looked away, trying to decelerate his racing heart.

"Fuck, dude, your wife is one naughty little angel." Lang touched the photo, looking at it a little too long for Brett's comfort.

"You ain't seen naughty... Look at this one."

Hunter then flashed another Polaroid, a pic of Madi with her lips around—assumedly—Hunter's dick, sea-foam green eyes burning into the viewer's as she looked up seductively.

"Jesus Christ, Hunt, you can't put that in there," Travis said with a snort. "You're gonna turn the whole damn team on." They all laughed, everyone save for Brett who was certain *he was gonna hurl now.*

In a flash of fury, he shot forward and took the pic from Hunt's grasp, watching Hunter's eyes narrow. "You son of a bitch," Brett growled, mad as hell with his best friend. "How dare you display pictures like this! She's your wife, not your fuckin' mistress. Have a little more respect."

After all, Brett knew Madison would be horrified if she knew what Hunt was showing them all.

"What's the matter, friend, you jealous?" Hunter crossed his arms over his chest, and all Brett wanted in that moment was to break the bastard's nose.

"Why would you put this in your locker?" Brett shook the photo at him.

"Oh, lighten up, Mr. Self-righteous; it's just to get me even more pumped about this whole baby-makin' thing. I see these, and it'll get me primed and ready for my wife."

Brett had never been more disgusted with Hunter. If this was his idea of a game or a joke, it wasn't funny. This should be private, not hanging up in public for anyone to walk by and see. Brett shook his head. "Take them down."

"Why? It's not like taking them down will deter anyone from desiring my wife. They covet, anyway. Don't they, Brett?"

It wasn't the first time Hunt had called him out like this, and Brett was getting sick of it. Brett had backed off a lot since Madi and Hunter had gotten married, but Brett knew Hunter would always have a problem with their close relationship. Brett had been there long before Hunter was, and Hunt was never going to be okay with that fact. He hated Brett and Madi's easy friendship; it was becoming more and more clear as time went on. Hunter could be friends with Brett, but he didn't want his wife to be. Was he threatened? Why did it matter so much? Madi was Hunter's. He'd won. Wasn't that enough?

They squared off, jaws ticking, eyes narrowed, a breath away from beating the shit out of one another before Brett said, "Fine. Go ahead and pin them up in your locker, but if Cavanaugh or Jerry see these, it's your ass."

With that, Brett threw the pic back in his face and walked off.

BRETT NOW HAD to make sure those pictures were taken down before Madi came in and cleaned that locker out; she would be appalled if she saw them. He'd be sure to hit the complex up when they got back and do just that.

For now, he stroked her hair and told her. "It's ok. It's not exactly something you announce to the world... unless, of course, your name is Hunter Thomas."

"Oh, God, he didn't."

"Yup, he did." The pictures flashed through his head again, and he tried hard to suppress his body's response as he recalled the sexual look in Madi's eyes. He'd seen them like that once himself; it had been so long ago, but he'd never forget that night.

"Damn him," Madi grated out angrily.

"He was just excited," Brett defended, not sure why he felt the need to justify Hunter's shady actions.

"That makes me feel worse. Now *everyone* knows I'm a failure."

"Hey," Brett took her face in his palm and brought her chin up. "Stop saying that. You aren't a failure. You've never failed at anything in your life. You're a fucking champion. Even your team." Brett trailed off as he said this, all too aware that the team was going to have a tough time this year with Hunter gone. He gulped, aware that he'd brought up a sore subject.

"I'm sorry," Madi said again.

"I want you to erase that phrase from your vocabulary. If anyone is sorry during all this, it has to be me. But we *have* to stop apologizing to each other, ok?"

Madi nodded. "You're right."

"Now, c'mon, we're in Cancun. No more tears. No more regrets. The day is stunning, and I wanna go to the beach."

Madi scowled, looking off and wiping at his wet shirt. "I'm still on my period."

"Well, I'm sure Val has tampons in a bathroom somewhere," Brett offered, getting a blush out of Madi. "Besides, we'll stay longer so you can enjoy it all the more, alright?"

Madi grinned, her mood a little lighter than it'd been in weeks.

"Why don't you go change, and I'll make us some smoothies to take out there with us?" he poked at her side, gently tickling her and she laughed.

When she acquiesced, he popped up and made them hearty smoothies with banana, kale, pineapple and mango, adding almond milk and vanilla powder along with some dragon fruit and oatmeal.

Brett ran up and changed into his swim trunks before Madi finally came down, hat on her head, a book in her hands and a towel over her arm. Her tall, tan frame was clad in a turquoise bikini that accentuated her ample curves and a pair of brown leather sandals, and he grinned.

"Damn lady, you are sexy," he simpered, getting a swat and an eye roll from her. He grabbed the smoothies and out they went to enjoy this amazing Cancun day they'd been blessed with.

"Sexy and bloated and *not* pregnant," she grumbled once they'd set their towels down on the sand.

"Hey, I can remedy that if you'd like." He winked again. She looked at him thoughtfully and his brows went up, then they both broke out into laughter.

Brett couldn't think of anything more perfect and as he looked down at Madi's bare belly, he imagined his baby growing there and smiled back at the woman who held his heart forever in her hands.

MADISON SPENT the next three days enjoying the beaches of Cancun and the food that chef Marcel came and made her and Brett for dinner. They spent their mornings working out and at the beach. They'd take long naps after a light lunch and a movie, then swim in the pool before a scrumptious dinner; tonight was fish tacos and Madi couldn't wait.

Brett elbowed her on the couch as they watched *The Predator*, one of their favorites.

"There should totally be a female predator. She'd be hot."

"Eww, gross. What would be hot about a female predator?" Madi wrinkled her nose.

"For one, it would be a bad-ass predator with boobs."

"I worry about you sometimes, Zeus. I think you need a woman in the worst way."

"Oh you do, huh?" The grin he gave her made her heart race. "You got someone in mind?"

He'd always been handsome, achingly so with his light brown hair and piercing emerald eyes, big smile, and even bigger body. He was the best features of both Channing Tatum and David Boreanaz... their big brother, on steroids, and with one of the best arms in the NFL.

Brett "Brickhouse" McFadden had stolen her heart long ago. That was until he'd broken it in two one night at a college party.

IT'D BEEN a fun night at the frat party at Omega Chi, drinking and dancing with her girls. Madi had decided she was finally gonna go for the gusto and show Brett how she felt after all the years of pining for him but being too afraid to make the first move. What if she was wrong? What if he didn't feel the same way? She'd gotten tired of waiting and decided she was gonna get hammered—or at least act like she was—and just do it; do what she'd been waiting to do for far too long, what she'd waited on him to do but he hadn't. Tonight was the night.

"Let's get out of here," she said and led him out the door.

He came willingly, and Madi made sure to sway all the way back to Delta Epsilon house, her sorority, so that he'd have a reason to touch her, hold her upright, and get her back to her dorm. She'd paid her roommate off so they'd have the place to themselves, at least long enough to make out, she hoped.

Madi hiccupped and giggled, and leaned into his broad, muscular chest as he opened her door. Brett was strong, so strong and tall. He towered over her, dwarfing her despite her own height of five-eight.

He sighed heavily as he pulled her into the room, closed the door behind them, and helped her to the bed.

She pulled him with her as she "fell" and her nose lingered at his chest. She inhaled him, loving his masculine scent. "Mmm," she moaned as her hands moved from his pecs to his waistline, fingers hooking through the loops of his jeans. Her face came up and she stared into his green eyes as he braced one hand by her head, keeping his weight off her.

"Damn, Sunflower, you're trashed," he scowled.

"Are you mad, Cap?" she asked him. Cap, short for captain, was her nickname for her favorite QB ever.

"No, I'm not mad, Madi. I'm glad you're here with me and not some jerk who'd just hurt you right now," he grumbled and attempted to pull his weight off her. She quickly wrapped her legs around his waist, stilling him, and arched her hips into his, feeling a hardness between them. She internally squealed, the squeal of victory.

"Mmm," she moaned again, "me too."

He visibly shuddered as she rubbed herself against his erection, mesmerized by the feel of it digging into her upper thigh. She'd never felt one before and was incredibly curious at its shape and size.

"M-Madi, you can't do that." He groaned aloud.

"Why not?"

The way he sighed and closed his eyes as she continued made her entire body shiver in electric spikes. She felt her sex awaken and his eyes darkened as she bit into her lip. He licked his lips, and she knew now was the time to act. She leaned into his chest and planted her lips on his.

The growl that escaped his throat was beastly and only spurred her desire on as her hand moved up his chest to his jaw and into his hair. His plump lips kissed hers back, much to her delight. She angled her head, deepening the kiss and thrusting her tongue into his mouth. Madi stroked her tongue across Brett's and when she did, she realized she'd started something she wasn't sure she was ready for.

The reserved Brett was gone and, in his place, a feral tiger prowled eager for his kill. Another deep growl hit his chest, and she felt it rumble as she gripped his shirt in her fist. His tongue moved rapidly across hers as he *kissed her like a man starved. He stretched his body out atop her own, pressing her into the mattress of her twin bed. Another moan hit her lips as he captured the back of her head in his palm and his lips and tongue tortured hers in an erotic dance of liquid electricity that jolted through her veins relentlessly.*

They were kissing—passionately, hungrily—and he was loving it as much as she was; she'd never been happier. He was insatiable as his tongue made love to hers. When she pulled back for a breath, she gasped as his hand grabbed for her breast and kneaded it with eager fingertips. Her body was on fire and she wanted to be engulfed by it, by him.

"Oh Brett," she whimpered as his mouth took hers again. "Yes, baby, I want you. I want..." she trailed off as he pulled back suddenly and abruptly.

His eyes were sad, regretful, distant as he began to pull his body from her own. She gripped him, feeling bereft as he began to untangle her legs from his waist.

"Madi, no. Stop! We can't do this right now."

The crushing pain that ripped through her being threatened to destroy her as she swallowed down her disappointment. She'd been wrong about how he felt about her. He didn't want her. Not like this. He was pushing her away. He was rejecting what she'd selflessly just offered up to him. He'd put her safely back into the friendzone, where she belonged. And her heart completely shattered.

He seemed to sense it and asked, "Are you ok? Are you gonna be sick? I'm sorry. I shouldn't have taken advantage of you, angel. I just—" he stopped talking and cupped her cheek. "I'll go now. Get some sleep, ok?" He popped up off the bed quickly, adjusting himself and looking completely miserable.

As he left her on her bed still reeling, he took her last shred of hope with him.

THAT WAS EIGHT YEARS AGO, and the pain of that rejection still swamped her.

"Madi," Brett's voice called to her and the light caress of his fingertips lit something back to life within her. How could his touch still do that to her? And with her being recently widowed? She felt guilty for it, didn't understand it, didn't understand her heart. Hadn't she been hurt enough? Hadn't she survived enough pain? Now her body had decided it wanted to go back down a road that'd been a dead end. She was angry all the sudden and didn't know why or how to respond to these yearning feelings she was having—yet again—for her best friend of twenty years.

His stroking on her skin made her sex tingle, and she moaned aloud. He stopped and gaped at her. "Am I hurting you?" he asked, pulling his hand from her arm.

Oh, dear lord, I really am *losing my mind.* "Uh, um, no, I uh, I think I just...I must be sore from our workout earlier."

Brett frowned, doubtfully. It hadn't been a strenuous workout or one she wasn't used to, but she played it off. She giggled even through a blush. "I guess I'm softer than I thought. A week in bed will do that, huh?" She shrugged.

"C'mon now, Wonder Woman. You got an image to uphold." He winked and again she felt herself swooning internally. *Holy shit, what's wrong with me?*

It could be that she missed being touched and held and kissed; having an attractive man around made her miss the physical side of Hunter. Or her feelings for Brett, the feelings she thought she'd tapped down years ago, were resurfacing. That thought scared her. She didn't know if she could handle the rejection again. Her heart couldn't take any more pain. *So, don't put yourself in a position to get hurt,* her inner strength demanded.

Just as she stilled her frayed nerves, the doorbell rang. She frowned at Brett, who smirked.

"Maybe Marcel forgot his key." Brett shrugged.

Madi looked at her phone; it was too early for Marcel. She pulled the blanket from her legs and stood.

The doorbell rang again as she strode down the hallway to the front foyer. She pulled the door open and gasped as she saw Travis Redmond and Skyla Larson grinning at her.

Madi covered her hands over her mouth in surprise and turned to see Brett coming around her side to face her, grinning from ear to ear.

"Oh my…"

"Surprise!" Travis and Sky said in unison.

"I invited them down. Sky had a couple days off from the trial, so they said they would come down and keep us company." Brett propped himself at the pillar next to the door.

Madi began to cry even as Sky launched herself at her, pulling Madi in for a tight hug. Madi squeezed her back, glad to see her friend. It had been since the funeral; she couldn't remember what she'd last said or if she'd even been cordial to her then. It seemed so long ago.

"The Mexican sun becomes you, lady," Sky said and pulled back, rubbing Madi's tanned arms.

"She's only sayin' that 'cause she's a ginger and can't tan." Travis joked and kissed Madi's cheek as he pulled her in for a hug.

"Watch it, Ares," Sky scolded. Travis smirked, sharing an intimate moment with his woman that wasn't lost to Madi and Brett. Madi envied their familiar exchange, feeling even more melancholy that she was on her period. Damn, her emotions were all over the place today.

"Come in, guys. Oh, I'm so glad you're here."

Sky entered the foyer and Travis lugged a duffle bag behind him, setting it down before they all moved into the living room.

"That view never gets old, does it, Zeus?" Travis motioned to the wall of glass in front of them.

"Oh, we're back to the god names again? My bad," Brett stated, rolling his eyes.

"This is our year, man. Gotta start early."

Madi felt a pang of regret seize her stomach and looked away even as Sky gave Travis a look. Sky gripped her arm and pulled her into the living room, away from the guys who were walking over to the bar.

Sky sat Madi down onto the couch and pulled her back into a hug. Madi reveled in the comfort she felt from the friend she'd only had for a few months. The girls had connected quickly after meeting one another the Sunday after Thanksgiving, forming a close bond.

"How are you, really?" Sky asked and rested her hand on Madi's arm as she pulled back.

"I started my period on Tuesday." Madi looked down, trying to hold the tears back again. Sky knew that she and Hunter had been trying to have a baby and would understand her disappointment better than Brett ever could.

"Oh, honey, I'm so sorry." Sky squeezed her again and let Madi cry on her shoulder. She did for a time before finally pulling back.

"I'm sorry, I'm not trying to spoil—"

"Hey, I'm here to be your friend, comfort, sounding board, anything you need. I'm sorry I've been MIA. This trial has been chaotic."

Giovanni Geraci's trial started the week after Hunter's death, and Sky had been in the courtroom nearly the whole time, Brett had told Madi. Madi knew what getting the crime boss charged meant to Skyla and Travis too. She nodded that she understood, despite that she didn't—not really. She'd seen court cases on television but had no idea the level of work involved in building a case.

Sky wiped the tears from Madi's cheeks and smiled at her. "Have you at least enjoyed getting away?"

Madi nodded and smiled. "It's beautiful here. How do Val and Linc ever leave?"

"Speaking of Linc and Val, they'll be here tomorrow to spend the day," Trav said from the bar as he poured himself a scotch. "They didn't wanna overstep; figured the boys would drive us all crazy if they stayed too long."

"Oh, nonsense. They're precious," Madi answered.

"Precious, demons, translates the same in any language." Travis winked, and Madi knew he was only kidding, he loved those twins like they were his own. "Val's words, actually."

"I think we need a girl's day when you get back home, Madi. Val needs a day. I say we let the boys babysit, go to lunch, and get mani/pedis," Sky offered with a wink over at her man.

"Fireball, you say the word and I'll play Mr. Mom. If that'll start the train rollin', I'm down. I can't wait to work on making Travis Jr." The lust that oozed from his eyes as he looked back at Skyla made Madison's uterus ache. Madi knew Sky was giving him a look, but she averted her gaze to keep the pain from ripping through her again. Travis didn't know, she couldn't fault him.

"What are you guys watchin'?" Sky asked, pulling the conversation in a different direction as she looked at Arnold Schwarzenegger shooting through the jungle on TV.

"Ah, we can go back out to the beach. You guys just got here. Let's go enjoy the day. We can watch TV anytime." Madi smiled and stood.

"Sounds good to me," Travis said. "Which room you want us in?" He asked Brett who suddenly looked back at Madi, a look akin to fear in his eyes that she didn't understand. He'd been acting different lately, and she couldn't pinpoint it. He was her best friend, and since Hunter died, things were just different between them. She was going to have to have a serious talk with him at some point, a talk they should've had a very long time ago.

Brett pointed to the room he'd been sleeping in. The housekeeper had just changed the sheets so they could've had either one, as far as Madi was concerned. But Brett was always putting her before himself, he always had, and she smiled back at him, thanking him without words. He grinned back and followed Travis up the staircase, presumably to move his things to Madi's room.

They'd slept together many times before now; they'd simply do so again for the next couple nights. Although, Madi's rapid heart rate stated it was going to be different this time. At least, for her anyway.

CHAPTER FIVE

"So, you told her yet?" Travis asked as they sat on the beach, sun beating down on them.

The girls were in the ocean, jumping the waves that crested in the distance.

"Told her what?" Brett asked wearily.

"You know *what*, Brett, don't be coy."

"You should tread lightly, Travis," Brett growled beneath his breath.

"Oh c'mon, man. I'm not tryin' to overstep here."

"Then you'll know that life is about timing as much as anything else, and *now* isn't the time!" Brett spat, whipping his sunglasses off.

"Easy there, Zeus."

"Stop fuckin' calling me that."

"Why?"

Because it makes me think of Hunter, he wanted to scream. Hunter who'd been thrown in his face far too much over the last three days. It was enough that he'd practically killed the man by being in the wrong seat at the wrong time. Now Brett was trying to pick up the pieces Hunt had left behind, including consoling the widow whom he'd failed to knock up. Brett was paying for that, too.

You selfish bastard. You had to go and die and leave me your messes to clean up, Brett wanted to shout to the sky. Brett felt a storm brewing, for he knew it was only a matter of time before the media caught wind of what happened back in Vegas last June, and when they did, he would be paying for even more. "You reap what you sow," his mother had always told him. So then why was Brett being punished for Hunter's fuck-ups?

"Hey bud, c'mon. I just see it on both your faces." Travis shoved Brett's shoulder lightly.

"See what?"

"Need. Want. Pain."

"Her fuckin' husband just died. She just found out she didn't conceive his child because she started her period three days ago. What am I supposed to do? Just waltz right in and have my way with her like none of that matters? No, I can't. No matter how much I want to."

"You love her."

"Yes, and I have for the last twenty damn years; that changes nothing. I'm not gonna be her rebound guy because that's exactly what would happen if I made a move right now. Besides, how the hell did you know, anyway?" Brett grumbled.

Travis looked him over and shrugged. "It's not that hard to see, especially now that I know what love is. What happened between you two? How did Hunter even come into the picture if you knew her first?"

Brett didn't wanna discuss this, not with Travis who'd never understood love until now. He looked into the distance, beyond the girls laughing in the surf, back to when he was a teenager, when his love for Madison Hope Taylor had been prominent and promising. Neither of them had dated anyone else, but they hadn't really dated each other either. They were good kids, Christian kids, growing up with big hopes and dreams. They were inseparable, always hanging out, always together. They never had to worry about the other dating because everyone just assumed they were together—and neither of them had ever bothered to confirm nor deny it.

Then it all changed come college, and Brett failed to make his move. He'd realized after their night in her dorm when they'd made out and he'd stopped her from going further, that something had changed. Madi was different with him, distant with him. And before he'd gotten the chance to even talk with her about it, Hunter was moving in and taking her away from him. It had all happened so fast.

"Why didn't you stop them from getting married if that's how you felt all along?"

It was as if Travis was reading his thoughts; how did he know? Brett sighed heavily and pulled his ball cap off, running a hand through his hair. "Fuck! Because I thought she loved him and was happy. Who was I to take that away from her? She'd never told me she loved me—not like that anyway. I just... I thought it better to have her for my friend than nothing at all. What if I told her how I felt, and she thought I was nuts and cut ties with me? At least at a distance I could still love her and have her in my life, even if it wasn't exactly where I wanted her to be. I know it doesn't make sense to *you* but, at the time, it was my best option."

"You got comfortable."

"Comfortable? *Fuck* no. I've never been comfortable. You think I'm ok with this?" Brett growled again, but it finally felt good to get it all out and in the open. He'd kept his feelings bottled inside for far too long.

"I know you aren't; it's written all over your face. That's why I'm saying something about it."

"Alright, Casanova, you're so good with all this shit, what would you do? Did you push Skyla into something you knew she wasn't ready for to serve yourself? Would you disregard it all, knowing she isn't mentally ready?"

"No, but a nudge in the right direction always helps," Trav smirked.

But Brett wasn't Travis. He knew Madi, better than anyone else did; he'd known her his entire life. She needed time to grieve for her loss. She needed space. She didn't need Brett confessing his undying love and forcing himself on her right now. It would be a mistake, and Brett had waited far too patiently for far too long to blow it—all because he simply couldn't wait any longer.

"Honestly Brett, I'm not being pushy. I just know what I see and you deserve to be happy," Trav insisted.

It had been so long since Brett had felt happiness, he didn't know what it was anymore. He'd thrown himself into the game, for if he couldn't be happy in love he could be happy with his accomplishments at least. Then Hunter had died, and his life felt like it had been upended and frozen. The emotions running through him were heightened to spiked edges. He now had Madi to consider over everything else. Not that he hadn't prior to that but, for the last five years, she'd been Hunter's direct responsibility; now, suddenly, she was his.

After Madi and Hunt had gotten married, Brett didn't call her as much as he used to or text or come by—which had been easier when they were in Denver. Once they'd moved home to Atlanta, he'd been there and, of course, had seen her almost daily at the complex over these last five years, but he'd tried very hard to give her and Hunter the space they deserved. Brett had always felt Hunter's subtle jealousy of his and Madi's relationship, despite his and Hunter's own closeness.

To say that Brett and Hunter had a hot and cold relationship would be an accurate statement. But how could another man really love the man who coveted his wife? Even if they had been like brothers. Hunter's intolerance of Brett's infatuation with Madi had become more and more evident as time had gone on, causing Brett to be even more cautious with her this past year.

Now, Brett could have a clean slate, with Hunter gone. He and Madi could go back to the way things had been, before Hunter... but they couldn't, not really. Not with Hunter's shadow always hanging over them both...and Brett realized that was the real problem here.

Even with Hunter gone, he'd never be truly *gone*.

And Brett hated that he hated that.

"Maybe it's *me* who should be committed," Brett stated and covered his face with his palms, misery etching his heart.

"Aww c'mon, man. Don't say that. He was your friend. He'd give you his blessing where Madi's concerned. What kinda selfish prick would he be if he didn't? I mean he could be a prick, but—"

"He did," Brett confessed, "give me his blessing, I mean. On his death bed. He knew, all along he knew. And yet he was still my friend. Fucked up, right? Could you be friends, no *best* friends, with me even if I was head over heels in love with Skyla? Tell the truth."

Travis gritted his teeth, air hissing through as he pulled in a breath. "Yeah, I'd probably wanna beat the living hell out of you, honestly."

"Exactly!"

"But you knew Madi before he did, so he kinda didn't have a choice in the matter. If he hated you, it wouldn't have made a difference, Madi was your BFF first. He *had* to accept you." Travis shrugged, his logic sound enough.

That was probably true. Madi had chosen not to cut Brett out of her life when she and Hunter hit it off, so Hunter *had* to accept Brett's relationship with her. Knowing Hunter, he'd kept Brett close out of necessity. What was that old saying about keeping friends close but enemies closer? Even still, Hunt could've forced Madi's hand—maybe he did at some point; but their friendship never seemed to suffer during Madi and Hunter's relationship of seven years, despite the imposed distance between the two of them. Perhaps it was Madison that bridged the gap, the glue that kept them all linked. It didn't much matter now, either way. Brett simply had to be glad that Hunter cared for him despite his secret love for the man's wife.

Brett remembered Hunter's dying words, "*I knew, and yet I was still going to have her."* Did that make him selfish? Yes. Hunt had known, and he hadn't cared. He'd known Brett was the right match, too—he'd said that also. Brett had Hunter's blessing, so why was he still so tore up about moving in and doing what he should've done all along?

"Know what I think?" Travis asked quickly as he saw the girls coming out of the water toward them arm-in-arm, laughing. Brett's brows arched in question. "I think you need to take Hunt completely out of the equation. He's gone now, buddy. Do what you would've done had he not been here. Because he sure as shit would've done the same if it had been you who'd died instead."

As much as Travis was right, it stung. Hunt, as much as Brett loved the jerk, was a selfish dick. If Brett had died and the roles had been reversed, there wouldn't be anything stopping him from taking what he'd always wanted if he were in Brett's shoes.

"That's true, but there's one thing you forget, *Ares,*" Brett grated.

"What's that, *Zeus?*"

"I'm nothing like Hunter. I've always put my queen first, and I always will."

"MARCEL, another delicious feast. I must say, I think I'll kidnap you and take you home with me," Madi cooed to their talented chef.

Marcel laughed and kissed Madi's cheeks, getting a giggle from her. "Muchas gracias! You flatter me, señora McFadden."

Damn that sounded good, Madison McFadden, but Madi was blushing. "Oh, no, I— were not…"

"You no married?" Marcel looked surprised even as Brett's big palm rested on Madi's back. "You two are perfectos juntos."

"Right. I said the same thing, amigo." Travis winked at them, and Brett rolled his eyes at him.

"Oh, you too, señor Redmond—pájaros del amor." Marcel pointed to Travis and Sky getting a blush out of them. He blew them kisses and moved back to flip the fish for their next round of tacos.

The food here was as amazing as the view and Madi had indulged on several skinny margaritas tonight, feeling her lips starting to numb. It was perfect outside with the warm, Caribbean breeze blowing as they listened to the sound of fresh fish charring on the grill, the ocean lulling them in the distance.

Madi smiled up at Brett who returned it. He seemed lighter too now that Travis and Sky were here—or it could be all the Coronas he'd been throwing back—either way it was good to see Brett break out of his serious-Captain-America shell. She nudged him and kissed his cheek, lingering a little longer than usual to inhale his aftershave, letting her nose hover at his scruffy jawline. He shivered and her body tingled as if striking an electric wire.

"I'm planning to propose to Skyla soon. Any ideas, Ms. CEO?" Travis asked as Sky walked inside to go to the restroom.

"*Already?*" Brett asked, surprised.

"Yes, already! Dammit. Y'all know that woman has me all kinds of crazy. I am *not* letting that sexy little spitfire get away before putting a ring on it. Beyoncé warns about that, you know? And don't say, 'She already has a promise ring.' That's not enough."

Madi giggled. It was adorable how Travis had gone from suave, I-need-nobody, bad boy Travis Redmond to swooning, love-struck Ares; it was endearing. There was hope for mankind, after all.

"Well, you know I'd say do it from the heart and not be extravagant, but I know you," Madi quipped.

"Yes, you do. And you know I gotta make it big and show-boaty. I was thinking of doing it at one of the games."

"Dude, seriously?" Brett scoffed.

"What?"

"That's so cliché."

"I don't care. I want it to be in front of millions... What?" he asked, looking at Madi.

"You know Sky isn't gonna like being the center of attention like that. The courtroom is one thing, but millions of fans is quite another."

"You also know how insecure she is. If I do it that way, she has no doubts as to my love for her," Travis reasoned.

He had a point. "Alright then do whatever you want. She's gonna love whatever you cook up, Chef Ares."

"Uh, that's why I asked for advice. You're a woman, you know these kinds of things."

"Alright, well, think more on it and get back to me with some ideas," Madi whispered before Sky came back into ear shot.

"So, you guys wanna scuba tomorrow? There's a shipwreck just down the beach a-ways?" Brett asked just as Marcel brought over another delicious-looking batch of grilled fish tacos topped with jicama slaw, chipotle mayo, and mango salsa. Everyone dug in and moaned aloud, savoring the sweet and spicy melding together in beautiful harmony.

"Jeez, Marcel! I love this man right here, but you're giving me serious doubts about matrimony." Sky licked the juice running down her fingers and moaned again as she bit into her taco.

"Hey!" Travis pouted and got them all laughing. "No fair, Aphrodite," he whimpered into her ear and began whispering, getting giggles as his big hand moved over Sky's bare arm.

Madi smiled at the love they shared and how they seemed so in tune with one another. Had she and Hunt been like that? Had their attraction to one another been that hot? She wasn't sure and the realization that her memories were starting to fade away hit her gut hard. She couldn't remember the taste or touch of Hunter's lips on her own. She couldn't remember exactly how he smelled; she couldn't remember the feel of his hands touching her. She gulped her last sip of the margarita down and stood to go make another, getting looks from the three of them as she did so.

"You ok, Mad?" Travis asked.

Madi nodded her head even as Brett stood. "I'm fine. I'm just gonna make another margarita."

"I'll do it." Brett began to take the glass from her but she pulled it away and shook her head.

"I got it. It's fine. You sit, finish your taco."

Madi turned, heading back through the screen door and into the kitchen. She poured some ice into a shaker and began measuring out tequila, triple sec, and Grand Marnier. She was adding the lime and fresh sours when she noticed Brett watching her from the door-frame. She gulped as he took a step forward, and she shook the shaker.

"You ok?"

"Sure."

She wouldn't be ok for a time, she knew. She was going to have to get used to her new normal, living the life of a twenty-eight-year-old widow. As Brett had told her time and again, it was going to take time, one day at a time. Time. Time. Time. It was all about damn time. Time was a thief. An enigma. Something that was relative; it could never be borrowed, some had too much of it and others would never have enough. It was never on anyone's side, and it healed all wounds. Time, to Madi, was an unmet promise. If she never heard the word again, that would be just fine with her.

"Does it bother you having them here?"

"No, why would it?" Madi frowned, not understanding why Brett would ask her that.

"They remind you of what you lost."

"*Everything* reminds me of what I've lost. I'm not envious of their love, Brett. They have something most people only dream about. I'm happy for them. Very happy."

"Me too. But that doesn't mean I don't want it, too."

The future. He was speaking to her about the future. Why? He'd never seemed interested in talking about marriage and children and all that before. Why was he doing so now?

"You'll find it, Brett. I'm certain. You're handsome, you're affec-tionate, you're giving. Any woman would love to have those qualities in a partner."

"You'll have love again too, Sunflower. Don't give up on it."

She frowned again, not understanding why he was saying these things. She cleared her throat as she poured the final margarita into her glass and took a sip. "So, you wanna go scuba-diving tomorrow?" she asked, wanting to steer the subject away from serious things.

"It might be cool to explore a shipwreck, don't you think?"

She grinned and nodded. "Maybe we should take a run in the morning after all these, huh?" She pointed to the drink and Brett nodded.

"I'm down."

"I don't mean to be a spoilsport, but I think I'm gonna go take a hot bath and go to bed."

"You aren't a spoilsport. Enjoy your bath. I'll be up shortly." He pulled her hand to his lips and kissed her knuckles. It made her shiver, but she tried not to let him see it.

Half an hour later, she'd soaked until she was pruney, trying to relax her mind and name all the things she had left despite her husband's death—Brett, her friends, her family, her job. All the things she loved. She was starting to go from the denial and depression phase of her grieving process and swing into the acceptance part. Although she felt she hadn't quite turned the curve yet, it wasn't as far away as she'd originally thought. Coming here to Cancun was a good idea, getting out of that house was a good idea, Brett had been right. Fresh air cleared her mind; while her heart was still heavy missing Hunter, she felt lighter. Her mood could be contributed to the margaritas she'd housed and the hot bath but, whatever the case, she felt better and her eyes less puffy than they'd been in days.

Madison got out of the tub and dried off, applied a coconut lotion of Val's she'd left there and inhaled it, loving the scent as it invaded her nostrils. It was the epitome of beach, sand, and sun and made her smile. She dressed in the shorts and tank top she'd left out for herself before exiting the bathroom.

She stopped dead in her tracks when she saw a half-naked Brett McFadden standing beside the bed. He'd been in the process of undressing when she interrupted. She gulped but couldn't still her eyes from taking in his massive frame: broad chest, toned arms, sculpted torso. Her eyes moved to the unzipped pants now falling down his legs and blue boxers, boxers that looked tiny on his muscular thighs and tapered hips. Her eyes came back to his chest. She'd forgotten how big he was, or better yet, not realized how big he was—*he'd not been this big in college, had he?*

Madi realized she was gaping and focused her eyes on the painting of surfboards to her left. God, how had she missed all those bulking muscles of his, those chiseled bands of thick coils covering every manly inch of him? And why was she suddenly so aroused?

It's because I'm on my period, she told herself. *I'm lonely, I—*

She'd only been with one man, her husband. And now he was gone, and she was simply admiring another man's physique. A man who also happened to be her and her husband's best friend. A man she'd once loved. A man she still wanted—*Oh lord*. Who couldn't want a stud that looked like that? She'd be crazy not to want him.

"I-I'm sorry," she stammered, realizing Brett hadn't moved, not even an inch.

"It's ok," cool and collected Brett said. How was he not as rattled as she was? How was that even possible? Brett moved into the bed and pulled the covers up, but only to his waist—*Damn him.* "I'm in."

Oh shit! He's gonna sleep in only *his boxers?* Madi's mind reeled. What would happen if he cuddled her? She would feel those hard muscles on his torso naked against her back. Had they slept that way the last few times? And how in God's *sweet* name could she possibly not remember!

"You comin', Madi?" Brett questioned. Madi was sure she appeared to be having a stroke, from an outsider's perspective, blinking rapidly and freezing in one spot only to move to another.

"Yeah, I uh, I thought I forgot something."

"All you need is me, Sunflower, and I'm right here."

She frowned again and looked over at him. He continued to say these things that confused her, things she didn't understand.

"Mad, baby, are you alright?" he asked again and turned, the big muscles in his throwing arm rippling with his movement.

I want to fuck the shit out of my best friend right now. No, I am indeed not alright.

She took a deep breath in and moved toward the bed. It was nerves, hormones, lack of sleep, trauma, guilt, grief. She ran through an entire list in her head of all the things this was, the emotions she'd been feeling since Hunter died, that's all it was, new emotions, new life, new...

But as Brett moved in behind her and pulled her into him, she felt peace, a serene knowing in her heart that she was right where she was supposed to be, in his solid, comforting arms.

Her thoughts quieted, her breathing slowed and she surrendered to the valiant knight who'd rescued her long ago.

"Hi, I'm Madi," a seven-year-old Madison Hope Taylor smiled to the tall, handsome boy. He looked nervous but handsome all the same. No-nonsense emerald eyes, light brown hair, lips tight. His face was oval-shaped, and she immediately pointed to the ball cap atop his head. It was their logo, the Gladiators, the team her father now owned and had for the last month. "I have one just like it."

That got a smile out of the quiet boy, whose perfectly straight white teeth made him even more handsome.

"Madi, this is Brett, Drew's oldest son. You'll be seeing a lot of one another. Drew's going to be working alongside me as our general manager."

"Will he go to school with me?" Madi asked.

"He will indeed. He's going to be in the second grade at Chesham Elementary," Mr. Drew stated with a smile.

"That's where I go!"

"I knew you'd be thrilled," her father said.

Brett looked up at his father and gave him a frown. *"Dad, she's—she's a girl."*

Drew and her father had a good laugh about that. "Son," Drew stated, "one day, you're gonna like girls, a whole lot. I promise."

"You don't like girls?" Madi's brows furrowed. Her father stepped up behind her and took her shoulders, but Brett answered her with, "It's not that. I just—"

"Brett," Madi's father ruffled the tall boy's hair. "Why don't you two go out to the field and throw the ball around? Let Madi show you what she likes to do for fun." Her father winked at the boy, who scowled back at him. Her father handed him a football, and he took it, wearily.

She and Brett moved off then, out of her father's office, and she led them to the elevators that took them out to the tunnel, the locker rooms, the weight room and the practice field. Madi already loved it here. It was her favorite place to be. She got upset if her father came here without her. She knew she couldn't come when she was at school, but she was here every second she could be.

Madi was different than her five-year-old sister, Brooke. Brooke was girly, liking dolls and makeup, and tea parties. Madi was a tom-boy; she preferred pants to dresses, hats and ponytails to curls, and would rather play football than babies any day—she hated playing babies, and that's all Brooke ever wanted to do.

"Whoa," Brett said as they passed through the locker rooms. "This is so cool."

"I know. Just wait til you see the field. It's huge."

"So, you can throw a football?" Brett asked doubtfully as they came nearer to the mouth of the tunnel leading out to the practice field.

Madi gave him a little laugh. "Yeah, can you?"

Brett gave her a laugh in return. "Yeah. My dad says I got a good arm."

"Maybe one day you'll play here, for the Gladiators." She grabbed the football, elbowed him, and ran off in the direction of the thirty-yard line. "Can you catch?" she asked and giggled again, launching the ball towards him.

He caught it roughly against his chest and looked at her like she'd just given him all the candy in the world. "Wow."

"Just 'cause I'm a girl don't mean I can't do what you can." She sassed and planted her hands on her hips.

It took him a minute to respond. He grinned a crooked grin and gripped the ball in his hand, lining the laces up and threw it back to her. He had what her dad had called "good form," making the ball fly in a spiraling straight line. Madi took a few steps back, shuffling quickly, and jumped, catching the ball against her chest with an, "Umph." She fell to the ground hard. Her tumble and the sound of the ball hitting her caused Brett to run over to her and extend his hand out.

"Oh my gosh, are you ok? I'm sorry I didn't mean to—"

Madi laughed, slapped his hand away and stood. "Got it. And that's a fair catch, by the way. I maintained possession." She cocked her brow, daring him to argue, using the words she'd heard her father use to impress the boy.

Brett laughed. He was pleased with her. The boy who didn't like girls was happy with her. It made her heart fill with joy.

"Wanna do it again?" she asked.

"Maybe we should do some tosses instead. I don't wanna hurt you."

"Pssh, you aren't gonna hurt me. Me and my daddy play catch all the time."

Brett seemed impressed with that and chucked her chin. "Ok, Jerry Rice. But let's run some routes, alright?"

"Ok." Madi jumped in glee and handed the ball over to him.

They played for a time, even getting a little physical with some tackles, but the boy seemed to enjoy her company so it made her happy. They had fun, and soon, the coach was calling them back in. Madi knew it was close to time for the players to come practice. She took Brett's hand as they entered the tunnel. She heard the noise before she saw the padded bodies coming at her but was too late to move. She was going to be hit, and there wasn't anything she could do.

She felt a tug on her hand and felt arms wrap around her as she crashed into Brett's chest. He tucked her head against him and turned, pressing her back to the wall of the tunnel, keeping them from being crushed by the giant football players entering the field. The noise of their running through the echoing tunnel seemed to go on forever before Brett pulled back some and looked down at her. Fear and relief painted his face—and she was sure her own. He gulped and ran a finger down her cheek.

"You-you saved my life. You're a hero," she said in awe of this boy who made her heart soar.

"That's what heroes do, right?" He winked, took her hand, and they headed back to her father's office.

CHAPTER SIX

Madi awoke to her phone ringing. It was Lathem Turner, their scout. She answered her phone on the third ring, "Hey, Scoop." He was called "Scoop" as he had a nose for scooping up the best catches. He'd found Pax and TJ two years prior, Langley last year.

"I got a guy you're gonna wanna look at, Madi. He's awesome. Fast. Strong. Gonna make a great fill-in for Hunter."

Madi's breath took. How had she forgotten that they'd have to fill his spot? Her heart raced, but she was able to keep her cool and her head about her. No tears came to her eyes. That had to be a good sign, right?

"Oh, um…yeah, great."

"I don't mean to spring this on you, but his agent called me first thing this morning. You can tell me to piss off. I know you're on vacation right now and probably not thinking about the team." Ha, she was always thinking about the team. It was her life and had been since she was seven.

"No, um, it's fine. If you think we should talk with him, then let's do so."

"Great. I already spoke to your father, and he wanted me to discuss it with you before we set anything up. His name is Quillan Layton; he was a TE for the Ravens."

"Yeah, I remember him. His wife died last year, right? And he left."

"Yes! But he's wanting to come back this year. And he's better than ever. His numbers at the Combine last month were impressive, Madi. I'm surprised someone hasn't already grabbed him up."

"Well then, talk to him and let's set up a meeting. You know I trust your judgement, Scoop."

"Good. Yes! I can't wait for you to meet him. He seems excited to get back to playing, and I think he'll make a great asset to the team we have now."

"That's great news. I'm glad we found someone who's got you so excited." Madi laughed. It felt good, really good to be able to talk about replacing her husband without being assaulted by anguish.

Lathem laughed on the other end of the line. "I know. But I'm telling ya, once you see him in action, *you're* gonna be the one excited. We're going to the Super Bowl this year, Madi. I feel it."

"I sure hope you're right. We got the talent, that's for sure."

"So, you want me to set something up for week after next? I'll inform him you're on vacation. I think he's taking his daughter to Disney World anyway, he said."

"Yeah, just let me know what time. We'll fly back before then. I need to get back to the complex soon anyway."

"I'm glad to hear it. And Madi, if you need anything…"

"Thanks, Lathem. I appreciate it."

She said her goodbyes and hung up the phone, feeling hopeful.

Brett stood by the window, arms crossed over his chest, his eyes questioning as Madi grinned up at him.

"Everything ok?"

"Yeah, Scoop found a replacement for Hunter." She tried not to let her voice waver when she said his name, but it did. Brett's reaction didn't help; his head fell and he looked upset. "Brett…"

"And you're ok with this?" he retorted as he looked back up at her, eyes narrowing.

"Well, I mean it's just a meeting. Of course I'm gonna see him in action and everything before we make the final decision."

"But you're ok with talking about this…so soon?"

"The draft will be here in a couple weeks, Brett. If we don't grab him up, someone else will. You know how it is."

Brett just nodded but Madi could see that he was still mulling it over. "Hey," she said as she shot up and stood in front of him. "Are *you* ok with this?"

"I'm fine. I just…"

"I know it's gonna be hard. I'm sorry." She rested her hand on his forearm and stroked him there lightly.

Brett gave her a weak smile. "Who?"

"Quillan Layton. He used to play for Baltimore."

"I remember him. Hell of a player. We won't regret signing him."

Madi smiled, and Brett returned it.

"You *sure* you're alright?" he asked again and moved to unfold his arms, a hand coming up to her cheek.

Madi simply nodded and smiled back, getting one out of Brett. "Let's take a run, then we'll go look for hidden treasure. I wanna know what it feels like to be a pirate."

With that Brett nodded and gave her a hearty laugh.

Hours later, Val and Linc were there with their adorable twin boys and everyone was on the beach, laughing, playing Nerf football, and listening to Bob Marley telling everyone to not worry and be happy. They all were simply enjoying this sunny day they'd been blessed with. The guys were sipping beers from the cooler, save for Linc, and the girls were drinking "mocktails." Madi knew Val didn't drink when Linc was around. He'd been an addict and alcoholic following the death of their daughter, Marly. When he'd given it up after trying to kill himself year before last, Val didn't permit the stuff in the house; she only drank when he didn't witness it. In her words, "If it's there, the temptation to pick it back up always will be." So, she'd eliminated that temptation. Although, Madi sensed that it wouldn't matter; Linc would never do anything to jeopardize what he had with Val and the baby boys he adored.

Madi and Brett had gone scuba-diving alone after their run this morning, leaving Trav and Sky the house to themselves—of which she was sure they'd done it on every counter, knowing those two. She hadn't found any treasure inside the old ship that rested in a watery grave fifty yards beneath the surface, save for an old Spanish coin. She'd been permitted to keep it, much to her delight. She was going to have it polished and appraised, not for monetary value, but for the fact that she loved history—especially when it came to nautical things. Exploring that shipwreck had been fun and a bit eerie. Seeing the ocean bed and sea life claim the centuries-old wreckage had been magical and a bit spooky. Madi had enjoyed every minute of it alongside her diving companion, who seemed to be as in awe of it as she had.

"Lennox, haul it over here, son. You need more sunscreen," Linc scolded even as he chased the cackling baby boy who was waddling toward his "Uncle Travis." His deep brown skin glistened in the bright sun that reflected off his neon green swim trunks.

Travis grabbed Len up and swung him around, making noises like an airplane, and getting giggles out of the adorable, curly-haired baby boy.

It was easy to laugh with the toddlers running around, all care-free and innocent. It lightened Madi's heart and even her mood, especially when Lofton crawled over to Brett and began pouring sand on his legs, getting a laugh out of the moodier one of the two twins. When Lofton leaned in to hug Brett, for no apparent reason, everyone gave an, "Awww."

"He never loves on anyone, save his mum, Brett. You should feel privileged," Valeria said, her Aussie, gold skin soaking up the rays beneath her white bikini.

Lofton surprised them further when he attempted to share his sippy cup with Brett, too. Even Brett gave a hearty laugh. Seeing him with the baby made Madi swoon even harder than she already had been. Once again, she was reminded of the fact that she was even further from having a child of her own with Hunter now gone. She was twenty-eight, soon to be twenty-nine, and her biological clock had begun to tick louder and louder. *Great timing too, by the way!*

"I'm sorry." Val patted Madi's leg as Brett and the men moved to the ocean to wash the sand off the boys, so Val could reapply their sunscreen. "We can go if they're bothering you. Sky told me about..."

Madi wiped the tears that ran down her face and vigorously shook her head. "No! Don't you dare. They're wonderful. I'm so glad y'all are here. They make me laugh and..."

"And cry!" Val stated pointing to her face. "C'mere you." Valeria pulled Madi in for a tight hug and kissed her cheek when she pulled back. "I'm sorry you aren't pregnant, Mad."

Madison shook her head and smiled at a frowning Skyla. "It's ok. Really. I'll be fine. I'm still on my period, so that doesn't help with these emotions." Madi fanned her face, trying to breathe.

"Why don't you ask Brett if he'll do the deed?" Sky winked over at Madi. "I don't think he would mind at all giving you a child." She looked over to Brett then, who was frowning back at Madi. "I swear, they have a language all their own."

"So, I've noticed. How long have you two been in love, Madi?" Val asked.

Madi literally scoffed. "What are you talking about?"

Sky rolled her eyes beneath a big straw hat planted atop her wavy, red hair, "Please! That man only sees you. How can you be so blind?"

"No, it's not like that. It's—"

"But it *is* like that. It always has been, hasn't it?" Val asked and patted Madi's arm. "It's alright. He'll confess in time, love. I'm sure he's simply biding his time."

"Want us to get you drunk so you can make your move on him? He's just itching for a reason to hike that sorry excuse for a skirt up and take you. Trust me, I know that look *all* too well." Sky bit into her lip as Travis made a kissy face back at her, his chiseled muscles rippling as he swung Lennox around like a rag doll.

"Gross," Madi feigned disgust, "I hope you two Lysol-ed the counters off after you *defiled* them."

"Of course, the table too. The couch was a bit harder to clean though." Sky winked and put her finger to her lips in a shush gesture.

"Wow, so it *is* true what they say about redheads," Val smirked over at Sky, who bobbed her brows.

"I dunno, blondes are supposed to have more fun," Sky stated back, flicking Val's blonde pony-tail, and they all laughed, even Madi.

"Seriously though, let's get them drunk so they can bone," Val insisted and handed Madi a pre-mixed margarita from the nearby Yeti cooler. "That's *exactly* what this Sheila needs. A good shag in the worst way."

"We could at least wait til she's off her period, Val." Sky wrinkled her nose. "But there *is* always shower sex." Sky rubbed her chin thoughtfully.

Madi couldn't remember the last time she'd had shower sex. The last several times she'd even done it, she'd had to monitor her temperature, ovulation, cycles, and plan it out like a football route. It had felt more like a trial for a lab than a sexual encounter. Madi frowned and looked down. "I dunno. It's not like it'd matter," she grumbled.

"What do you mean?"

"In college, I made a move on him. He didn't..." she gulped the disappointment down.

"Come again?" Sky asked, surprise lacing her voice.

"He, uh, well...we made out. It was hot. Really hot but then...he stopped."

"Well, there had to be a damn good reason for it," Val insisted, brows shooting up beneath her dark sunglasses.

"Well, I mean, I made him think I was drunk." Madi felt her cheeks flush as red as Sky's red bikini then.

"Why?" she asked and pulled at Madi's hand so she'd look at her.

"I was trying to get us away from the party. I wanted him *alone*," Madi confessed.

"Well, that's why he stopped, silly. He thought he was taking advantage of you."

"I dunno," Madi argued.

"Madison Thomas, look at me. As much of a gentleman as Brett is, he would *never* take advantage of you. I bet he always opens the door for you, holds an umbrella over your head, walks to your outside. He's probably even leery about his language in front of you, am I wrong?" Sky asked, and Madi shook her head. "There, ya see. He would never publicly grope you and, even behind closed doors, he wouldn't force himself on you if he thought you were shit-faced drunk!"

It all made sense; Sky was right. How had she ever been so stupid? She'd been so sure of how Brett felt about her that she'd underestimated his moral code. Of course he wouldn't allow their first time together to be a drunken roll in the hay.

"So, he's a good kisser, huh?" Val asked and shoved at Madi's shoulder.

"Oh, stop it. She's a recent widow; she needs some time."

And it was true; as handsome as Brett was, she wasn't ready to jump right into another relationship. It was too soon. The death of her husband was too new. She was still mourning him and would be for a while longer. But that didn't dampen the fact that there was hope for a future with Brett.

Madi smiled big for the first time in a long time. Her life wasn't over, as much as she'd told herself it was in the beginning. She wasn't going to be alone. She was going to be okay.

MUCH TO BRETT'S DISMAY, they left Cancun sooner than he thought Madi needed to. But her spirits seemed high and she seemed really excited to meet Quillan Layton, their potential new TE at week's end. Langley had seen him on television and called Brett, worrying about his position. Brett had reassured him; besides, it was out of his hands anyway. Just because Brett was the QB didn't mean he got to call the shots. Even Madi, as CEO, didn't have full run of everything —nor did her dad, the owner. Although they each had a fair amount of pull...and Brett did too, if he were being honest with himself.

Brett enjoyed his vacation with Madi; snorkeling, swimming, working out, and generally just having no set plans. But it was now April; off-season training would be starting, and it would be back to the grindstone. Practice would be on him soon enough, and Brett wanted to get back to what he loved—football.

It had been fun hanging out with Trav and Sky, Linc and Val and the babies even if they'd only stayed the weekend. Madi and Brett had spent the next six days alone, and Brett had silently gone back to his room when Trav and Sky left that Sunday. Madi seemed fine either way, which disappointed Brett a little. She also seemed more content than she had before they'd left for Cancun, something he was grateful for. He was glad he'd been right to bring her there, it was good for her mental health and well-being. She was better being away from the house that reminded her she was a widow, alone and childless.

Even now, he begged her to come back to his house with him. She kindly declined.

"I need closure, Brett. I'm ok now. I can take it from here."

Was she dismissing him? Had he missed his chance? Was she saying she didn't need him?

"I love you. Thank you for everything." Madi leaned in and kissed his cheek, lingering there for a time before taking his hand.

Why did this feel like she was saying goodbye? He gulped. And tried to stop himself from panicking. "I'll be around, if you need anything, call me."

"You know I will. I just need to be alone right now. I love you." She told him again.

"I love you, Sunflower. So very much." He pulled her to him for a tight hug and held her close, propelling his strength into her.

When she finally pulled back, Brett felt his heart fluttering. He'd been with her for weeks now, slept in the bed with her, had her close by, this was going to be difficult, not being with her constantly. She seemed to feel it too, and reluctantly let his hand go. She gave him a soft smile and turned, heading into the house. Brett had already taken her luggage up to her room, so he was left useless. He nodded and headed back to his vehicle.

He was leaving for California tomorrow to give a speech and film a commercial. He'd be there in LA for a few days before attending the mini-camp he'd scheduled for disabled kids next week back in Atlanta. He'd be missing Madison like crazy before he got to see her again.

He couldn't wait to see her again... God, he was pathetic.

CHAPTER SEVEN

Madi spent the next three days alone combing through Hunter's things, having multiple bawling sessions, and drinking wine at night as she watched sappy movies that reminded her of him. She knew her mom and sister—and Brett—were worried. Every one of them had texted her, including Val and Skyla, but she reassured them all that she was fine. And, she was; she just needed time to adjust and let go.

She and Brooke went to lunch the following day and for mani/pedis. Life was returning to normal, she could feel it. It had been over a month since Hunter was gone but each day was getting a little easier, her heart lighter, her head more focused.

On Saturday, she returned to Gladiators Headquarters and got hugs from all the staff there. They welcomed her back, and she felt good meeting with the new defensive coordinator, the rest of the coaches, and newest members of their organization who'd been called to their meeting that day. Her father and their GM, Josh O'Connell, were glad to have her back; they were eager for her meeting with Quillan Layton tomorrow, and she was too—eager and anxious. Now that the day was almost upon them, she was starting to feel her gut tighten to meet the man who might potentially replace Hunt.

Quil was a powerhouse; she'd seen his film highlights Scoop had gotten together. He looked promising as both a TE and a WR, and she knew he would fill either position well. His numbers were impressive as Lathem had said, eighty-five receptions for eleven hundred yards and eight touchdowns. He was going to be a force to be reckoned with.

"Another god of the gridiron," Madi said with a laugh. Now to figure out a title for him; she'd let the guys handle that for they were so good with the nicknames.

She went home and cried that night, talking to Hunter in their bed as if he were still with her. She told him how much she missed him, his laugh, his banter, even his cockiness. She felt lonely and alone. At one point, she considered calling Brett and begging him to come back. He'd been right, this house wasn't good for her, too many memories, too much left unspoken between her and Hunt. She'd gotten mad and yelled at Hunter then, letting her emotions run their course for, perhaps if she did, it would start the next stage of the grieving process.

Madi was late to work the following morning, feeling groggy and depleted, despite that Sundays weren't really her regular days in the off-season. She tried to keep her days in line with the players, Tuesdays being her off-days. She lived, ate, and breathed work. It was her life, and now it was what would keep her sane and grounded.

Her eyes were puffier than usual from the crying she'd done, her head foggy from the wine she'd consumed last night, and she wasn't as focused. She'd taken her time getting ready; showering longer, taking more time to apply her makeup, and stopping at Starbucks to get the largest coffee she could. Her secretary, Kathryn, just smiled at her as Madi strolled in, hiding behind a big pair of Oakley sunglasses.

She peeled them off as she approached her desk and sat down in her large leather executive chair. After logging onto her computer, she texted Quillan's agent, Chan, that she'd arrived and apologized for running behind.

Chan: No worries. We're on our way now. See you in ten.

Madi got on her phone, calling her father so he could be in attendance, too.

She was heading up the elevator to his office to greet him when her phone buzzed.

Brett: I'm home :-) Wanna do lunch?

Madi couldn't contain her smile and texted back with, "Absolutely! Meet me here at noon. :-*."

She hugged her father, who complemented her dress—a simple, crimson Vera Wang V-neck. She thanked him, and they entered the boardroom with just enough time to get seated before Quillan and Chan joined them.

She was unprepared for the six-foot-six-inch dreamboat clad in a gray suit and blue tie who walked through the door. She even came close to stumbling as she moved forward to shake his hand, but was able to right herself just in time to keep from launching herself into his chest.

Quillan Layton was tall, deeply tanned, dark, and gorgeous. He had eyes the color of caramel, jet black hair, thick eyebrows and a trim beard that covered a square jaw.

"Mr. Layton, it's a pleasure." Her father stated, looking up to the tight end.

"I assure you, Mr. Taylor, the pleasure is all mine." Quil shook her father's hand then turned to Madi, giving her a bright smile that made her knees weak.

"This is my daughter, our CEO and VP, Madison Thomas."

"Wow, you're even more beautiful in person, Mrs. Thomas. I was so sorry to hear about Hunter. Truly."

Madi's heart tore at his words. Would she ever get used to hearing people apologize for the death of her husband? She shook it off and smiled back. "Thank you, Mr. Layton. And my condolences on the death of your wife, as well." She gave him a look that only the victims of loss can understand. He held her gaze for a moment before giving her a subtle nod.

"Please, call me Quil, señora." His handshake was firm before he pulled his hand back, and Madi motioned for them to sit.

Her father started the conversation off thanking them for reaching out, stating how grateful he was, talking about the stats of their team and all the necessary jargon before he gave the floor over to Madi.

Madi then proceeded to run down her mental checklist, asking what Quil needed from the team, what he planned to contribute, how long he planned to stay, where he saw himself in the coming years, etc.

Quillan informed them that he was a single father who'd planned to stay home with his daughter until she inspired him to come back. She'd been diagnosed as a baby with a rare blood disorder that required her to be in the hospital frequently. Her strength in fighting this condition had made him realize he wasn't quite done in the NFL. It was amazing how much hope Madi took from his words, and she found herself tearing up as he talked about his love for his child. He simply wanted another chance to prove himself on the gridiron. He knew their team was all about family and wanted to be a part of what they were doing.

"I want you to know that I don't intend to replace Hunter. I know that isn't possible. I only wish to be a valuable asset to a team that's well on the way to their next Super Bowl. I saw what your boys did last season. I was impressed, inspired, hopeful... and I want in. I want to be a part of your organization." Quillan gave a nod, and Madi and her father followed, smiling.

Quillan Layton was a beacon of hope in their sullen world, and Madi was ready to get him signed. She smiled at her father, who seemed to share her feelings.

They talked longer than originally intended, bringing up old stories, family, the team values, how they ran things, and what they expected from each of their players. Each topic brought deep talk from either herself or Quillan. Madi felt confident that he was going to be among one of their elite.

She was taken off guard when a knock came at the door frame. Brett, clad in a light green Ralph Lauren polo and dark khakis, grinned at her and waved.

Her excitement at seeing him overruled her professionalism as she ran at him, threw herself into his arms, and greeted him. He laughed even as he returned her hug, and they both blushed when her father cleared his throat.

"I apologize. Quil, this is—"

"Brett McFadden. Wow! Zeus in the flesh. Nice to finally meet you, jefe." Quil stood and shook Brett's hand.

Brett smirked the term Zeus off as he always tended to do. "I've heard great things about you, Quillan."

"Likewise. I'm eager to join your ranks, man."

Madi had a thought then. "Would you like a quick tour, Quil? I'm heading down to the locker room before Brett and I have lunch. Which, we'd love for you to join us!"

"Oh, of course. I'd be honored."

Brett looked put-off but quickly recovered with a nod.

Chan and her father stayed behind to discuss more numbers, and their team lawyer headed in then while the three of them got into the elevator. The two men had a stare-off, sizing the other up, Brett seemed especially charged with tension for some reason that Madi couldn't pinpoint. He'd just met the man, were they seriously comparing penis sizes? Why did men do that? Sheesh.

"And here we are, Quil. 'The Colosseum,' as the boys like to call it." Madi laughed as she showed Quillan around. Brett just followed, big arms crossed over his chest.

They moved through the training and rehab area, the spas and meditation rooms, workout room, and finally the locker rooms before she showed him out to the outdoor practice fields. He seemed happy with what he saw, and soon, they were coming back into the air-conditioned locker room.

Quil heard his phone ding and excused himself. "I gotta take this. Can I meet you guys upstairs?"

"Of course. We'll be up in a minute. I just need to grab something."

Quil nodded and walked off, leaving Brett and Madi alone.

"So, what do you think of him?"

Brett shrugged. "He seems excited. Won't know until I'm playing with him."

"You don't look so eager to play with him," Madi fished.

"You're reading too much into it."

"No, I just see an alpha squaring off with an alpha."

"I'm the QB. I'm the *only* alpha," Brett growled with no conviction, getting a laugh out of her. "I missed you." He pulled her into his arms, and Madi couldn't stop her heart from racing at his closeness. "I was hoping we could have lunch alone, but then you go and invite the newbie."

Madi grinned at his pout; it was kinda sexy to have him jealous. She enjoyed it, she realized. "Oh, c'mon, you get me to yourself all the time. I just wanted us to have some time with him. I'm gonna sign him. I want to make sure I'm making the right decision here. I want you to tell me what you think of him. I value your opinion, you know."

The way he was looking at her had her insides tightening up. She licked her lips because she felt like he was about to kiss her. Then she remembered why she was down here. Hunt's locker.

She moved out of Brett's embrace, toward it confidently. She could do this. She needed to do this. It was part of her closure.

"Mad, uh, are you sure you wanna do this now? It's 12:15, I'm hungry."

"It won't take but a minute," she contended and stepped in front of it.

"Madi..." Brett grumbled and placed his large palm on her shoulder. "C'mon. Let's do it later. Please? It's not going anywhere."

"Jeez, Brett." She huffed and turned as he pulled at her. "What's your deal? Give me just a sec." His eyes burned into hers—flashing some uncertainty she couldn't place—but he protested no more and stepped back, removing his hand.

Madi moved the dial around, remembering the numbers, for they were the same as their alarm on the keypad at home. When it popped open, she braced herself. And stepped back in horror at all the pictures of herself lining the inner door. She gasped and covered her mouth in shame.

"Oh my God." Nude pictures, *shocking* pictures of herself doing sexual acts on her husband, disgracefully greeted her eyes. She quickly pulled them all down, one by one, each worse than the last, and when the final one was in her hands, she looked back to Brett who had braced himself for the hit. "You—you *knew* about these!" It wasn't a question. Of course he did. They *all* did. She fell, hitting her knees.

Brett was there, grabbing her before the shame ate her up and swallowed her into the ground. "Madi, listen to me."

"Why? Why did he do this? Everyone...*everyone* saw these! How could he do that? This is—" She was speechless as she rambled. Her husband had taken something sacred and intimate between them and turned it vile. She felt sick. She felt horrified. She was pissed! "That asshole!"

She threw the pictures back into the locker and slammed the door shut, snapping the lock and turning the dial. She attempted to rein her anger in knowing her fight wasn't with Brett; it was with the dead man who'd tarnished her image in front of the team she loved like her family. She was their CEO... and her husband had made her look like little less than a porn-star, a hussy, a prize. A prize—that's all she'd ever been to him. It stung. It ripped her apart. It made her want to pull his carcass from the ground and beat him bloody.

"Madi, I'm sorry," Brett offered, looking into her eyes as he continued to hold her up from the pit of despair. "For what it's worth, I tried to stop him."

She shook her head. She didn't want his apology.

"It's fine." She pulled back and adjusted her dress, wiped the tears at her eyes, and held her chin up. "I'm signing Quillan Layton. We'll have lunch with him and after, if you have any reservations about him, let me know. Otherwise, he gets Hunter's locker...and maybe even his number."

"Madi!" Brett stated with shock. "Surely you don't mean that."

Oh, I mean it alright, she wanted to say. *And maybe, just maybe Quillan'll get his* wife *too!*

"HE DIDN'T! Oh my God, what a donger!" Val gasped in surprise.

"Why would he do that?" Sky asked.

"What did Brett say?" Brooke inquired.

"He said that Hunt said it was to, and I quote, 'Pump him up for our baby making.'"

"That's some bullshit!" Brooke said. "He just wanted to show the guys what he had in the bedroom—a little sex kitten." Brooke pinched Madi's leg and meowed, getting an eye roll out of Madi.

"Have Linc and Travis said anything?" Madi looked down, embarrassed. She knew their guys had to have seen those pics, *all* the players probably had at some point.

"No, but they wouldn't. They love you, Madi. Don't let this bother you, hon."

But how could it not *bother* her? Hunter had made her look like a floozy. Those scantily clad pics of her had fed wild imaginations; no wonder some of the guys looked at her like they did. Now she understood why!

The girls comforted her as best they could, but Madi had come home and swore up a storm. She wasn't much for cussing, but she'd never felt more humiliated in all her life. She was so glad Quil had gone upstairs before she'd opened that locker. The mortification would have been tenfold.

"So, tell me about Quil," Brooke said, bringing the conversation back to a lighter topic, something she was known for. "He looks like a well-bred Spanish stud."

"Oh he is," Madi agreed and they all giggled. She began to tell them all about what Quillan said, about his daughter, how excited he was for the team and how Brett had reacted to him.

"Well, duh," Brooke added, "He sensed competition. Don't you remember how he acted when you first brought Hunter around?"

For a moment Madi was taken back years ago, to college, where she met the cocky and attractive Hunter Thomas. Brett's reaction had been similar then. "Wonder if he'll let it get that far this time before he intervenes," Madi wanted to say but held her tongue. He'd been all over her at lunch, holding her hand, dropping his palm to her back, pulling her hair from her face, throwing his arm around her as he sat next to her—if Quillan had any ideas, they would have been quickly shelved. That or there would be a pissing match at some point. Quil seemed to take the hint though and had been professional and grateful for the invite.

"Well, too bad I'm not into football players, or I'd have to let him score with me," Brooke laughed heartily.

Sky's brows went up, surprised. "Girl! I think I'd make an exception to that rule, at least this one time." Her freckled cheeks blushed.

"Daddy said he could only take one of his girls being with a football player. Besides, I'm more into the Christian Grey types…if you catch my drift." Brooke winked.

Val rolled her eyes. "Money is money, whether it's earned on the field or in an office shouldn't—oh, oooohh," Val finally caught Brooke's drift and winked back at her, getting a laugh out of the rest of them. "Hey, for all you know, he's got a secret room."

Brooke shrugged. Madi wouldn't tell her secrets. Brooke had been bisexual for a long time and never planned to settle down. If she ever did, it would surprise the hell out of Madi.

"So, who's down for a round of Heads Up?" Sky asked and stood, pulling her phone from her PJ pocket.

They all raised their hands and began to play their favorite game together. Madi was glad for their company and glad they were all having a sleepover. It was long overdue. She was grateful for these friends of hers, grateful for their advice, their input and support. They made a bad situation lighter and helped her understand her husband even more. Madi felt bad about being so angry with him; she couldn't stay angry with a dead man. She'd never understand his reasons and never get answers, but being resentful was only gonna hurt her in the long run. She had to let it go, especially since the team was holding a memorial for him soon.

Madi had loved Hunter; he wasn't perfect, but he'd once made her happy despite his flaws, despite his shortcomings. She was going to remember the good he brought into her life. She was going to remember the Hunter she'd fallen in love with and let the past be just that.

CHAPTER EIGHT

May came and the mini-camps started. The draft had brought them six new players with multiple trades in the works. Contracts were negotiated, renegotiated, and signed. Numbers were flying like the hub of an airport, and Madi stayed busy, grateful for the distraction.

She and Brett had seen a lot of one another, and as great as things were, Madi was still holding her breath for him to make a move that didn't come. She could sense his hesitation and understood it, but it didn't take those lonely nights away. So, she announced that very morning she was going to sell her house. Her family was shocked, especially her mother; but, as she'd told Brett, she didn't feel it was home. It was too big, too grand, and not her taste. Hunter had needed all that, not her.

Brett had offered to let her stay with him and she agreed. She always loved his house and felt comfortable there. Even if she and Brett didn't get "together," she'd find somewhere else. For now, she needed to get out of the house that still held too many painful memories.

Today was the day of Hunter's memorial, and Madi's emotions

were high. She was tired of talking to lawyers, looking at contracts, and sending emails. When Brett came to get her at five PM, she was already dressed and ready.

He literally fell a step back when he saw her. She'd dressed in Hunter's favorite yellow dress, the one that complemented her hair color and pinned it up atop her head in a twist. Her makeup was light, and she wore the single diamond necklace he'd given her on their honeymoon.

"Wow, Madison. You're stunning." Brett's eyes echoed his words, and Madi smiled as he pulled her to him for a kiss on the cheek. She took peace in his company, grateful for the solid foundation he was and had always been in her life. But even now, his touch was starting to awaken her hibernating womanhood.

She had started to miss sex a great deal. With Brett's overly masculine allure, it wasn't difficult to imagine how incredible—and dominating—he'd be in bed. She imagined an alpha with an intense gentleness who knew exactly when to be rough. She cleared her throat, attempting to calm her tingling body as he took her arm and escorted her to the black limo in front of them.

She'd not touched herself, although she'd been tempted to do so many times over the course of the last two months. It wasn't that she had an issue with masturbation, she simply knew it would be unsatisfactory. Orgasms weren't what she missed, she missed the intimacy of the act itself. She mostly just missed being touched and, as Brett's big palm came to her bare back, she shivered and moaned aloud.

His eyes darkened as she looked up, surprised by her own reaction to him. She gulped and didn't miss his Adam's apple bob as he did the same.

He looked so gorgeous tonight, his big frame clad in a dark gray suit, white button down, and crimson tie with the Gladiators logo on it. All the guys would be wearing them tonight. Brett's light brown hair was trimmed and spiked with gel. His face was clean-shaven, accentuating his perfectly-prominent square jaw, straight nose, and emerald green eyes with lips that simply begged her to kiss them.

Despite that this party was to memorialize the accomplishments of her husband, Madi's focus was simply on not bawling her eyes out or feeling any more shame about the fact that the entire football team had seen what she looked like spread eagle. She now knew what a Play Boy pinup model felt like—or *did* she?

Brett seemed to sense her reserve and a thick knuckle grazed her cheekbone. "Sunflower, you ok?"

Madi grinned and nodded, pulling willpower from the fact that she had her own streak of accomplishments to list, and being Hunter Thomas's whore wasn't one of them.

"Just ready for a drink," Madi stated and allowed him to help her into the car.

"Well then, enjoy a glass of champagne on me." He winked and settled in beside her, grabbing a bottle of the chilled libation he'd just mentioned. He poured her a glass then one for himself. "Here's to Hunter. May he be catching deep passes in Heaven."

Madi smiled and nodded. She was still hurt by what her husband did and knew she'd get over it, eventually, but that didn't change the mood she was in now.

"C'mon, Mad, what's the matter? What aren't you sayin'?"

"I'm sorry, I just... It's hard to face all these people now, knowing that...that they know what my insides look like." She held back her sniffle even as the tears hit her eyes.

"Oh, Madi. I'm so sorry. I begged him to take them down. I begged him to stop putting them up. It made me sick to..." Brett trailed off, but his free fist clenched at his side. She could tell he'd had a big problem with it but, just like every other wrong Hunter had made, Brett couldn't pay for the other man's sins.

"I can't help but be angry. I know it's stupid, but it still hurts that he would hold me in so little regard."

"He made poor decisions, often. He was full of himself, but he also had a big heart too."

"A heart as big as his ego."

Brett laughed. "Still, you meant the world to him, Madi. You have to see that."

Madi attempted to rein her emotions in again. "Nobody's perfect."

"No, they're not. So, tonight, let's focus on the good that was Hunter. The Hunter that made us laugh. The Hunter that we loved. Not on his many flaws, alright?"

"Spoken like a true best friend." Madi toasted Brett and said, "To Hunter."

"To Hunter."

They pulled up to the banquet hall and Brett got out, assisted Madi, and escorted them both inside.

She smiled and greeted those around her: current and former players, their wives, administrators, coaches, big names in the NFL, her in-laws, her parents and her sister.

Travis and Skyla, Val and Linc, Coach Haskins, Coach Cavanaugh, everyone looked great in their formal attire. Pax came up and kissed Madi's cheek, followed by Langley, Josh, and TJ. Many players she recognized, some she didn't—the old, the new, former players from other teams. Her face grew tired from smiling so much, and Madi was glad when Brett pulled her into a dance, grabbing another glass of champagne for her. He knew exactly what she was thinking, he always had, as if they had an unspoken language between them...like Travis and Sky had in Cancun, which made Madi's heart flutter.

Soon, they were being ushered to a podium and Brett was giving a speech, following the commissioner and her father.

Brett looked to Madi as he spoke, his eyes piercing her soul. "Hunter Thomas was my best friend, and as many of you know, one of my favorite targets for the thunderbolts I throw." He got a roaring cheer from the crowd and grinned big. "But Hunter was more than just a great wide receiver; he was like my brother. I loved him, and I miss him." Brett looked down and Madi could see this next part was hard for him. "I was with him when we were hit, and I was with him when he took his last breath. I made pro—" He sniffled, lowering his head, and Madi had to look away from him to keep from breaking down, but looked back after a moment. "I made promises to him, promises I intend to keep; promises I take very seriously. I know that if he were here today to see all of us, he would be thrilled with the football team we have in place. I'm looking forward to practicing with you all and making us a team worthy of the title of gods." Another roar bellowed through the crowd. "I'm gonna make Hermes proud. And I'm dedicating this year to him. I promise to give you my all, Gladiators. Follow your QB, Zeus, because we're going to the Super Bowl. This memorial is for you, brother."

Brett kissed his two fingers, tapped them on his chest where his heart was, and pointed up to Heaven as he looked up. Madi closed her eyes against the tears that came, and applause exploded around them. Brett approached her, pulled her in for a hug and embraced her, then kissed her cheek. "I love you, Sunflower."

She sniffled and pulled back. "I love you, Cap."

She approached the podium, looking through her thick tears onto the faces before her. "How can I follow *that?*" she asked with a laugh and got one out of everyone else. "Seriously though, I want to thank all of you—this team, my friends and family—for all your love and support in this difficult time. Hunter would've been very appreciative and glad you've all come together like this for him. He—" she sniffled. "He, uh, loved being the center of attention. Although," she laughed again through her tears and looked up, "you didn't have to do it like this, love." Her eyes fell back to the audience. "I miss him. I miss his funny, crazy side and even his sarcasm. He had a gift for being a goofball and was full of boundless energy. Anyone who knew Hunt, knew he never ran out of *that.*" Everyone laughed at that. "He loved this team. He loved this sport. He loved you all." Madi glanced around at all the faces that held back tears, like she did. "This means so much. This memorial to the man and football player he was. May his spirit forever live in all of us. His free, loving, benevolent spirit; a spirit that shown so brightly. I pray his soul is at peace. I pray we continue to remember him. And again, thank you so much for being here and showing what Hermes meant to you. God bless you all."

The commissioner and her father approached her with a trophy-like statue in the shape of a player catching a ball. Madi took it, shook the commissioner's hand, and thanked him then hugged her father. She turned with the trophy and held it up, getting a round of applause that roared through the crowd.

Soon, the trophy was being taken from her to be cleaned—it would go on display at the complex. People began to separate into groups, talking, dancing, and milling around the beautifully decorated banquet hall with ribbons, bows, and drapes of crimson and gold.

Madi moved to speak to her girls, Brooke, Val and Sky, who oohed and aahed over her dress and her speech. Having them there made her heart happy; their friendship meant the world to her. After more drinks and talking, she was pulled into a dance with Travis, then Linc, TJ, Pax and finally Lang. She was starting to get tired and eager to exit the hall, especially when Langley's hand came up to cup her cheek.

"You look amazing tonight, Madi," he murmured as his big brown eyes gazed into hers.

"Th—thank you."

"You do. I hate that we have to have this party under these circumstances, but I'm glad to have an excuse to see you in a dress like this."

Madi glanced up at him sharply.

"Sorry, but it's true. You're a very beautiful woman, Madison." His eyes, usually puppy-dog like and playful, were now roving her flesh—more bare than cloaked at the moment—in unabashed approval; it gave her the creeps.

Madi gulped. How much had Langley had to drink? She looked around. Where was Brett?

"Madi, I'm gonna be forward for a minute: I'm here for you. I know you're lonely without Hunter." Langley's hand moved down Madi's uncovered arm, and she shivered, feeling her gut tighten in alarm. "Given the chance, I can make *all* of you shiver, angel. A woman like you doesn't need to be alone. You need a man, a man with only your pleasure in mind."

Madi cringed as Langley's hand began to move down her waist. She glanced sharply around. Where the *hell* was Brett—or Travis? Or Linc? Trepidation inched up her body, seizing her heart as Lang's plump lips hovered at her ear.

"It's no surprise that I want you, baby girl. Let me show you."

Oh my God! She could feel the head of his erection poking into her thigh and attempted to pull back. Her eyes caught Brett's suddenly, and they said everything without her speaking a word.

Zeus moved through the crowd quickly, a stealthy QB breaking through the line of defense. His eyes held hers and darkened as he took in the scene before him.

"Is there a problem here, Lang?" he growled, taking charge and jerking Madi away from Langley's surprised grasp.

"Uh no, man. We were just talkin'." Lang looked to Madi with a smirk. "Everything's good here." He winked and briskly walked away.

Brett gently pulled Madi to him, attempting to keep the order and not make a bigger scene than he already had. Her hands moved up and around his neck, and she stared back into the green pools of solace that eased her heart in that moment. She loved the feel of his big arms around her as he held her, the power of his presence. He was larger than life and had always had a formidable force about him. He wasn't the biggest man on the team, nor the tallest, but he was the captain, the alpha, the backbone of the bunch; and he'd shoved his dominance in Lang's face tonight. It had been relieving and—to her surprise—arousing all at once.

"Madi, what did he say? What did he do?" Brett's lips curled angrily.

Madi's head reeled as she tried to calm her breathing. If she told him, Brett might literally kill Langley. "He's just had too much to drink, I think. Let it go, Cap. Let's enjoy the dance."

Brett's snarl reverberated through her ears. "I don't like other men touching you... gazing at you like he was."

Her eyes snapped up to his once again, and he held her gaze, realizing what he'd just said.

He softened the fierceness on his face and leaned his head down next to hers, his nose running the length of her jawline. She shivered. "He'll never get that chance again, I promise you, Sunflower."

She gasped as she sought his eyes—emerald spheres that held hers in limbo. They were full of promise, and she gaped up at him. What was he saying? Her world spun. She'd had too much bubbly tonight—that or her emotions were just getting the best of her. Hope filled her but dread also; she feared more heartache coming her way. She'd always loved him, but couldn't take rejection from him again.

"Take me home now, Brett."

He nodded and did as she asked, taking her back to his house.

THE NEXT MORNING Madi had a dozen missed calls and thirty text messages on her phone, but it was the call she got from her sister that woke her up.

"Are you up?" Brooke hastily said.

"I am now, thanks to you." Madi grumbled and tried to orient herself as she sat up in the guest bed of Brett's house.

"Don't turn the news on or check Facebook. In fact—don't even look at your phone right now!"

"Why?" Madi huffed even as she pulled the comforter from her hips, getting out of bed.

"Are you sitting down?"

"Brooke!"

"Ok, so there's this very credible picture of Hunter with two women taken last year..."

"Vegas!" It all came back to her: the way he'd acted after returning from the trip, Brett's distance. Something had happened during that trip—something bad—and Madi's nauseous gut was telling her she was about to find out.

"Yes. I'm on my way to you right now. Just hang tight for a second, ok?"

"Brooke, what does it say?" Madi whined; her heart couldn't take any more heartache, disappointment, anguish. "Just tell me, please?"

"Are you sitting *down*?" Brooke repeated again.

"Yes!"

Madi clomped into the kitchen, looking out into the pasture at Brett's beautiful roan bay horses. She pulled out one of the bar stools at the island and sat down, feeling her stomach clench before Brooke muttered the words, "He had an affair, sister."

CHAPTER NINE

Brett laughed at Travis as he made fun of the defensive player from the tape once again; TJ, Quil, and Lang joined in. They'd just come from their showers. They'd had an early morning offensive meeting and a workout, and were dressing in the locker room when Travis stopped moving, frowned, and stared at something behind Brett.

Brett turned and was surprised to see Madi standing there in gray shorts and an old Gladiators t-shirt. Her hair was up in a bun, tears ran down her red face, and she had a newspaper in her hands. Brooke stood in the doorframe behind her.

"Madi?" Concern ripped through him as he approached her. "What's wrong?"

"Please, *please* tell me that you didn't know?" she pleaded, her face crumpling.

"Know what?"

Madi shoved a newspaper at his bare torso. "This!"

Brett swallowed hard as he jerked the paper from his stomach, and Madi folded her arms across her middle. All he needed to see was the headline, "Deceased NFL Star, A Vegas Playboy?" and the picture—Hunter with the two girls from the casino on either of his arms taken in the hallway on the way back to his room—and he knew his worst nightmare had just come to life. His face dropped.

She shoved his bare chest but didn't budge him, not an inch. "You knew!" she shouted and jerked the paper from his hands, shoving it into his face. "He cheated on me, and you fucking *knew*. How could you not tell me? You're supposed to be my best friend."

"Madi, I—"

"No, don't you dare! Just answer the fucking question."

Madi was really mad; she never swore, and she'd said the F-word twice now.

"Did you know?" she growled out.

Brett gulped and closed his eyes briefly. With his nod, he sealed his fate.

"I never want to see you again."

Brett went to grab for her, but she pulled his hand from hers and swatted it away.

"Don't touch me! You don't *ever* get to touch me again."

The words bit into his heart like a giant set of fangs, stealing the life from him. He watched her beautiful face contorting in anguish that he couldn't heal, for she'd found out the one thing Hunter never wanted her to know—and for damn good reason.

She stalked out of the locker room. Brooke gave Brett a sad smile and followed.

Now, Brett was once again left to pick up the pieces of Hunter's mistakes. And this time, he wasn't sure he could fix this one.

"Man, talk about wrong place, wrong time." Travis clapped Brett on the back.

Brett looked at Travis, feeling completely dejected.

"Let's go hit up a bar. Looks like you could use a few beers."

Brett threw his shirt over his head, and he and Trav grabbed their gym bags and headed out.

THUNDER RUMBLED in the distance as Brett pounded on Madison's door—when ringing the bell five times in a row didn't get him the result he wanted.

Brooke answered looking unhappy and anxious, her green eyes peering hard into his.

"Hey," he grumbled.

"She doesn't wanna see you," Brooke stated without conviction and moved to let him enter.

"I know, but ask me if I care," he smarted back, the booze gushing through his veins.

"I figured you didn't, just wanted you to be aware in case—"

"What are you doing here?" Madi's angry voice called to him, echoing in the marble-tiled foyer.

"I need to talk to you. You don't just get to turn your back on a twenty-year friendship without hearing me out."

"I have nothing to say to you, besides something you don't wanna hear." Madi's red face contorted in anger.

"You don't get to talk. I do, dammit, and I have lots I wanna say."

"Start with, 'I'm sorry, Madi, for being the *worst* best friend in the world.'"

"You wanna do this? Here, in front of your girls?" Brett pointed to Sky and Val who stepped up behind Madi.

"Hell, I have no shame left. The whole world has seen *everything* I have to offer now. So, go ahead. I got nothing else to lose, Brett." Madi's cry rang out through the high ceiling, making his ears hurt.

"We should go," Val murmured and grabbed Sky's arm. Sky nodded and turned to Madi, a pained look on her face.

"We *all* should. Brooke, c'mon." Amelia's stern look pierced Brett's eyes with daggers. She stopped and looked up at him. "The only reason I'm not stopping this is because I know there are things that need to be said, things that need to come out into the open. Tell her what you need to tell her." Amelia's brows went up in finality.

Brett didn't confirm what he would or wouldn't say. He was buzzing and ready to unburden his heart. But whether he did or didn't tell Madi how he felt—how he'd always felt—wasn't why he was here. He needed to tell her what happened in Vegas.

When all the girls had left, Madi looked up at him from her perch at the table centered between the two staircases. Her lips quivered, her fists clenched at her sides, and in a flash, she moved forward. He thought she would come into his open arms, but instead she slapped him as hard as she could across the face. His head snapped to the right, and if it weren't for all the drinks he'd consumed, his jaw would've stung from the blow.

Tears flowed down her cheeks as he looked back at her, his heart breaking in two at the disappointment and anguish smearing her face.

"Madi, I'm so sorry."

"How, *how* could you not tell me?" Her rage battled with her pain, but he held his ground. If she needed to hit him to get it out, then that was better than her ignoring him.

"I wanted to. I was going to but…"

"Was it really two girls? *Two!*"

Yes, it'd really been two. Yes, it had really happened. Yes, Brett had threatened to kill Hunter when he'd seen him with them.

"What happened?"

"HUNT," Brett called as he watched his best friend walking out of the casino with a girl on each arm. "Hunter!"

Hunter's face was red, as if he were embarrassed—and his snockered ass should be.

"What the hell are you doing?" Brett frowned.

"Havin' some fun. We're in Vegas after all, right, brother?" Hunt smirked. But Brett's eyes narrowed as he took in the two sluts all over Hunt, clad in mini-skirts and tube-tops.

"With these two?

"They've promised me all the amazing things they can do. How can I pass up the opportunity to have a threesome?" Hunter laughed then held his

hand out in a gesture of truce. A threesome? Why hadn't he done that shit *before he'd gotten married. "I'm being selfish, sorry. I guess you can have* *one of 'em. I don't mind sharing." Hunter thrust a brunette his way, but Brett pushed the girl away with his forearm and gripped Hunt's collar.*

"Have you forgotten who you're married to?" Brett growled.

"Oh, don't give me that religious crap about holy matrimony. I'm a *football star. You should be surprised I haven't cheated before now. I've had* *ample opportunities."*

Brett literally snarled thinking of how much he'd pined for Madison Thomas, and here her sorry-ass husband was throwing her love aside like it meant nothing—all for one night with two skanky whores.

"You're forgetting who her father is, too. And who I am. I'm her best *friend. Do you honestly think I'm just gonna let you walk out of here* *without telling her what the fuck you're up to?"*

"Yes. Yes, I am." Hunt pulled Brett's hands from his collar and threw his *chin up. "You wanna know why, big shot? Because I know your dirty little* *secret. You think I'm oblivious to how you feel about my wife? No. I've* *hidden in the shadows the last six years watching you ogle her like a love-sick puppy and guess what? I don't fuckin' like it. Not much I can do* *though, huh? Or is there? Hmm." Hunter smirked, the grin of a hunter* *catching his prey in a snare. "If you so much as think about outing me, I'll* *make you out to be no better than some sick stalker. You won't be able to* *walk down the street. I'll ruin your reputation so bad you'll be jerking off* *for the rest of your life because no woman—or man, for that matter—will* *want to be anywhere near you. So, you go right a-fucking-head and you* *call Madi. But if I go down, your sorry ass is going with me,* friend.*"*

Brett continued to eye the man he suddenly hated with everything inside *him. "What makes you think she'd believe you, even if you did?"*

"Because I'm her husband! Who do you think she'll believe?"

Brett shook his head, feeling his blood pressure shoot up so high his ears *could've blown smoke. "You son of a bitch. You'll regret this. Go ahead and* *have your fun, but this is so far from over. I swear if it weren't for hurting* *Madison, I'd fuckin' kill you right now."*

"Idle threats, Brett. You're all talk and no action...which is why you're

not with *Madi right now. Let me know when you grow a set, and I'll meet you outside. Until then, get the fuck out of my face."*

Hunter shoved him away and gave him a final devious smile before grabbing the arms of the women. Brett watched him head down the hall, unlock the door to his room and enter it, all the while debating on whether he was gonna let the bastard live.

He slammed his hand against the wall. "Fucking Hunter."

He knew this was going to come back and bite him in the ass, but God help him he could never jeopardize how Madi saw him. The fear that Hunt would make Brett's love for Madi out to be something crude outweighed everything else. He prayed no one ever found out about this...especially Madi.

BRETT'S HANDS shook as he moved to the bar and poured a glass of whiskey into a highball glass.

"Don't you think you've had enough of that?" Madi's tone was cautious, and he looked back at her, frowning, confused. Why did she seem fearful?

"As far as I'm concerned, I haven't had *near* enough. But, if it bothers you, I'll be done." He set the glass down and saw relief hit her eyes. Then anger ripped through him as a sudden thought occurred to him. "Wait... Hunter never got violent with you when he was drinking, did he?"

Madi looked down. Brett moved fast and gripped her arm, turning her to face him. She was crying, and Brett felt a punch to his gut. "Madi, you'd *better* tell me." Brett felt like he was about to explode.

"He...he got loud and occasionally aggressive. He never hit me but...in bed, he..."

Jesus, Brett thought and wanted to punch a wall with the fury that seized him. *That motherfucker!* He needed to go puke; he wasn't ready for any more damn surprises today.

Brett turned, covering his face with his hands, attempting to hold his rage inside. He moved away before he roared so loud he scared her.

"Brett?" Madi asked. He could hear her closing in.

"Give me a sec, Madi. I just need to…" His entire body shook, and he took deep breaths in, moving to the couch to sit down. He wrung his hands. "God, I could literally rip him out of that grave and kill him right now." Brett didn't miss the flash of lightning that glinted in the window.

"I felt the same way today," she said, bowing her head as she sat down next to him.

He looked up at her, at her pain, and his anger began to dissipate. "I'm sorry he hurt you. In more ways than one. I never should've…" he trailed off, knowing *she* didn't need any more surprises today either. He had to ease into telling her how he felt and tonight wasn't the night.

"You saw him…with them?"

"I mean, I didn't actually see him *fucking* them, but I saw him go into the room with them. Then the next morning, I saw them leave, so…"

"Did he talk to you about it afterward?"

"No. I think he knew better than to bring it up."

"I guess I shouldn't be so surprised, huh?"

"What do you mean?"

"For me to be naïve enough to believe he wouldn't cheat on me."

"Oh, Madi…"

"No, it's true. Isn't that typical for celebrities and athletes?"

"Not *all* athletes," Brett defended. "You're more than worthy of having a man devoted solely to you."

"Apparently not."

"C'mon, Madi, Hunt lived for the fame. He wasn't like you and I, he didn't grow up with it. He basked in his stardom. He was a show-boat. Men like him can't be true to themselves, let alone anyone else. Don't take his shortcomings personally. He obviously sucked at being a husband."

"Or *I* sucked at being a wife," Madi whimpered and covered her face with her hands.

This was what Brett had dreaded, Madi blaming herself for what Hunter had done. How could he convince her she was amazing? How could he prove to her she'd always deserved better than Hunter Thomas?

"Please don't blame yourself, Sunflower." He pulled her to him then, grateful the anger was gone but sad that dejection had taken its place. "Madi, please listen to me. I know that if Hunter were here now, he'd hate that you knew; he'd hate himself for hurting you like this. He'd tell you how sorry he was and how it wasn't worth it."

"You're just saying all this to make me feel better."

"No, I know it's true. He wasn't perfect. But he loved you, even if he had a shitty way of showing it."

Brett let her cry then, cry for the past, cry for Hunt's wrongdoings, deep down knowing Hunt had been right about one thing. Brett had been all talk and no action, too terrified to tell her he loved her. Well, if Brett had learned anything in the last few months, he'd learned that life was too damn short to drag his feet. Life had given him a false start—or was it Madi who'd been given the false start? Either way, Brett wasn't going to let this opportunity pass him by. He'd been given a second chance and he wasn't going to waste it. Soon, he was going to tell Madison Hope Thomas how he'd always felt about her and hope like hell he wasn't too late.

CHAPTER TEN

Madi moped for two days after finding out Hunter had cheated on her last June at a football conference in Vegas. Once she'd seen the newspaper article, she'd let her anger overtake her and allowed the blame to settle on Brett. It still bothered her that he'd not told her when it all happened and not answered the question as to why he hadn't. Madi let it go. Maybe guys had a guy code that caused them to refrain from telling on each other. Maybe he'd just never knew how to tell her. Maybe Hunter had never given him the opportunity. Whatever the reason, Madi knew that Brett had to have a good one. Brett valued honesty at all costs—honesty and loyalty—and he'd always been both to her. He'd never done anything to break her trust, never done anything to make her doubt him, never been anything but on her side, always.

But what she couldn't let go of was how inadequate she suddenly felt. Hunter had been the only man she'd ever been with, and he'd cheated on her. With not one but *two* women at once…presumably. Was it because Madi's sexual performance hadn't been satisfactory? Had he been seeking more action in the bedroom because Madi was boring? Was she bad in bed?

She'd never had low confidence, but right now her self-esteem was reeling...and badly.

She'd spent the first day in bed, again—yes, she found peace in sleep. And Brett took the hint, leaving her to wallow. But by the second day, he'd come and got her, made her shower, and taken her to his house.

He was right, she had to get rid of her house; it was bad for her. The memories were destroying her.

It wasn't until she was getting out of the tub and dressing for bed that Madi got an idea, an incredibly awful idea, that embedded itself into her brain. Brett was her best friend. If anyone could understand, it was him. And he owed her this much.

Madi pulled her clothes off, looked in the mirror, and took in a deep breath. She headed into the bathroom and donned the silky white robe hanging behind the door. When she exited the room, she made her mind up. She was putting herself out there once more, putting her heart on the line. She was braving the prospect of rejection once again, but she had to know; had to know if *she* was the reason Hunter had cheated.

And Brett was going to be the one to tell her.

BRETT SLIPPED into a pair of boxers following his shower and crawled into the freshly cleaned sheets. He grabbed his phone to text Pax back.

They were excited about him practicing with Quil tomorrow, but Brett found himself nervous. As angry as he'd been with Hunter, his best friend had also been his favorite receiver. He and Hunter had meshed well on the field together. Whatever had been going on outside of work, when they were on the field, nothing existed but the game. Brett and Hunter had been on the same page; they read each other well and were always in sync. Brett would call for the snap, Hunt would get in position, and somehow that pigskin always made its way into his hands. It was as if Hunter had a target on him, and Brett's arm always managed to hit that target. And when 83 got that ball, he aimed to score—or do his damnest to get as close to the red zone as possible.

Not that Brett feared Quillan wouldn't have that same drive; he was a great football player. But Brett felt somewhat lost without his best friend. And being on that field for the first time without Hunter there was going to be difficult.

A knock came on Brett's open door. He looked up to see Madi, still in makeup and hair curled from their dinner earlier. She'd seemed miles away as they ate together, but he let it be; he knew she was still hurting over what Hunter had done—*Hell, who wouldn't be?*

She had a white silk robe on and wore a look of apprehension on her stunning face as she stopped in front of his bed.

"Hey, Sunflower. You ok?" He would be glad when he could stop asking her that question. Far too often lately she donned an expression of sadness, regret, or pain on her face; each time he asked, he feared the answer for he knew she wasn't really ok.

"Um, I—" Madi wrung her hands, looking far more insecure than she ever had. "Brett." She took a step forward and leaned her hip against the post at the end of the bed. "You're my best friend, right?"

"Right." Of course he was. He always had been, and she'd been his.

"So, you'd do *anything* for me. Right?"

Brett smirked in amusement. "Of course I would, Madi. But…I'm not digging up Hunt. I know we were pissed at him, but that's just too damn morbid, sorry."

Madi seemed to miss his humor and looked down instead, gulping. Perhaps that comment was too premature; Brett gritted his teeth in regret.

Were her cheeks flushing? "I need to ask something of you. Something I've never asked. Something I…I need you to do for me." She was stumbling over her words. Why did she seem so off?

"Madi, baby, what is it? C'mere." He opened his arms, beckoning her to him.

"And you'll do it, right? It has to be you, Brett. I trust you more than anyone else, and this is...this is *big*."

"Madi," Brett gave a chuckle. "Whatever it is, I'm in. You know I'd re-sink the Titanic for you. You mean everything to me."

"Good because...I ...I need you to... have sex with me."

Brett's brows shot up just as Madi pulled the robe from her shoulders and let it fall to the floor.

Anything Brett had been prepared for hadn't been this. She was completely naked beneath the robe. Completely, superbly naked. Madison Hope Thomas in the nude, in the flesh, was the most gorgeous thing he'd ever seen in his life—as he'd always known she would be. He couldn't keep his desperate eyes from descending her shoulders, down to her perky, plump breasts with their light pink nipples—utter perfection, not too big and not too small but just the right size to be a handful. He took in her athletically trim waist and curvy hips to the little blonde triangle of hair pointing to the place he knew would be the closest thing to Heaven he'd ever get. Her thighs were muscular, and he longed to grab them and spread them open, lose himself in the depths between. His mouth literally watered as his eyes ascended, retracing their pleasurable excursion, back up to her twinkling, sea-foam green eyes.

She was more exquisite than he'd ever dreamed, and his immediate arousal banished all thoughts from his head. He was helpless and speechless as she slowly moved toward him. Was he dreaming? He had to be dreaming. This was definitely a dream, he knew. As the woman of his dreams moved onto his bed and began to crawl atop his lap, he indulged in this perfect fantasy.

His erection pressed painfully into her inner thigh as she straddled him and looked deeply into his eyes. Her soft hands moved slowly up his forearms to his shoulders. He shivered as he rested his own on her waist, his eyes moving from her breasts back to her eyes.

He felt her nipples touch his pecs and grunted, loving the feel of her bare flesh against his own.

"I haven't been ok with all this, not really. I need to know if I'm the reason that Hunter cheated. He's the only man I've ever been with, Brett," she whispered, shamefully. Then the beauty on his lap looked down, biting hard into her lip. "I have to know. I have to…"

What was she saying? His thoughts were running a mile a minute, and all he could focus on was how good her sexy body felt pressing against his. Some part of him knew he needed to stop this, knew he should be a gentleman and look away from the splendid physique that enticed him so; but, God help him, he simply couldn't. He'd done the right thing for far too long where this woman was concerned. He'd held back, stayed quiet, hid in the shadows, and right now, all he wanted was to shout out his claim for the one he'd privately adored all his life. He'd never been selfish with her, never pressed for more, never made his desire for her known—tonight that was all changing.

Before he could protest, before his subconscious mind kicked in and shut this tantalizing scene down, he made the move he'd always longed to make. He leaned up and kissed her just as she was moving her head down to do the same. His palm cupped her head and pulled her face to his, angling his mouth as he deepened the kiss and took what he'd always wanted. Her lips were just as soft and sweet and delicious as he remembered back in college. The moan that escaped came from him, and when she fell into him, he ran with this incredible feeling humming through his veins—the need to make her his, finally.

Her tongue moved across his, and he flipped her over onto her back, the urge to be buried deep inside her taking over him. His hand moved to cup a breast, and he kneaded it like his life depended on it, loving the sounds escaping her throat as his other hand moved to her thigh, gripping it tightly. Madi moaned as her hands gripped his biceps, and when she pulled back for a breath, his mouth descended to her throat. He licked and sucked and had her hips arching up against his, making his desire for her rage like a fire fed by kerosene. He growled as he thrust back, scowling at the barrier of his boxers separating their bare flesh.

Her head flew back, and she gasped when his lips moved lower where he gently bit into the mound of her breast. "Oh, yes, Brett," she practically whimpered.

Her desperation fueled his own as his hand moved up the back of her thigh to grip her bottom, but a little voice in the back of his head grew louder and louder and finally screamed. Suddenly, he stopped and looked back at her face.

His hand moved from her breast to her cheek, and he cupped it gently, letting his breathing calm some before he spoke. He frowned at her questioning face and said the most honest thing he'd ever said to her, "Not like this, Madi. We can't."

She gulped, shame reddening her features.

"I want to. Trust me! You can *feel* how much I wanna be with you, angel." He thrust his raging boner softly into her pelvis. "But not here, not like this." Brett shook his head. "I won't be the man you fuck to prove something to yourself. I'm sorry."

Madi's lip quivered in humility, but he wasn't done.

"When I make love to you, it will be because you want me to. You can't allow this insecurity you're feeling right now to do this to yourself—to me, to *us*." When Madi frowned, he finally confessed the secret that had threatened to suffocate him for so long. "I'm too in love with you to have waited this long for a simple one-night stand. I won't be your rebound. I won't be second any longer, and I sure as hell won't be the one to compare you to another woman." She swallowed hard, and he did too. "Don't you see, Madi? It wouldn't even be possible because no one holds a candle to you in my eyes. They never have."

He watched her face go from surprise, to acknowledgement, to acceptance. She looked away and fought the tears that came to her Caribbean blue-green eyes. He knew she was rife with mortification, but he couldn't have their first time be under these circumstances.

He didn't want her just for tonight, he wanted her forever, for always—and having sex with her on these terms would only hurt them both in the long run.

"Fine," she scoffed and lifted her chin, looking back into his face. "If you won't do it. Then I'll find someone who will!"

It made so much sense now. All of it. How Brett had been acting all this time...hell, all their lives. In high school, in college, at her wedding... Brett's ex-girlfriend, Hailey, showing up to her office the morning after they'd broken up, telling Madi she was a, "very lucky woman." It was as if a veil had been uncovered, the revelation to a magic trick, to every action and reaction Brett had ever had.

Madi felt her heart soaring even as Brett smirked, "Oh, I don't think so, Sunflower. Maybe you didn't hear me. I'm in love with you, and I don't plan on sharing you. Not now. Not ever." His eyes sparkled, brighter than she'd ever seen them.

He was in love with her, and he was confessing it—and damn the confession felt surreal, amazing. She gulped.

"You won't be finding *anyone* to do your dirty deed."

Madi had no time to respond as he brought her hands up and over her head, pinning her wrists with his big palm. She grunted, but before she could speak, he was kissing her again, eagerly, slowly, sipping her lips as if they gave him his very life. She moaned as his other hand came to her breast and squeezed possessively.

"Mmm, Brett," she cooed when he pulled back for a breath, his mouth moving to her cheek, her jaw, her throat.

"Brett isn't here, Sunflower. I think I should show you the owner of the lair you've entered." Brett's grin was triumphant as he shifted and opened a drawer of the nightstand, pulling a tie from it. He began to loop it around one of Madi's wrist and tied it to the bed post. He pulled another tie from the drawer then did the same with the other wrist. "Tonight, you're here with Zeus, darlin'."

"But you said…" Madi gasped as Brett gripped her breast tightly again in his big palm. He lowered his head to her nipple, pulling the hardened peak into his hot mouth and teasing the tip with his tongue. He nipped and sucked and licked her into a quivering stupor while his other hand tortured the opposite breast.

"Mmm, you're delicious, Sunflower," he murmured as his eyes flashed jade fire.

Her hips began to arch up against him even as he chuckled and switched breasts, overwhelming her in sweet torment.

Finally, he pulled back just enough to look up at her, his hand moving down her side. "I said I wasn't being the man you fuck to prove something to yourself. I said *nothing* about not worshipping your body as I've always wanted to do. After all, you came to me. I'd be a fool to refuse such a sexy little goddess, wouldn't I?"

"Oh, God," Madi stated as his hand moved down her belly to her thighs and in between, his finger sliding through her slit.

"Mmm, that's Zeus to you, love." He winked as he brought his finger to his lips and sucked it into his mouth. He moaned before he taking her lips for another searing kiss that made Madi's sex drip with desire; she could taste herself on him and the eroticism of all this made her entire body tingle with electricity. "As sweet as a peach." He licked his lips and arched a brow as he began to lower himself down her body. He kissed the underside of her breast and nuzzled it tenderly. His nose moved over her skin, to her navel, where he licked a trail achingly slowly to the delta of her thighs. She literally quivered in anticipation, loving the feel of his large palms roving her body like he was a sculptor attempting to memorize every inch before replicating it.

She gasped when his mouth centered over her womanhood. Her head flew back as he connected with her aching flesh. "Ohh," she cried out in pleasure as he licked her sex like it was an ice cream cone, pushing her into exquisite madness. His thick finger moved to the entrance of her body and slid inside her as he all-out made out with her clit.

Madi began to rock her hips against his face and thrusting finger, yearning for the searing release burning inside her to be quenched. "Oh, God, oh yes, oh, oh," she whimpered and begged. And he gave, his tongue beating a frantic rhythm against her throbbing bud as his finger dove faster and harder into her, his other hand moved to her breast and fondled her.

"Damn, I love hearing how good I make you feel, Madison," he said, his smooth, deep voice unfurling ribbons of pleasure along with his ministrations. "Are you gonna come for me, baby? Tell Zeus."

"Mmm, yes," she answered. "So close. So good, oh it feels so good."

"Then let go, Sunflower. Yield to your king."

Something about the way his sexy eyes darkened and the determination in his face drove her over the edge. Her mind split as her body soared across the heavens, to Mt. Olympus where Zeus worshipped her like an empowered goddess, loving her womanhood with all his might. She gasped and moaned and whimpered like some love-drunk banshee before returning to earth to see him straddle her waist. He was pumping his thick cock—*damn it was big, bigger than she could've ever imagined*—with one hand and squeezing her breast with the other. He made sexy moans and growls of his own as his head lolled, and he bit into his bottom lip. Her sex still clenched and oozed desire as his pace quickened and his groans filled the empty air.

"Oh, Madi, baby, you're so gorgeous." He licked his lips as she watched him stroke himself, jerking hard and fast. "Mmm, I'm gonna come."

And he did, practically roaring as he spilled himself onto her belly, his seed shooting up her torso and onto her breasts. He grunted as he continued to milk himself, his eyes watching her reaction. She could've begged him not to stop, for she was so turned on again it was embarrassing. He finally ceased his tugging and looked at the mess he'd made, grinning in post-coital bliss. "I'm a messy god, it would seem. Let me go grab a towel." He leaned in for a soft kiss before moving off her.

He walked to the bathroom, his firm ass more impressive than she'd originally assumed it to be. He retrieved a towel and came back to her side, removing the remnants of his passion from her midriff. She stifled a moan as the towel swept between her legs, and he wiped the dampness there. He threw the towel down and moved atop her, aligning his body to hers.

"That wasn't exactly what you had planned, I know, but I don't want to rush this," he said, his tone serious. He kissed her again, gently, and Madi swooned even as she felt her wrists being unburdened. She relaxed her arms down, around his neck, pulling herself closer to him as her thighs wrapped around his waist. God he was massive, his frame so big and broad. She was completely turned on by his size and his kiss, the noises he made, everything about this bigger than life god-king. He moaned then chuckled before pulling back. His eyes roved her face and he smiled big, cupping her cheek. "I love you, Madison. I've always loved you. You know that, don't you?"

When Madi shook her head, he frowned as if confused. "I thought you didn't want me that night in college...after the party."

"Oh, Madi. You know I did. You felt that kiss; it was as powerful then as it is now." He kissed her again just to prove his point, and she was the one moaning this time. "See, it wasn't because I didn't want you. It was because I wasn't going to take advantage of you. Just like I can't take advantage of you now. I want nothing more than to bury myself inside you right this minute and never come out, but I can't. You're still so vulnerable, love. I have to wait. You aren't ready."

She wanted to argue with him and sass that it wasn't his place to tell her when she was ready, but she knew he was telling the truth. She only nodded and blushed. "Why didn't you ever tell me?"

"I was always afraid to."

"You weren't afraid to ten minutes ago," Madi smirked.

Brett chuckled heartily. "No, I guess not. Seeing my perfect Hera in all her goddess-like beauty forced all my inhibitions out; there was nothing left to hold back. I'd lost too much time already. It was time to throw the cards on the table and see what happened."

"Hera, huh?" Madi smiled big into her Zeus's handsome face. "I like that."

"Well, I mean, if I'm *Zeus* then that's who you are, Sunflower."

Madi smiled big, loving that he was claiming her—and as the queen of the gods too. Then a thought occurred to her. "Hunter knew, didn't he?" she asked, guilt hitting her gut at that moment.

Brett nodded and bowed his head. "I wanted to come to you and beg you not to marry him. Beg you to choose me instead, but I loved you too much to put you in that position. You were in love with Hunter, not me. I couldn't do that to you, no matter that it meant ripping out my own heart in the process."

"Oh, Brett, I'm so sorry. I should've—"

"No, Madi. No more wishing to change the past, no more regrets. We have here and now, and we have each other. Let's just start from where we left off. That night in college would be a good place, don't you think?"

Tears of joy came to Madi's eyes and she smiled big, loving how at peace she felt in the arms of the man she loved...the man she'd always loved.

"How do I look, buddy?" Hunter asked Brett, even as Brett scowled, looking at his best friend in the mirror. How could Brett be his best friend when he wanted Hunter's bride for himself? He was horribly sick to his stomach, wishing that this day had never come. Yet here it was.

Despite that this was one of the most beautiful places he'd ever seen, Ireland, today was the worst day of Brett's entire existence. All he could think about was how he'd failed, how late he was, how dumb he was. Madison Taylor would no longer be his—not that she'd ever really been in the first place. She would no longer be the love of his life because she would belong to another man. And Brett would have to—finally—let her go.

How the hell was he going to just be able to stand there and let it happen? How could he possibly hold his tongue when the priest asked if anyone had any reason why the two shouldn't be joined? Witnessing his sweet Madi promise herself to Hunter Thomas was going to destroy him.

Brett took another swig of whiskey as he tried to hide his true feelings from Hunter. He nodded and sighed, "You make a fine bridegroom, my friend." It was an honest statement. Hunter had cleaned up nice compared to their late night in an Irish pub singing with the locals in Irish Gaelic neither of them understood, drunkenly pissing in a giant trough in the bathroom, and reminiscing on the "good ol' days."

Hunter approached him then, looking fairly stricken himself. "Brett, I don't mean to get all sappy on you right now, but it's my wedding day and I want you to know that I'm really glad you're here. I'm glad I met you. I'm glad you were my QB, and I've enjoyed knowing you for the last four years. I know we haven't always seen eye to eye, I haven't been the greatest of friends, but you've been the best friend I've ever had. You've been there for me through everything. You mean the world to me and to Madi. I'm not perfect, not by any means, but I'm gonna try my damnest to love her the way a better man would."

Brett frowned. Better man, huh? Is he talking about me?

"What I'm trying to say is: I love you, like a brother, and I'm honored to have you for my best man."

How could Brett say anything to discourage that? "You too, man. Glad to be here for you." You fuckin' liar!

"You're family, man, always."

"You too, buddy."

Hunter pulled him in for a hug and Brett returned it, patting his back, all the while wishing he could earnestly not hate the man. Hate and love, the space between the two was where Hunter took up residence in Brett's heart: best friend, favorite teammate, worst enemy all bundled into one.

"How's my bride?"

Brett gave him a little shrug when he pulled back, wanting to be hammered drunk by the time the ceremony was done so he could numb the pain this day promised.

"Why don't you go check on her? I know she'll be sweatin' bullets, worse than I am, I'm afraid."

God, please no? Why would I torture myself even more than I am now?

But he simply nodded and left the room.

Brett wasn't sure how long it took him to get there, or how long he stared at the door to the bridal suite, before he finally got the guts up to knock. He felt his heart bleeding torrents of emotion before the ancient wooden door opened and Brooke smiled at him, a brow going up.

Brett came in, his heart racing and his breath hitching as his eyes fell on the most beautiful sight he'd ever seen. Madison Hope Taylor in an elegant, white lace gown. He could have fallen to his knees before the shining angel that stared back at him.

Tears hit his eyes and he covered a hand over his mouth as he took her in, a vibrant smile across her gorgeous face.

"Wow, Madi, ho—" He was speechless and had a difficult time swallowing.

"I'd say I look pretty good by your reaction."

He shook his head. "Good? Good doesn't even cut it. You're stunning, Madi, absolutely the most beautiful thing I've ever seen. Hunter's gonna..." he trailed off.

This should be my moment, *he thought.* Not Hunter's.

Every cell in Brett's body, every thought in his mind, urged him to beg her to call this wedding off. To reconsider the match between herself and Hunter, to choose him instead. As broken as his tattered heart was, he couldn't bring himself to utter the words. Today was Madi's day. And because he worshipped her, loved every fiber of her being, he wouldn't do anything to hurt her.

Even if that meant hurting himself. Even if it meant never telling her the truth—that his heart was, and always would be, hers.

She approached him then and took his hands. She kissed his cheek and the warmth of her lips made his suffering all the more poignant.

"You're the most beautiful bride ever, Madison Hope."

His eyes held hers for the longest time. No amount of wishing or wanting could change the heart that wasn't his to take. She wasn't in love with him, and Brett had to accept that.

"Hunter Thomas is the luckiest man alive, and I pray with everything in me that today he realizes it."

Madi beamed up at him, her seafoam green eyes speaking words only his heart could hear. "Tell him I love him, and I'll meet him at the altar," she finally said.

His lips came to her cheek, and he savored the final moments he had with her. The final moments he had to absorb that he'd made the gravest mistake of his life by not coming clean before today.

He'd live to regret staying quiet, being the perfect gentleman, staying only her friend.

He planned to get shit-faced drunk by the time the reception started; after that, he would try to move on with his life. Somehow, he would find a way to live a life without his heart.

But for now, he had a wedding to attend... a wedding that marked the demise of true love for Brett McFadden.

BRETT GRINNED, hearing the birds wake him before his alarm had a chance. The sun streamed through the plantation shutters and shimmered down on his sleeping queen, lighting up her blonde ringlets. The sunlight that shimmered among the golden curls made her look like she had a halo around her head, but Brett didn't need a reminder that Madison was an angel; he'd always known. He leaned in, kissed her cheek, and laced his fingers through the hand that laid on his chest, stroking his fingers up her forearm. The sexy little moan that escaped her lips made him rock hard in seconds. He longed to pull her hand to his erection and let her torture him even more than she already had last night.

Seeing her naked in front of him, exposed to him, as vulnerable as she'd ever been to him, made something inside him finally snap; it had been his resolve. He'd always regretted not talking to her about that night in college, always regretted not coming clean about his feelings before Hunter swooped in like a hawk and carried her away from Brett, always regretted not having another chance. Last night, he'd had that chance and he'd taken it.

Now, he was so glad he did. Madi knew how he felt, she knew he loved her, and she knew he wanted to make her his. He'd finally been given the opportunity to show that to her, even if he'd not officially made love to her yet. He'd gotten to love the body that had always haunted his dreams, worship her as she always deserved, and made promises he couldn't wait to fulfill. She'd been completely his to command last night, and he'd eaten up every sexy second of it. He felt alive for the first time in so long, feeling as if he'd truly woken up on Mt. Olympus.

Madi must have shared his thoughts because she was grinning seductively at him.

"Good morning, stud," she cooed and pulled his stroking hand to her lips to kiss and suck his fingers, making him groan in anticipation of her mouth on his stiffening cock.

"Careful, my goddess, you'll disturb Zeus's slumber, and we both know he's a very dominating god."

Madi giggled and peeled down the sheets; Brett swore he'd never wanted anything more in his whole life. "I liked Zeus...a lot."

"Hmm, I'll have to summon him more often then." Brett moved and pulled her into his chest, wrapping his arms around her and lowering his lips to hers. He kissed her soft at first then aggressively and possessively, thrusting his pelvis into her thigh to show her just how much he wanted her.

She ate it up, and when he pulled back, she was breathing hard and looking at him like he was a big piece of meat and she the dog salivating for it; it made him feel good, damn good. He stroked her cheek and watched her eyes as they moved over his face. Having her look at him like this was new, and he was going to indulge a bit.

"That was the first time I've ever been tied like that," Madi confessed, and Brett saw her cheeks pinken.

"Oh? Did you feel helpless?"

Madi bit her bottom lip and shook her head. "I felt..." she searched for the right word a moment then said, "Empowered. Sexy. Aroused."

"Mmm, you'll be feeling that a lot, I'm afraid. Get used to it, my queen."

Madi giggled again and took his lips. She moved her hands down his shoulders to his chest and stroked him as if she were testing his solidity. When her hands began to lower, he growled a warning. "Easy, Sunflower."

"I wanna touch you. When do I get to touch *you*?"

Brett grinned deviously. "When I can fully have every inch of you. That's when." When she huffed, he explained. "Madison, I've been a patient man for a very long time, but the minute I feel your hands on me, I'm gonna claim you, and God knows when or if I'll be able to stop. For now, Zeus is in control and he'll stay that way." Brett winked, and Madi pouted. He nibbled that pout away and began to stroke her body, loving the sounds that escaped her as he did. He had her melting like ice cream in his palms before he stopped and shot up off the bed.

"Brett? Where are you going?"

He smirked. Having Madison Hope Taylor aching for him might be the hottest fucking thing ever; his dick was swelled to bursting. "I gotta go to practice, baby. Remember, Quil and I are running drills today."

Madi sat up, brows drawn, arms crossing beneath her perfect breasts. "You get back here and finish what you started, Zeus, or so help me..."

"Oh, Hera, you sass the wrong god, my queen. Better not finish that statement." He shook his finger at her. "Whose bed is that?" Madi simply huffed back, and Brett ate it all up. "That's right. Zeus will have you when he wants you, and unfortunately, our fun will have to continue later."

"Is that so?" Madi's brow cocked, and it was all he could do not to jump back into bed and beg her to lash him with that delicious tongue of hers. "Well then, *Zeus*, two can play your little game."

With that, she threw the covers off and began gathering her robe.

Brett chuckled and said, "Hate to see ya go, darlin,' but *love* to watch you leave." It was true since her tight little ass was utterly bitable, and he couldn't wait to have her apologizing for her behavior later.

Yes, indeed Brett McFadden was fully awake and fully alive. Now to go continue that streak on the field. He laughed as he moved into the bathroom to shower.

"AGAIN," Haskins huffed and growled at Brett.

Dammit, couldn't Haskins see this wasn't working? Why did Brett and his offensive coordinator clash so? If he'd have watched any of Quillan's game highlights he would have seen that Quil moved best from the left, not the right. This was the fourth time they'd ran the same route, and Quil hadn't even come close to catching the bullets Brett had thrown him. Quil was off. Or was it Brett?

He was anxious, highly anxious. He thought he could do this. He thought he could just come onto this field, start running plays, and everything would be back to normal. Well, dammit it wasn't and Brett wasn't sure when or if it would be.

Some of it was Brett's guilt. Not only was he still feeling guilty for driving the damn McLaren, he'd gone and messed around with Hunter's wife last night and now he was sure he was seeing him on this very field.

It was if Hunt were standing in the end zone, out of the corner of Brett's eye, flashes of that damn jersey—number 83. Hunt was mocking him, haunting him, harassing him for taking the life he'd left behind. Brett had just swooped in after all and taken his place, right?

Brett's stomach tightened as he called for the snap from his center, caught the ball hiked to him from the shotgun position, and pivoted his right leg out waiting for Quil to get downfield. His right arm came up, and that's when Quil's practice jersey morphed from an 87 to an 83. Brett panicked and moved back a step or two. The sun was playing tricks on him. It couldn't be Hunt. When Quil turned, it was indeed a three not a seven, and Brett's arm fell, defeated.

The ball fell from his grasp onto the turf, and he just stared back down field.

Hunter was waving his arms, ready for the catch that would never come again.

Brett watched with bated breath. He had so much to say to his best friend. So many things to apologize for. So many wrongs to right. But it was too late, and slowly reality set in as Quillan Layton ran back to Brett and pulled his helmet off.

"Brett?" he asked, frowning. "You alright, man?"

"What happened?" Josh asked, looking down at the football on the turf.

"What the fuck, McFadden?" Haskins growled, coming over to them.

"I can't do this right now." Brett moved quickly away from the two of them, toward the tunnel.

He was going to be sick.

CHAPTER ELEVEN

Madi grinned as she looked out onto the field from her desk. It was good to see Brett back in his element, even if it were bittersweet. Hunt would be proud, Hunt would be excited, and Hunt would be glad that Madi was finally starting to move forward with her life. Brett had nodded when she'd asked if Hunter had known about Brett's feelings for her. Madi wasn't sure how or when he'd known; maybe he'd known all along. But it didn't really matter because she was happy, and she knew deep down that Hunter would be happy for her too. It had been four months since his death, and she was finally starting to be able to talk about it and not have her insides rip when she said his name aloud to others.

Last night had seemed like a dream, being tied to the bed, and having the man she'd secretly desired most her life kissing, licking, sucking, and touching every part of her was an erotic fantasy come true. There was a small part of her that felt guilty moving into another man's bed so soon after her husband's death, but it was Brett; it felt right and so damn good having him do those things to her. And, she reminded herself, they hadn't had intercourse. *Hell, close enough,* her brain reminded her. She blushed as her father entered her office, so glad he couldn't read her mind.

"Hey Dad," she said as she looked up from the computer screen where she was working on budget totals.

"Hey, pumpkin, wanna do lunch?"

"Oh, Brett was gonna..." she trailed off blushing again and her dad looked away with a smirk.

"You and Brett are together a lot lately, I see."

Madi just nodded; she didn't know what to say to that. It was true after all. They spent almost every waking moment together. "Is that a bad thing?" she wondered aloud then frowned when her dad shook his head shocked the words had actually come to her lips.

"Not at all. I'm glad to see you really smile again." He took her hand and his gray eyes burned into her own. Her father was a handsome man; his once blonde hair had turned white along with his mustache, but he was spry for a man of sixty. "Well, can we see you for dinner?"

"We're going to Brett's folks tonight, but we're free on Thursday," Madi recovered and got another grin out of her old man.

"Looks like I'm gonna have to take ol' Zeus golfing and have the same talk with him I had to have with the wide receiver who once had my daughter blushing like she is now." Her father's brow went up, and she could've choked on the coffee she was still sipping.

Her father assumed it to be that he'd mentioned Hunter, but she was choking because she was suddenly mentally thrown back into that bed where *Zeus* had been ravishing her body.

"I'm sorry, honey, I didn't mean to..." her father apologized.

"No, no it's ok, I forgot how to swallow all of a sudden." Madi gave him a laugh and stood. "Wanna go see how our QB is doing today with Quil?"

"I'd love that. I was about to head down myself. Wanna check the mirror first though?" he gave her a wink, and she ran to grab her compact in her drawer.

"Dad, I thought I had something in my teeth, don't do that." She scolded him and got a laugh in return.

She took his arm as they walked out the door and down the hallway, toward the elevators.

"You and Brett were destined to be together, Madi. I'm glad to see it finally coming to fruition." When he smiled over at her she returned it and they hopped onto the elevator. "I knew it a long time ago. Long before Drew told me that as a child Brett told him he'd found the girl who would one day be his wife."

"Brett told him that? When?" Madi asked in awe.

"The day he met you, Drew said. And it made Drew laugh but Brett was dead serious. Which is why it always surprised me when he didn't intervene between you and Hunter."

"Brett's a gentleman, you know that father." *Although he wasn't a gentleman in the bedroom last night*, she thought. "Besides, he didn't want to impose on my happiness for his own selfish gain."

"That's true. He's never been selfish where you were concerned. Which is why he has my blessing."

Madi grinned big as the elevator dinged, their destination reached, and leaned in to kiss her father's cheek. "Thanks, Daddy. That means so much."

"Tell him I said, it's about damn time." He chuckled and they moved through the training room to see a grumbling Coach Haskins.

"I can't deal with this bullshit today." Haskins threw his clipboard onto a bench. To say he overreacted on occasion was an understatement. The man lived football, ate it, breathed it, slept it, and most times needed a stress reliever in the worst way. Madi was surprised he hadn't blown a coronary with how worked up he got. Not that the rest of them didn't take football seriously, but Haskins had a cork up his ass 97% of the time.

"Now Haskins, let's just relax," Jerry said.

"Why don't you tell that to your QB? He's the one who needs to fuckin' relax." Haskins huffed off in the direction of his office and slammed the door behind him.

Madi knew if Haskins was going into his office, Brett was no longer on the field.

"Let me go see what's going on. I'll meet you on the field." Madi leaned in to kiss her father's cheek and moved to the locker rooms where she found Brett leaning forward, elbows on his knees, hands covering his face. He wore a sweat-stained gray muscle shirt that hugged his big frame, black workout shorts that came past his knees and new cleats. "Brett," she whispered and rested her hand on his shoulder.

He breathed in deeply but didn't move.

"Are you ok?" she asked. It was rare to see Brett upset, even after a loss. Their QB, their captain, was as solid as a rock, never getting rattled. The first time she'd seen Brett cry was when Hunter died; he wasn't one to show emotion or theatrics.

He pulled his hands from his face and looked up at her, a mixture of fear and anguish in his eyes. "I saw him."

"Who, Brett?" Madi squatted, glad she'd worn a pant suit today instead of a dress.

"Hunter," he whispered and looked around, making sure they were alone.

"What do you mean?" Madi asked, trying to understand.

"I think he's haunting me, Madi. I can't throw a pass today to save my life. It was as if he was there, on the field with me, instead of Quillan. I kept seeing his number."

"Brett, you're stressed. That's all." After all, he'd been soothing her and not really grieving himself. They'd known this was going to be hard. Having Quillan, someone new, was just getting to him. "I know this is hard."

"No, you don't."

Madi frowned. "Of course I do."

"No, Madi, you don't *know*. You weren't the one in the car beside him watching him die, in the ambulance watching him die, in the hospital *watching* him die…all the while being in love with his wife. Now, he's come back to haunt me for it." Emerald green eyes pierced her heart.

"Oh, Brett," Madi sighed.

"It's fucking true. There was a part of me that was somewhat glad, how sick is that? I don't deserve you."

"Stop this!" Madi commanded, taking his face in her hands. "You listen to me. You are the best man I've ever known. I don't know where this is coming from, but Hunter wouldn't take this away from you. This is your own mind feeling guilty, Brett. He loved you. I know he did."

"How could he? You know how angry he'd get with me."

"Your relationship was rocky at the end, I know that, but he—"

"He was jealous of me."

"Yes, he was. Very much so. But he never hated you, even when you thought he did." Her eyes pleaded with him to listen to her words and take them in. "You remember what you told me about him loving me? I doubted it at first too but I know now; I *know* in my heart that he loved us both as much as he possibly could."

Brett gave her a crooked grin even as she pulled him to her, kissing his lips softly. "I love you, Madi," he said when she pulled back.

"I love *you*, Cap. Now you get out there and show Quillan Layton that cannon of yours. You are Zeus, thrower of thunderbolts, and as your queen I demand to see your power in all its glory."

Brett's eyes sparkled, he nodded, and they both stood. Brett took her hand and they made their way out to the practice field.

THE RIDE WAS silent on the way to Brett's parents' house that night. He was reeling from his poor performance. It hadn't improved with Madison's speech, or her presence, of which he'd been certain would help get his mind in the game. By the tenth toss, he'd called it and he could see Quil was disappointed too. It made the humiliation so much worse. Brett had never had an ED problem but assumed this would be what it felt like for a man who did. It fucking sucked.

Madi was gracious enough not to follow him into the locker room and make excuses for him, apologize to him, or give him some BS encouragement that would only make him feel like more of a sorry excuse for a quarterback than he already did. That was yet another thing he loved about the woman who'd always been his best friend; she knew when he needed advice and when he needed her silence—tonight was that night.

She'd simply taken his hand and they'd left the complex around five. His parents were expecting them for dinner, and despite his foul mood, he was eager to see them. It'd been weeks.

When they came up to the door, Brett's mom, Sophia, answered it. She gave her son a bright smile and opened her arms for a hug. It didn't matter how old he got, he would always feel home in this woman's loving arms.

"Hey, Momma," he stated as he pulled her against his chest, cradling her head.

She squeezed him tightly. "Oh, there's my boy. It's good to see you."

"You too." He pulled back to look at her lovely face with its distant Italian roots, her hazel eyes and deep brown hair pulled up in its usual bun.

"Madison, child, you get more beautiful every time I see you. How are you, my sweet girl?" His mom moved to Madi and grabbed her, kissing her forehead and embracing her tightly.

"I'm good. Really good. Thanks to your son."

She patted Brett's bicep as Sophia released her. Sophia's eyebrow rose, and she gave Brett a knowing look. "Something you two wanna share?"

Brett couldn't help the blush that came to his cheeks. "Well, uh... we..."

"We're taking things slow but," Madi looked up into his eyes and he literally swooned, "we're...well, we're together now."

Sophia laughed and jumped up and down. "Oh, thank God. It's about freaking time."

"Mom," Brett scolded but laughed as she patted his cheek, tears coming to her hazel eyes.

"You two were meant for one another, if I can be so bold." His mom pulled them all together in a group hug. "We mothers know what makes our children's hearts complete. Madi always completed you, Brett. And it looks like you've finally let her in on that secret."

When his mom pulled away, she was wiping tears from her eyes.

"I'm sorry I'm emotional about it, it's just... I'm so glad something good can come from this tragedy. We start to see what really matters in life when we lose those closest to us." Sophia had lost her sister when they were just teenagers. Bianca had been in a car accident right before she graduated high school; his mom had always revered her big sister. She'd see Bianca in every butterfly that flew by, thus why her kitchen was literally overflowing with them—well not real ones, figurines, wallpaper and depictions. Bianca had always been obsessed with butterflies, so Sophia surrounded her life with them, even released them at her and Drew's wedding in commemoration of her sister.

Madi leaned in, kissed his mother's cheek, and the two women hugged again. Brett's heart swelled to bursting. He'd always loved how close Madi and his mother were.

"How's my two favorite kiddos?" Brett's father, Drew asked as he walked up at that time.

Brett smirked, even as he pulled his old man in for a hug. "I'll be sure and tell Brock and Bridger that, Dad."

"Nah, it's our little secret," his dad joshed. Brett knew his father didn't actually have a "favorite" despite that Brett was the only one who'd followed in his dad's footsteps as far as football was concerned. Brock was an engineer and Bridger was in finance.

Brett was the oldest of three boys and man, they'd been *all* boy.

141

All out, all the time. Wild, reckless... broken limbs, cuts, skinned knees constantly. Brett wasn't sure how his soft-spoken petite mother had done it; she'd always been patient and never raised her voice to any of them. God bless her little heart, literally.

"Drew," Madi said and pulled Brett's dad in for a hug.

"Madi, honey, you look great. My son have anything to do with that smile?" Drew winked, and Brett was certain he'd overheard their conversation in the foyer.

Madi just grinned back and they all moved into the living room. Before she could even sit down on the couch next to him, Brett's mom was playing hostess, of which Madi politely joined her in the kitchen to assist.

Drew took his usual recliner and muted the television; it was set to ESPN, like always.

Brett was grateful for the moment alone with his dad when he said, "So, you being with Madi the reason you're feeling so guilty?"

How could he possibly know that...unless...?

"Jerry tell you about my shitty-ass practice?" Brett blushed.

"Nope. You've always worn your heart on your sleeve, son. I can see something's bothering you bad. The chip on your shoulder is mighty heavy."

Brett's father had always had a sixth sense about people. It was one of the reason's Jerry Taylor loved having him for a GM; he could smell a rat from a mile away, Jerry'd said. Drew McFadden had been as serious a man as Brett back in his heyday. He was tall and broad like Brett too, although he'd gotten a bit softer—and more easy-going—in his fifth decade on earth. Drew's eyes were dark green, his brows thick, hair thinner and lighter than Brett's and his tolerance for games an all-time low.

When they'd gotten in trouble as children, Brett and his brothers had known better than to beat around the bush. They could've gotten away with murder around their prim mom, but their dad was a hard-ass and didn't abide disrespect, disloyalty, or disobedience; his strong Scottish roots ran deep.

"I couldn't make a single pass to Quillan today, Dad. I felt like a rookie all over again. It was damn embarrassing. Talk about making an ass out of oneself."

"We all have off-days, lad."

"Not like this. I can't get my mind right. I felt..." Brett shook his head, unable to convey his thoughts.

"You were in the car with him when he was injured and with him when he passed away. That affected you. Probably even more than you know. Now, barely months later you're moving in on his wife. You're feeling guilty."

Brett wasn't "moving-in" on Hunt's wife. It had been Madi who'd come to him, but he wouldn't get into the rigors of it with his dad. Still, that fact did bother him when he looked at the big picture. He knew he hadn't intended to do what he'd done with her that night she'd propositioned him, but it was bound to happen. Their connection, their draw to one another was simply too strong to resist. It was why Brett was attempting to take it slowly, but he also knew his old man wasn't being accusatory, just being a sounding board.

"It was as if Hunt were there on the field. As if I could see him, his jersey, feel his presence. It was..."

"Have you visited his grave since the funeral?"

No, come to think of it, he hadn't. Wow! Some best friend he was.

"I know your relationship with Hunter was shaky at times and perhaps that's bothering you, too." It was true, although other than Madi he'd not really discussed their issues with anyone else. Again, Brett wasn't surprised his dad had picked up on it. "Son, perhaps you need to go and have a little chat with him. Ease your mind, your conscience, your hesitations. Just go talk to him about how you feel. You've been so focused on Madi's grief that I bet you haven't really had time to do much of your own, have you?"

Brett looked at his father as if he'd just revealed the holy grail. He was spot-on; Brett had not taken the time to assess his feelings, aside from letting the guilt consume him. Yeah, he'd cried, he'd prayed, he'd let the emotions run their course, but he was still stuck in the middle of his own grieving process. No wonder Madi was ahead of him. She'd faced the toughest part of the road and forced herself to battle it out when she'd taken some time alone. Brett hadn't done that. He'd run from it; he'd not faced it head on. He'd cowered in a corner, and when the time came to move forward, he'd shoved the truth down; allowing a "ghost" of his former friend to upset him.

"You're right, Dad."

"Of course I'm right. I'm old and wise." He winked over at Brett, getting a smile out of him. His father might be "old and wise," but he was incredibly far from feeble. At just fifty-five, Drew was in great shape, barely graying, and had the stamina of a thirty-year old. He ran every day and could run circles around Brett's brothers. Brett hoped he aged half as well as his "old man."

They had a delicious dinner of roasted veggies, steak, and salads and the conversation was easy. Brett felt better talking to his father and even his mother.

As he and Madi left, he felt lighter than he had in weeks. He was planning to go talk to his best friend. Despite knowing that he could've talked to him anywhere, he knew it would help to visit Hunt's gravesite and let go of some emotions he'd held in for far too long.

He hoped doing so would change things.

CHAPTER TWELVE

Brett's mood was atrocious a week later. He still hadn't been able to sync with Quillan, nothing was working. He couldn't focus, couldn't get his mind right, couldn't ease his heartache, couldn't stop seeing Hunter...

And he hadn't been to the gravesite. He couldn't force himself to go. There was something holding him back, some unseen force keeping him away.

He and Madi had slept in the same bed together, but they hadn't messed around. He hadn't even kissed her and was starting to feel guilty about that. She seemed to understand he was off but that didn't make him feel better. *So, you're feeling bad about messing around with your best friend's wife but then guilty about* not *messing around with her. Make up your fucking mind, Brett!*

He was pumping iron hard the next afternoon, during the scheduled time when the defense was supposed to be working out and some of the guys looked at him like he was nuts. He didn't care, he ignored them. To hell with them! Yes, he'd already worked out today, but the only other thing he could think of to get his frustrations out wasn't an option. He wasn't having sex with Madi, not yet. He couldn't afford anything else to be remorseful about. And if it came to making himself feel bad or Madi, he would choose himself. She had enough on her plate still too and he wouldn't burden her by "unburdening" himself. So, it was workouts and running. That's what he did, since his arm didn't want to cooperate.

He was even off with Travis, and The Ram didn't have the patience Quil seemed to. Brett was soon to get the horns, he knew, because Trav was frustrated too. He was anxious about proposing to Sky soon.

Brett's aggravation was at an all-time high when Pax came up and frowned at him.

"Dude, take it easy, will ya? You're gonna throw your shoulder out." Paxton motioned to his right arm as Brett lifted yet another rep in an overhead press. It was heavy and yeah, he was struggling, but the anger blinded anything else. He set the weight down loudly and jumped up, brows drawing as he faced off with the big linebacker.

"Mind your own business, *merman*," Brett growled.

"Easy, Brett. C'mon man, you're not the only one missing him, you know?" Pax whined. To be so broad and strong, he was a damn teddy bear.

Brett shoved him. Perhaps sparring would help lift some of the tension he felt. "What'd you say to me?"

"C'mon, Zeus, stop." Pax held his hands up, gentle giant he was.

"Don't fucking call me that!" Brett grumbled.

"It's who you are!" Pax argued.

"Some great fuckin' god I am. I can't even throw a damn football right now. You haven't seen it, you don't know." It was true. He'd only practiced with the offense. Defense had different camps this week.

"Even Zeus wasn't perfect."

Jesus, these guys took this Greek god thing *far* too serious. Brett rolled his eyes.

"What?"

"You! You just don't get it."

"What don't I get? He was our friend too, Brett. And I'm not going to stop calling us gods because we are. We proved that last year. You proved it. I did. Hunt—"

"Don't throw his name around," Brett warned, finger out.

"Why? Does it bother you?"

"Watch yourself, Pax," Brett cautioned again, knowing his anger was about to erupt.

"He believed in us, too. Just because you've chosen to bury his legacy along with his body, some of us aren't so quick to do so."

"How dare you fuckin' say that to me!" Brett grabbed Pax's shirt collar and gritted his teeth in the man's face. "You have no idea how I feel, what I've gone through…"

"Whoa, whoa, whoa," A deep voice and big hand on his shoulder brought Brett back from the ledge. He felt himself being pushed back as Quillan Layton came up in between him and Paxton. "Breathe, Cap, just breathe." Quil looked into Brett's face and pushed at his shoulders again, sitting him down on a nearby bench. He then turned to Paxton and whispered something.

Brett felt his entire body shake as adrenaline coursed through his veins. He'd been ready to tear his LB's face off. *What the hell is wrong with me?* Brett covered his face in his hands as he attempted to calm his rage. He needed a soak, a drink, a fuck, a swim… something!

"You alright, ese?" Quillan asked as he sat down next to Brett and patted his shoulder again.

"I dunno. I'm not so sure right now to be honest," Brett answered, truthfully.

"Death is hard. And just when you think you have a handle of it, it slaps you back down to the ground."

That's right! Quil's wife had died, under what circumstances Brett wasn't sure. If anyone could understand, it was Quil.

"I'm sorry, man."

"Nothing to be sorry for. You and Pax'll be joking around about it before the week's out."

It was probably true, but it didn't make Brett feel any better about how he treated his friend.

"He didn't deserve that."

"Sometimes we focus our anger on people who don't deserve it when we're at our most vulnerable. Don't worry, he'll forgive you."

Brett wasn't worried about Pax forgiving him. Pax was easy, cool, light-hearted. He'd realign his chakras or whatever, meditate, and be over it in no time, but Brett would have the stigma for a time. That was what he did best. Hold grudges.

"You aren't the only one in pain, Brett. Just keep that in mind."

Brett nodded. He knew that, he did; he just was so consumed with his own at the moment.

"We're gonna find our groove, man. Ok? We will. Zeus isn't done here." Quil smirked and elbowed him. "I just want you to know that I'm patient. I'm not gonna stop working at it. It's gonna take time. But we *will* get it. I believe in our spirit. We got a lot of people counting on us, and we all have the talent."

Brett looked his new teammate over. Despite his dark brows and serious demeanor, there was a lightness to him, a man who shown with promise, a man who knew about second chances, a man who'd also stared death in the face and not let it swallow him up. It gave Brett pause, and he nodded again.

"Thanks for the bout of confidence, Quil. I'm gonna go shower now and head home."

"Rest is as important as work, amigo. Make sure to take care of yourself."

"You too, ace." Brett stood and began to walk away, only to hear Quil say, "Remember, we got a Super Bowl to prepare for."

When he turned back around, Quil winked and gave him a smile. Brett smirked back. If only he had that same conviction.

BRETT HEARD the doorbell ring and looked to Madi who blushed. He'd noticed she was making more food than usual—who had she invited to dinner?

Quillan's deep voice called from the doorway, and Brett internally sighed. Why had she brought him here? Madi gave him a hug, which irked Brett to no end, but then Madi squatted down and her voice softened. Brett frowned and moved toward the door, his curiosity getting the best of him.

He stopped when he saw the cutest little girl he'd ever laid eyes on. Beautiful, brown hair, eyes and skin just like her father's. She was definitely Quillan's child, there was no denying it. She couldn't have been older than six, wearing a princess-type gown that looked more like a costume.

"And who's your favorite Disney princess, Quinn?" Madi asked her, tapping her lightly on the nose. The little girl giggled, and Brett couldn't help but grin.

"Pocahontas," Quinn's eyes got big and her smile brightened. "She's Native American like Daddy is."

Quillan step forward then, pink hitting his cheeks as he took Brett's hand. "Hope we aren't imposing."

"Of course not. You're my teammate. Mi casa su casa, brother." Brett tried to lighten his mood. It'd been a while since anyone on his team had been to his house. He was overdue.

"And a beautiful casa it is, amigo." Quil looked around at the kitchen with its white cabinets, granite countertops, dark wood floors, shiplap walls, and high, beamed ceilings. Brett's home had the whole farmhouse style down, and he'd gotten many compliments on its authentic feel; he'd said Joanna Gaines could have decorated it for how close it was to her vibes. He was proud of the work that had been done to this old house. He truly loved it here.

"Can I get you something to drink?" Brett offered and showed him into a little sitting area where they sat down in Queen Anne chairs that looked into the kitchen.

"No, thank you. I'll wait until dinner," Quil answered then

nodded to the little girl who held Madi's finger and looked up at him. "Brett, meet my daughter, Quinn."

Brett smiled at the precocious little girl with the Jack-o'-lantern smile. "Hi there. I'm Brett."

"He's also called Zeus."

"Zeus?" Quinn asked excitedly. "Like the king of the gods?"

Brett's brow rose in surprise. How'd this kid know about the Greek gods?

"She's a history buff, not unlike her nanny who likes to read all kinds of things to her that she probably shouldn't." Quil explained.

"'S ok, Dad," Quinn lisped. "Tia Nita just enjoys a good hero story." She shrugged, getting a laugh of the adults. "Why do they call you Zeus?"

Brett grinned again, but it was Madi who answered, "Brett here is our quarterback. He throws the football to receivers like your dad. One of his teammates coined him that because he's really good at it, saying how he throws passes like Zeus threw thunderbolts."

That got a giggle out of the little angel and they all laughed again.

"Want some juice, Quinn?" Madi asked and Quinn nodded her head. "I hope you like spaghetti and meatballs."

"Are you kidding? This kid's grandma is half Italian, she loves meatballs," Quil answered.

"My Nonni makes sweet spaghetti sauce, it's *so* good."

Brett smiled and looked up to Madi who looked apprehensive all of a sudden. "Uh oh, I hope my sauce can even compare. You'll have to let me know, ok?"

"Oh, don't worry, Ms. Madi. Nonni calls me a food critic." The six-year-old's chin went up at that, getting yet another laugh out of the adults.

"She obviously doesn't get her sense of humor from me," Quil shrugged. "How about you just eat Ms. Madi's cooking and keep your opinions to yourself, kiddo?"

"But Daddy…"

"No, listen, reinita" Quil whispered loudly. "This lady here is my boss, I don't need you getting me fired."

Madi stifled another laugh as she leaned into the back of Brett's chair. He took her hand and laced his fingers through it, loving the sound of her enjoyment. It had been so long since he'd seen her this light and stress-free and he absorbed it himself.

She smiled down at him, eyes sparkling, and he longed to shoot up, pull her into his arms and kiss her breathless; but he held back, if not for the kids' sake, for Quillan's. He might get jealous. Ha, who was Brett kidding? He was slightly intimidated by the six-foot-six-inch "beef-cake" as the girls had referred to Quil, seated across from him. He'd heard the ladies whispering about Quil when they didn't think the other guys noticed. In all honesty, from a guy's stand point, Quil was pretty—for a dude—so Brett could kinda understand why they all thought that.

Soon, they were eating dinner, and Quinn was approving of Madi's cooking, much to Madi's comical, overdramatized relief. It was an enjoyable meal, and Quinn was quite entertaining discussing numerous topics that left Brett stunned. This kid was gonna be a genius...and a man killer. Quillan had his hands full.

The guys cleaned up as the girls moved into the living room to watch Disney+. He and Quillan worked in companionable silence, Quil washing while Brett dried and put dishes away.

"Thanks for having us over, Brett," Quil said after they'd finished.

"Glad to have ya, Quil. Thanks for helping clean up."

"Quick hands make light work, my abuela always said."

"Thanks for helping calm me down today, too." Brett cleared his throat and looked away, guilt eating at him over how he'd treated Pax. He needed to call him, maybe suggest they hit the golf course one day and apologize, make things right.

Quil patted his shoulder, and Brett looked up at him. "You know, I thought my life was over when Rian died. It had been hard with her drug addiction and raising Quinn practically alone, but then her death was yet another feat I had to overcome. It was like God was slapping me in the face. I was angry with everyone, especially Him. My daughter was ill, my wife loved cocaine more than her own flesh and blood, and I was pushed out of doing the one thing I'd always wanted. Life ceased to exist for me."

Wow! Brett had had no idea this had happened. All he'd known was Quil's wife had died and he left the NFL, nothing more.

"I went into solitude. Me and Quinn. Hoping to raise my daughter away from the disgrace of what her mother had done to humiliate us both. My daughter's six. She didn't really understand it all, but she knew something was off. We can't protect them from everything." Quillan shrugged. "But soon I saw that I wasn't cut out for early retirement. My father was a hard-working man. He was a single father who worked long hours as a lumberjack to provide for me and my grandmother, who cared for me. I guess that value extended to me; I found myself floundering without football to keep me grounded, and Quinn saw it too." Quil grinned. "One day she looked at me and, point blank, asked me why I'd "given up." That opened my eyes. I realized that I *had* given up. Everything. Hope. Love. Life. I knew then that I owed it to my daughter, who's a stronger fighter than I've ever been, not to stop fighting for what I love. Football. That was what I loved—aside from her and her mother. And I wanted to inspire her to follow her dreams. To seek her goals and never stop pursuing her passions."

"Well, she's a good kid, Quil," Brett said with a smile, hearing the little squirt giggling in the background.

"She's the only thing keeping my feet here on the ground. I don't know what I would've done without her. She's my everything."

Brett understood that statement all too well. It was how he felt about Madison. That angel in the room next door was the reason he was breathing every day. He couldn't do life without her in his, which was why he'd made the choices he had.

"I can see Madi loves you, Brett, and you her."

Brett's eyes warned Quil off, but he didn't heed it.

Quil's hands came up in surrender. "I'm just saying, you can't feel bad about what happened to Hunter. It wasn't your fault. Just like Rian's death wasn't mine. Bad things happen and it's out of our hands. We have to keep going though...for them." Quil pointed to the room next door. "Don't let your regrets and guilt and pain keep you from the Heaven we're given here on earth. You both have hurt enough over what happened. Embrace the good that's been left behind."

With that, Quil clapped a hand to Brett's shoulder and gave him an understanding smile.

He moved into the living room, leaving Brett to ponder what he'd just said.

Brett let Madi see them out and waved to his new teammate and the adorable little girl of his. Madi looked down then before approaching him, and he felt his heartbeat quicken.

"I...I'm gonna go to bed, I think. I'm really tired."

"Madi," he pleaded and reached his hand out to her.

"Thanks for being a good sport." She gave him a weak grin and turned away.

Was she mad at him? Upset? Had someone told her how he'd acted at the complex today? Why was she being so distant with him?

Great, as if I didn't have enough shit to deal with, he thought and decided to hit the treadmill again.

MADI'S EYES were sore and slightly puffy as she made her way downstairs to the weight room to work out the next day. She was surprised to see Brett pumping iron, all swoll and sweaty, and sexy as all get out.

Dammit, her womanhood was soaking up the smell of his musk like he was freaking heroine and she, an addict. Her desire was full throttle and had been all week as he'd been so close yet so far away. She understood his distance, she knew why he was being this way, she'd heard about his temper in the weight room yesterday and she hadn't been surprised. Mr. Cool and Collected had always held his emotions in and now he needed to expel them somehow—and as a football player, physical combat was the only thing he'd ever known. Brett was an alpha, an apex predator, and when he didn't have prey he went stir crazy. It didn't help that he'd felt inadequate all week with his poor skill during passing drills or the fact that a newbie had shown up to take Hunter's place—or the fact that the sexual tension between him and Madi was crackling like a lightning storm on a summer day.

No, they needed some way to expel their stress; sex was what should be doing it, but Brett was holding back. Madi understood that, too. Hunter wasn't even cold in the ground yet, and Brett felt like he'd swooped in on the "damsel in distress." She got it, but that didn't mean her body wasn't aching for the loving she knew he could give her. The way his mouth had possessed hers, the way his hands had moved over her, the way his fingers had dominated her body; she was dripping wet at the prospect of having him. And as she moved past him while he bench-pressed an impressive amount of weights and huffed out, she made her mind up.

She watched his eyes linger on her ass, scantily clad in a pair of bike shorts and when he looked up, his eyes sought hers as he re-racked his barbell and rose. She could have moaned aloud at how the shiny, sweaty muscles in his arms and his chest rippled with the movement. His masculine strength called to every cell in her feminine body. She wanted to rip his clothes off him and succumb to his domination in any way he wanted to take her.

She made her move. She turned and began to pull her shirt over her head, revealing the sports bra beneath, then she began removing that too. He inhaled sharply as she threw it aside and moved toward him. When she stopped directly in front of him, she peeled the tight shorts off her frame and stepped out of them, watching his eyes stop at the delta of her thighs. He licked his lips as if he could remember what she tasted like; it made her mouth water.

She moved to straddle the bench and held his gaze for a moment before her hands moved to the hem of his shirt. She had it up and over his head and thrown to the side in a matter of seconds. Then her mouth descended to his as her hands moved to stroke his damp muscles. He groaned hungrily, and her sex tingled in anticipation. She felt her womanhood oozing want as his hands moved to her back and pulled her closer. They kissed like they were crazed, starving for one another as their tongues fought for control.

"Oh, Brett. Mmm." Madi whimpered as his mouth moved to her throat, and her hand fell to grip his hard member, held captive within his shorts.

"Oh God, Madi. Shit. That feels so damn good, baby girl."

She struggled with the hem of his pants and grunted when she couldn't get it down like she wanted, getting a chuckle out of him.

"What's the matter, my queen? Can't get to what you want?" The smirk on his face turned her on even more.

"You *know* what I want, now stop stalling." She moved a hand through the wide leg of his shorts and cupped his scrotum, getting a hiss from him. *Ha, victory!*

"Mmm." He took her lips again and squeezed her breast while she stroked his sex to its full potential, feeling triumphant. She was going to have him. Finally. "Tell Zeus what you want." Brett's brow rose, his lips puckered, and Madi saw the prize—*so close.*

"Oh, mighty Zeus," she cooed. "I want you in my mouth." She licked her lips slowly, watching his eyes as they darkened and he growled, a hungry lion about to devour his prey. "I want to taste your want for me. I want to take you deep down my throat."

Then suddenly she was thrown backward, her breath whooshing out of her chest. His big palm cupped the back of her head as his tongue licked her from her ear to her jawline, and she shivered at how much she wanted him inside her.

"My queen will *always* get what she wants."

Madi gasped as she was pulled upright and watched in awe as Brett stood and began jerking his shorts down. Her eyes settled on his impressive manhood, jutting up at her eagerly, as she went to her knees before him. She wanted nothing more than to pleasure him as he'd pleasured her not so long ago, but she wasn't so sure she was good at this. She'd only done it to one other man—what if she was bad at it? She hesitated so long she was sure Brett would give up on her, but he had the patience of Job as he watched her battle within herself.

His hand moved into her hair, and he gripped her ponytail in his fist and twisted, pulling taut. "Are you intimidated by the size of your king, Hera?"

Afraid, no? Turned the fuck on? *Hell* yes! She hesitated no longer as her tongue delicately licked the crown of him. He shivered, and his head fell back. *OMG, I did that? Yes. I did that!* The encouragement spurred her on as her lips encircled the tip of him and sucked gently.

"Oh, shit," Brett swore as he gazed down at her, his eyes watching hers as she looked up at him. "You're so damn sexy with my cock in your mouth, Sunflower."

Again, her confidence soared, and her hand came up to the base of him, squeezing as her mouth moved, taking his shaft slowly down her throat. She relaxed, relaxed her jaw, relaxed her hesitations.

"Oh, my..." he trailed off as his body quaked and his eyes closed. "Madi, Jesus, your mouth, baby. Holy..." She left him speechless as her mouth and tongue and hand moved simultaneously to love his manhood—the way a queen loved her king, the way she'd been longing to since that night in his bed days ago. She moved a hand to cup his scrotum and soon, he was attempting to pull back, but she held him fast. Her hands moved to his ass in a death-grip, her head moving as his hips thrust. "Madi, please? I'm gonna..." he trailed off again as he groaned in climax, pumping into her as his grip tightened in her hair. He gasped, and groaned, and shuddered as he continued to thrust into her mouth, spilling his seed deep down her throat. "Oh, oh, God, baby."

"Mmm," she moaned as she continued to suck and stroke until he finally stopped her and pulled back, quaking. "Was that ok?" she asked and wiped at her mouth.

"Ok?" he smirked. "What do you think, my queen? You had me literally sputtering."

Madi grinned deviantly. "I did, didn't I?"

His smirk soon turned into a frown. Uh oh, serious Zeus was back—and gripping her ponytail again. Her sex clenched. "Is that funny, Hera?"

"No, my king."

"I think you should suffer for your mockery, you naughty little goddess."

"Mmm, what did my king have in mind?" Madi purred, and Brett all out growled, his cock jerking to life again, making wetness drip down her legs.

Madi gasped as she was pulled to her feet and cradled in his arms. He took the stairs two at a time, Madi swooning between want and excitement.

He practically threw her on the bed and moved to his drawer of secrets. Madi gaped as he brought out a leather collar with a chain leash...and her dildo. "Brett! Where—? How did you...?"

"Perhaps you shouldn't leave your toys laying around, my sweet. They might be used against you." His brow went up, and she gulped in anticipation, the thought of having him fucking her with her own vibrator made her insides flutter. "Now, where were we?" He put his hand to his chin in thought then smirked again. "Ah, yes, I remember now." He dropped the sex toy to the bed. He opened the collar, wrapped it around her throat, and clasped it shut. "Now, lay down like a good girl and spread your legs."

"What if I don't wanna be a good girl, Zeus?" She brought her finger to her mouth, feeling naughtier than she ever had in her life.

Brett's face contorted into something sinister, and Madi's tummy fluttered in desire once again. She loved this side of him. How had she never known he was such a dominant alpha male? How had she never known this side of herself? What the hell was he doing to her? And why was she loving every second of it?

"Well then, darlin', you'll be spanked if you disobey your king. Do you defy me?"

Mmm... God, yes! She wanted to defy him. She'd never been spanked, and the thought of it turned her ravenous for him. Her brow went up as he gripped the chain of the collar and pulled it taut. "Mmm," she moaned as his finger trailed her body, going from her breast to her side, to her ass.

"Turn and bend over," he coaxed. "I'll show you the penalty for defiance."

Madison obediently turned and bent over. She felt his body press into hers from behind, feeling his erection digging into her ass, yearning to have him buried deep. She wanted to beg for him to do so, then felt his thick finger enter her and gasped on a moan.

"Mmm, so wet... You make my mouth water, Sunflower."

His big palm cupped her head, and he pushed it gently, down to the pillow. She jutted her ass out as his finger thrust in deeper.

Suddenly, he pulled it out, and she felt his palm smack her ass cheek. The bite was as erotic as painful; she gasped even as she moaned in bittersweet pleasure. Another smack came before she felt the head of her toy being pushed gently inside her. "Oh, God," she whimpered and reached for Brett's thigh, grasping and digging her nails into his muscular quad. His hand reached around her leg, and his fingertips moved to the aching bud between her thighs. He began to use the dildo on her, pushing it in and pulling it out, moving it faster and deeper inside her, eliciting strangled cries from her before turning it on to vibrate. "Mmm," she whined as he spanked her again and gripped her ass hard as he fucked her with her vibrator.

"Does that feel good, naughty girl?"

She responded with gasps and moans as the rhythm increased inside her and his finger tortured her wet folds.

Suddenly, he pulled the toy out, and she felt his mouth sucking at her aching flesh. The vibrator moved to her clit, where he stroked it ever so lightly, then tapped it against her flesh, "spanking" her with it.

"Oh, oh my God," she whimpered then screamed as her orgasm came violently upon her.

Before she could even come down off her high, she was being pulled up and flipped over onto her back, Brett moving to the head of the bed, on his knees. He opened her legs, sliding a hand down her inner thigh, and she gasped. She felt the leather tighten around her neck as he gripped the chain, and he began to tap the cold metal gently against her swollen folds. He moved forward slightly to straddle her face as the dildo moved back inside her. She gripped his erect shaft tightly in her fist and stroked him as she tilted her head back, sucking the head of his member into her mouth.

"Oh, my sweet goddess. You sure know how to please your king."

She moaned around his shaft as he turned the vibrator on high and went to town on her.

Soon, she was gasping and groaning in pleasure as her climax came once more. He followed, thrusting against her sucking mouth as he grunted and spasmed.

After they caught their breath, he pulled the vibrator from within her and turned it off as she leaned her head back against his thigh, exhausted.

"Did I wear you out, Sunflower?" he smirked, and her eyes looked up as he stroked her cheek with a knuckle.

She attempted a nod, and he moved off her, coming to her side to kiss her lips.

"You cum a lot," Madi said bashfully.

"I do, huh?" He seemed pleased by this news. "More than a mouthful?"

She nodded. "I just find it surprising. I didn't say I have a problem with it," she confessed.

"I mean I *am* Zeus, just sayin'." He shrugged, and she elbowed him. He laughed loudly and pulled her into his chest, kissing her breathlessly. "Thank you," he said when he pulled back. "I needed that."

"Touché, monsieur."

"Hmm, talk French to me, mademoiselle." Brett went in for her neck then, licking, kissing and sucking, getting giggles from her before he planted his lips back to hers. He kissed her slowly, languidly, pulling her desire back with his ineptly skilled tongue. "I think I like the French kisses the best, myself," he quipped and fondled her breast, getting a moan out of her. "Mmm, mademoiselle likes them too, I see."

Madi laughed. "Mademoiselle likes everything you do to her, handsome."

He smiled but then his smile faded suddenly. "I'm sorry."

"For what?" she asked and cupped his cheek.

"Last night."

She pulled her brows in, not understanding what he meant.

"You were upset before you went upstairs."

"That wasn't you. That was me, feeling sorry for myself."

"I'm sorry," he said again.

"You said we weren't doing that anymore, remember? Apologizing to one another."

"I did, didn't I? Ok, let's start that over again." He gave her a big smile, and she swooned. God, she was so in love with him.

She pulled him in for another sexy kiss that lasted longer than the last one before he pulled back.

"Madi, I'm going to the gravesite."

Madi's brows went up. "Oh? You want me to join you?"

He was shaking his head. "I need to go alone. I need to talk to my best friend." When Madi pouted, he corrected, "My other best friend." He winked and grinned, kissing her pout away.

When he moved his tongue in, she forgot all about his indiscretions and moaned before she pulled away, running her hands down his chiseled torso. "Go, get things off your sexy chest. Because mademoiselle will be impatiently waiting for your return."

Brett smirked. "Oh, really? Hasn't that greedy girl had enough yet?"

Madi's brow went up and a braver side of her surfaced. "You haven't seen a greedy girl yet, my king."

"Mmm, I can't wait to see what Hera has in store for me."

BRETT WAS solemn as he approached the grave. It was a clear and beautiful day, almost June now and he felt an ache hit his gut, the nagging guilt that he couldn't repress no matter how many days passed.

The mound was still slightly raised, now covered in grass where the last time there was fresh dirt atop it. Flowers sat in vases, brilliant colors and various kinds, perched on the base of the headstone.

Seeing Hunter's name carved into the stone sent daggers through Brett's belly; it halted him in his tracks. He'd lost count of the number of times he'd come by here and hadn't stopped; it was on the way to the complex, but he hadn't had the balls to face the reality.

Birds called overhead, butterflies flew, and the clouds rolled all while Brett felt like his life had stopped. It was a strange feeling.

Finally, Brett squatted and touched the headstone, a cold shiver running down his spine.

"HI, I'M HUNTER THOMAS." The young, spry receiver stated, shaking Brett's hand. He was a transfer from the University of South Carolina, and rumor had it he was really good.

"Brett McFadden, good to meet ya."

"Oh, a fellow southern boy, huh? Where you from?"

"Tate, Georgia. You?"

"Charleston, South Carolina."

"Welcome to UGA, buddy."

"Thanks man, I appreciate it. Good to be here."

"You'll love it. It's a great school, great team."

"I've heard." The smile that graced the young man's face looked playful.

He was almost as tall as Brett but leaner, less broad. His eyes were a light brown, hair a dark brown, and he had a deeper tan than Brett's. "Say—you got one hell of a cannon, Cap."

"Thanks." Brett was proud of his arm; it was gonna make him a starter this year. The scouts would be coming around soon, and he aimed to get seen.

"You must work out," Hunter smirked and shoved at him, getting a laugh out of Brett.

"Oh, you a jokester, huh?"

Hunter nodded. "Hell, life's too short to be too serious. Don't you agree?"

Brett shrugged. Sure, but a man had to be serious in their sport, if he wanted the pros.

"Damn, who the hell is that?" Hunter's head motioned over to where Madi stood, talking to her fellow cheerleaders.

She was gorgeous today, as always, clad in her daisy dukes and a tight tank top that accentuated those perfect breasts of hers. He should know, he'd felt them for himself days ago. The wind caught her golden-blonde hair, and she pulled it back into a ponytail, waving over at him as she caught his eye. He could feel his body floating on a cloud as he waved back, he was swooning.

"Dude," Hunter nudged him, awakening him from his reverie. "Who is that? She's fine as hell."

Brett immediately scowled.

"What? That your girlfriend? Sorry, man, but she is." Hunter blushed.

"Her name's Madison Taylor."

"Mmm, maybe I'll have you introduce me to her later, huh?"

"Easy, Romeo. Go set up. I'm gonna make you a target first. Let's see what you got, alright?"

"Alrighty there, gunslinger," Hunter gave him a hick accent and moved to set up at the line. "The name's Hunt by the way, Cap, and I'm about to blow your mind with my moves." Hunt gave a wink and puckered his lips.

Brett rolled his eyes even as he called for the snap.

. . .

THE MEMORY of that day burned hot into Brett's mind, and tears ran down his face as he recalled how well-matched they'd been from day one—the QB and his receiver. They'd had a connection, friends from the get-go—that was until Hunt had met Madi and Brett's hopes and dreams were dashed in an instant. The young man whom Brett considered a friend suddenly became his enemy and he didn't even know it, not for years to come.

Brett wished he had his time to do over again. He would've introduced Madi as his girlfriend, and that would have been that; but he'd hid his true feelings. Instead of discussing what happened after the party, he'd avoided the conversation all together, too scared to find out the truth.

The fact of the matter was: he'd been fearful Madi's bold actions had been a drunken reaction—not a representation that she loved him—and he couldn't have tolerated it if that had been true. He should've known their magnetism went far beyond that.

Either way, he'd rather have gotten a pissed Madi, who would've gotten upset with him for claiming her as his girlfriend, than to allow Hunter to swoop in and take her away from him as he'd done.

Now, Brett was left with the pang of regret that flooded his entire soul.

"Dammit, Hunt, I'm sorry. I'm fucking sorry it happened. I'm sorry I was driving your damn car, and you were the one to die because of it. I'm sorry I took your life. I'm sorry that I can't move on because I feel horrible about it all. You would still be here if it wasn't for me!" He was bawling like a baby now. He stood and began to pace. "I'm sorry that I'm in love with your wife, and I always have been, God help me, but I can't apologize for how she makes me feel. How amazing it feels actually being with her, touching her, kissing her. I need some sign that you're ok with all this. I know what you said on your death bed. I know you told me to take care of her, to give her babies, to love her like you couldn't but…

"I—I keep hesitating because I haven't told her that I actually spoke to you on your death bed. And it's eating me alive. As if I don't have enough shit to feel guilty about. I'm sorry we fought so much in the end, but I still loved you even though you fucking cheated on her. Damn you, you *had* to know she would find out!" Brett crossed his arms and yelled down at the grave. "God, do you know how fucking hard that was—how upset she got? She fucking propositioned me. And I was able to *not* have intercourse with her. Shows you how much restraint I have! Right? I know, I was just as shocked as you are."

He laughed, knowing Hunter would have if he'd been there. If someone walked by, they'd think Brett had lost his damn mind talking to a gravestone like it was a person, but it made him feel better. "Dammit, Hunt, do you know how much we miss you?" he whimpered as he hit his knees before the grave and leaned against the headstone. "I miss you. I miss my brother. The one who told me to suck it up when we lost a game, the one who had my back and always knew where to be on that field. I can't fucking throw, man. I can't. I don't know what the damn problem is. Yeah, I do. It's because my boy is gone and I'm not throwing him bombs anymore. You took those with you, didn't you?"

The wind blew then and ruffled Brett's hair.

"You'd give me your blessing, give Quillan your blessing, right? You'd like him, Hunt. He's a good guy. He's got the cutest little girl." Brett began to cry again. "I think it hit Madi hard, seeing that little girl, the life y'all were supposed to have." He looked up at the sun that beamed down on him then. He smiled, feeling it warm him, fill his hollow heart.

"I want to give your wife the life she deserved to have with you. I love her, you know how much I love her. It's just this guilt that I can't shake, Hunt. I need your forgiveness. I can't move on without it. Tell me you forgive me for killing you. I'm so sorry. I'd do anything to turn back time."

Brett held his breath and waited. Waited for redemption, even retribution. Retribution from a dead man. From a grave. He sat down on his butt, feeling defeated, feeling somewhat crazy for thinking he could come here and receive answers, a pardon.

Just as he started to rise, he heard a voice calling, "Son, what are you doing?"

Brett turned, surprise and awe filling him.

A little boy in a crimson Gladiators jersey came forward with big, chocolate brown eyes and a baseball hat hanging off his little head. He stared at Brett in surprise, holding his gaze for long moments before looking down and pointing. Brett's eyes fell to see a tortoise walking over Hunter's grave and he gasped, thinking of a conversation between Hunt and the team when Linc told him that the god Hermes was associated with a tortoise, from one of the fables they'd found online.

Well, then you named me after the wrong god, Lazarus. I'm far more comparable to the hare, Hunt had smirked to Linc and waited for Linc to deny his claims.

Linc and the rest of the guys had laughed big then, including Brett, for Hunt's speed on the field was undeniable.

Linc had crossed his arms over his chest. *There's more reasons for why I named you Hermes, including that you're a trickster and you're fast, thus why I drew wings on your damn cleats, Speedy Gonzales.*

Remembering that conversation had Brett tearing up before he smiled back up at the little boy, now giggling down at the tortoise on the ground.

"C'mon, champ, let's go. Mommy's waiting."

Brett nodded at the boy's father, realizing he knew who he was and looked embarrassed that his son had interrupted Brett's moment.

When the little boy turned, Brett covered his mouth. He had on Hunter's jersey, number 83.

CHAPTER THIRTEEN

"A tortoise named Hermes. It's only fitting," Linc said as he moved over to the aquarium filled with dirt. "But he would have named it something else, ya know?"

Brett laughed and sipped the beer in his hand. He shrugged. "Probably Speedy."

They all laughed and Pax shoved at Brett. "You better not have too many of those, Zeus. We got practice tomorrow."

"You perfected your pose yet, merman?" Brett flicked at Paxton's cup.

Pax scowled. He didn't like Brett calling him that, but it was appropriate, especially after he'd caught him practicing his new victory dance while filming himself on his phone; everyone else had found it equally as hilarious.

"Drink your Kefir and zip it, hippie boy," Trav smarted and playfully punched at Pax's bare chest.

"I'll have you know this is one of the healthiest—"

"Yeah, yeah, we've heard it! Lighten up, will ya? It's Independence Day. Have a damn cerveza." Quil grumbled and rolled his eyes, getting another laugh out of the rest of them.

Quillan had really hit it off with the team. Brett went to practice the day following his visit to Hunter's grave, and it was as if everything just clicked. They took to the field, Brett threw a deep pass and hit Quil right between the numbers. He, in turn, took it into the end zone for a fifty-yard touchdown. It was as if the minor hiccup they'd had the entire week had never occurred. After that, they were on fire and had quickly formed a bond. They'd been practicing with the rest of the offense for the last few weeks and camp was starting next week. Their practices, routes, and routines were gonna get rigorous, so they were sucking up their last hoorah before their bodies and minds would be put to the test. But Brett felt good about his team, good about this year, and he planned to dedicate his to his best friend, Hunter Thomas.

Brett saw TJ looking around and stifled a smirk. He was looking for Brooke, Brett knew, Madi's younger sister. Brooke was attractive in her own right, with straight brown hair, brown eyes, and deeper tanned skin than Madi's; but Brooke was a loose cannon. She was admittedly open to both sexes, male and female. Hell, Brett wouldn't put it past her to sleep with transsexuals. After all, she was much more liberal than her conservative sister and prided herself on being in the spotlight any chance she got; she was a model and pushed the envelope with her poses and stages of undress. She loved attention, good or bad, and that made her "dangerous" in Brett's eyes.

Brett had first noticed TJ's appraising eyes on Brooke at the memorial they'd held for Hunter. Every get-together or event they'd had since, TJ had watched her but hadn't spoken to her much since Brooke made it known that she wasn't into football players. Brett considered warning his OT about Brooke's shiftiness, but knew TJ would figure it out on his own. It wasn't Brett's business anyway.

"She's happy, really happy, Brett." Pax nodded over to Madi then, elbowing his QB.

Madi was laughing at something Skyla was saying, bouncing Lennox in her lap on the pool stairs. She looked stunning in a bright yellow, lacy bikini that complemented her lightly tanned skin.

Brett smiled. She was, and he was too; incredibly happy, happier than he could ever remember being. They were in love, completely and desperately, despite that he still hadn't made love to her yet. He wanted to, he wanted to so badly, but he was waiting. He played the part of the ever-present gentleman he'd always been with her, courting her like a man was supposed to court a woman: taking her out to dinner, shows, and on trips. He sent her flowers, love notes, and gifts for no reason other than to see her smile.

She'd moved into his house, and they slept in the same bed together…and they'd done amazing things together, all except intercourse. He didn't want to impose on her; he wanted to make sure she was ready for the next step of their relationship. Hell, it'd just been four and a half months since Hunter's death, and Brett didn't need anything else to feel apologetic for. He was just now starting to feel whole again.

Madi had sold the house; this was their last weekend hanging out here before the movers came. Most of the furniture was being donated, some was going into a storage unit, and the clothes were going to Brett's. It had been Madi's idea to give the house a farewell party; that just happened to coincide with the fourth of July.

"Daddy, are you getting in the pool?" Valeria swam over with Lofton as she looked up at Linc, eyes hinting like she might refer to him as Daddy when the boys weren't around too.

"Yes, sexy mama, I'm coming," Linc confirmed and shrugged at the guys as he moved to the edge of the pool.

Brett continued to man the grill and smirked as Langley laughed.

"Can't say as I blame him. Blondes have more fun anyway, right, Brett?"

Brett frowned at the conviction in Lang's eyes.

"Hell, he wouldn't know," Trav mumbled under his breath, but Lang caught it and Brett could've punched Travis in the mouth. Trav saw it and immediately apologized, "Sorry, man, it's just…when the hell are you gonna take the plunge? Don't tell me you still feel guilty?"

"I forget my girlfriend is friends with yours," Brett grated, annoyed, and Pax laughed.

"Gotta take her out of the friendzone, man," TJ suggested with a shrug of his big shoulders.

"Right? Thank you. I mean, can you really even *call* her your girlfriend? Just sayin'." Travis put his hands up as Brett gritted his teeth and lunged forward.

"Looks like we might have Trav dogs instead of beef franks." Brett bawled up his fist and pointed it at Travis in warning.

"Easy, Zeus," Pax patted Brett's shoulder.

"Fuck all y'all. We're dating, we're together. I don't need to stick my dick in her for it to be official." He huffed. "You know what? You guys wouldn't understand anyway. Linc, how would you feel if I moved in on Val before you'd barely even started to rot in your grave, huh?"

At that, all five guys balked.

"Yeah, that's what I thought, so back off." Brett turned the dogs and kept his eyes low. He didn't need them to tell him what constituted a relationship. None of them had ever been as patient as he'd been, so how could they possibly understand waiting to make love to the woman of their dreams until she was over her husband's death? They couldn't. Furthermore, there was nothing wrong with waiting for the moment to be right. Brett intended to make love to Madi, but he wanted it to be perfect. He wanted to marry her, too. And he had no idea when she'd be up for that again. Besides, it was really none of their business.

Brett's eyes looked over at Lang suddenly, who was intent on Madi's bikini-clad frame as she handed Lennox over to Skyla. Her breasts bobbled precariously as she righted her low-cut top and blushed at the near-exposure. A flash of jealous, angry heat shot through him at the memory of a similar encounter not long ago:

. . .

"HEY, MY BOYS," *Madi cooed as she ran up to them, smiling. She was clad in workout gear, a tight gray sports bra and black shorts, her blonde hair curly and pulled back in a ponytail. She looked sexy as hell, and Brett wasn't the only one to notice—or appreciate—her outfit as he greeted her in turn.*

"Hey, baby," Hunt grinned like he'd just been given the winning lottery ticket.

"Have a good practice. I love you both." She blew kisses to both Hunter and Brett before moving off to the edge of the football field for her morning run, breasts and bottom bouncing.

"Mmm, damn you, Hunter Thomas! You get to hit that fine ass tonight."

Brett was two seconds from reaching out and grabbing Langley in a chokehold for his words, only to hear Hunter laughing victoriously beside him.

The two sets of eyes that roved Madi's retreating backside had Brett feeling murderous. Lang and Hunt were eating her up like she was a free buffet—and he was absolutely livid.

"Correction, dude, I'm gonna hit that fine ass here in about an hour when we get a break," Hunt replied, brow arching as he glanced at his Rolex.

Brett felt his stomach pitch, appalled that Hunter would allow Langley to talk about his wife, and boss, in such a lewd manner.

When Langley walked ahead, Brett grabbed the back of Hunt's shirt and held him fast.

"What kinda man says such things about the woman he's supposed to love, honor and cherish, huh?" He gritted through his clenched teeth. "How dare you allow that bastard to disrespect your wife that way!" Brett's gaze bore holes into Hunter. Hunter looked taken aback, remorseful, and ill-equipped, but it was anger that he answered Brett with.

"Why don't you mind your own damn business? Seeing as she's my wife, after all, and not yours! You tend to keep forgetting that, Zeus."

THE MEMORY WAS poignant as Brett remembered Hunt's poor treatment, and poor defense, of Madi. He realized, once again, how wrong Hunter had been for her.

A throat cleared bringing Brett from his reverie, and he looked back to Lang who was entertained by the baby now in Linc's arms.

They all stood there, quietly sipping their beers, Pax his Kefir, before Quil calmly said, "You know what, Brett? I personally commend you. I think it takes a strong man to be able to hold—"

"Fuck you, Quil."

"Yup. So, about practice tomorrow..."

Everyone laughed then, even Brett, who playfully shoved at Quil. Travis patted his shoulder in apology, and all was right as rain again. That's how dudes were, fighting one minute, joking the next. He loved these assholes and couldn't wait to play ball with them.

MADISON GRINNED OVER AT BRETT, taking his hand in hers as they waited for the fireworks to begin. Lofton and Lennox looked up from their blanket at the ones they could see in the distance, and their little baby blabber tickled Madi's heart. They were so precious, and she wished she had one of her own. One day she would. With the man who held her heart in his massive hands.

He leaned in to kiss her, and she reveled in the feel of his masculine presence. They'd not made love yet and, as eager as she was, there was also a side of her that was relieved they hadn't gone all the way. She hadn't planned to move on so soon after Hunter had died, but life was funny that way; it still didn't take away the slight hesitations she had though, even if it were Brett she was falling in love with.

Madi leaned into him and he wrapped an arm around her, pulling her closer into his embrace. He smelled like sunshine, sweat, chlorine, and a scent that was all him, both sweet and manly; she couldn't get enough of him. His nose moved along her jawbone, and she shivered as his mouth settled on her throat. He made her feel safe and loved. These past few weeks with him had been amazing.

He seemed to get the answers he'd sought that day at the gravesite when he'd brought the tortoise home; whatever he'd been seeking, he'd found, despite that Madi didn't understand where a turtle came to play in all of it. She simply let him have his symbolism and reaped the benefits.

The fireworks went up and the babies clapped even as Travis whistled from the opposite side and tackled a squealing Skyla to the blanket. *Jeez, those two.* Skyla would be the next having a baby and, as wonderful as that was, it also made Madi extremely jealous. She couldn't get over her issue with the whole lack of a child, and she wondered if it was because her biological clock had started to tick. She tried not to overanalyze it as Brett kissed her passionately and grabbed at her breast. She grunted and swatted his hand away—albeit playfully—interlacing her hand through his as she looked up at the explosions of red, blue, and shimmering white lights blasting through the onyx night sky. It was beautiful and made her feel happy, despite that this was their last night in this house.

It would make a fine home for the family coming in, but it didn't feel like home anymore to her. She was glad to be shutting this door in her life. She'd loved Hunter, but it was time to finally say goodbye; this house was the endgame of that closure.

Brett was kissing her again, drawing her desire out as his tongue stroked across hers. His hand moved from hers to her breast again, and she began to scold him only to stop as his hand descended her body, coming to rest on her thigh. He nudged her legs open and moved his hand into her bikini bottoms, dipping a finger in between her folds. She stifled a moan, watching the brilliance of lights dance over his handsome face. He thrust his finger inside her slowly, then removed it and brought it slowly to his lips, sucking it into his mouth, savoring it and making her lust for him increase tenfold. He then leaned in to kiss her again and rubbed the essence of her across her taste buds. He loved to bait her, and she wondered how long he would hold out before he finally put out.

They made out for a time, touching each other subtly and erotically while the fireworks lit up the summer sky, but soon they were over and everyone was talking again.

Madi's pulse quickened when she heard Skyla squeal in delight and turned to see Travis on one knee, proposing.

"Holy shit, he's actually doing it," Brett whispered before closing his mouth abruptly as Madi's finger went to his lips. Tears came to her eyes as she watched Travis, more emotional than she'd ever seen him.

"Skyla Lynette Larson, I love you. Eight months ago, I went into a cabin in the woods a broken man and I came out whole thanks to you." Travis wiped a tear running down his cheek but grinned back at the redhead covering her mouth. "I didn't know how lost I truly was until you found me, Fireball. I love what you do to me, how you make me feel, how amazing life with you every day is. I want that to go on forever. Say you'll be mine. Say you'll marry me. Say you'll make me a husband and a father. Say…"

"Oh, shut up and let me say yes would you, you stubborn ram?"

Travis busted out laughing and nodded, and Sky replied with a, "Yes," before he placed the big solitaire on her finger and pulled her into his arms.

Madi stood quickly and turned away from the scene as applause rang out all around her, her emotions too great to stay.

She was breathing hard as she moved into the kitchen from the patio, holding her chest as she attempted to calm the panic attack coming on. This had happened several times when Hunt had first died, and she'd let the grief almost consume her. She still had them on occasion, but they weren't as frequent now as they were in the beginning. She continued to move through the kitchen, finally stopping in the butler's pantry and leaning against the counter. She closed her eyes and told herself to relax.

Soon, she was able to see without spots and breathe normally, but just as she turned to rejoin the party, Lang stood in her way, giving her a disturbing grin that stilled her blood. She gulped as he stepped forward.

"You ok, Madi?"

She nodded and made to move around him. He caught her arm and pulled her into his chest, backing her into the counter.

Panic rose in her gut. She gulped again as his knuckles moved over her cheek and his eyes appraised her body, clad in nothing but her bikini and the thin cover-up that did *nothing* to cover anything up at this point.

"You're so beautiful. I think I know what you need, baby doll." He motioned down to his crotch which she could feel was stiffened against her.

She stifled a whimper, hoping someone would be stumbling in to check on her very soon.

"It's been a long time for you, I heard. Perhaps it's time to remedy that, don't cha think?"

She couldn't move as fear held her captive, Langley's face coming down on hers. His lips were rough as they moved against her own. Her attempt at pulling back did nothing, for there was nowhere for her to go.

Madi struggled to scream even as he lifted her and braced her hips with his own. She was resisting and pushing against his chest even as she heard the zipper of his pants give way. She screamed loud as she shoved with all her might, but to no avail. He was simply too big and too strong for her to fight him.

This wasn't happening. He wasn't going to do this. He wasn't—

"Lang, dude, what the *fuck* are you doing?" It was Pax.

Oh, thank God! "Paxton—" she began, but he was already moving, his big arm reaching for Lang's shirt and pulling him backward. Madi fell abruptly to the ground with an, "Umph," as Langley's grip immediately loosened around her.

"Pax, what the—?" Brett asked and frowned as he realized what had just happened. Suddenly his eyes turned murderous, and he lunged for Langley's throat. "You motherfucker, I'll fuckin' kill you!" The roar that escaped Brett's lips was animalistic, and Madi stood to stop him from murdering Lang.

TJ grabbed Brett's arm before he made it to the man's throat, and he and Pax moved in to hold Brett back, for they were the only two as broad as Zeus was. Quil, Travis, and Linc were there then, grabbing Lang even as Brett fought to get to him. Brett was as furious as a bucking bronco, and Madi came forward to try and help, cupping his cheek and telling him to look at her.

"Calm down, baby. I'm ok. I—"

"Let me go, Pax. Fuckin' let me go, right now or I swear to God!"

"No can do, bro. I can't win a Super Bowl if my QB is injured. It's not happening." Pax held tight, but Brett's adrenaline was fueling him, giving him inhuman strength.

Quil and Linc took Lang out of the room even as Brett yelled to him. "You filthy bastard, I'll fucking kill you if you ever touch her again. You sorry piece of shit!"

"Brett, baby, it's ok," Madi cooed and finally got him to stop struggling; Pax and TJ looked exhausted.

"Call the fucking cops, Trav. He ain't getting away with that shit this time. Madi, baby, did he hurt you?" His eyes softened for a brief moment as his focus moved back to her, then he erupted again. A volcano of fury. "I'll fucking kill him, I'll—"

"Shh, I'm fine. He didn't hurt me." Brett's eyes flashed with pure rage, but Madi reassured him once more. "Brett, I'm fully clothed."

All the while, Madi was shaken to her core, fearing the man was going to rape her. She was grateful he hadn't gotten any further than he had.

Brett looked her over carefully, assessing for any marks before she finally got him to relax a little. TJ released Brett first, but Pax wasn't apt to let him go too soon. Brett swore he wasn't going to attack Langley, but Madi wasn't so sure. She threw herself into his arms when Pax finally let go, knowing that her presence calmed her captain.

"Oh, Madi, baby, look at me." He pulled her face up and touched her, his eyes darting her body for any sign of harm. When he was satisfied, he sighed heavily. "Are you ok?"

She held her tears and horror back, drawing every ounce of her willpower out as he pulled her back into his arms and kissed her softly yet possessively, treating her with delicate hands as if she were fragile cargo.

He sighed once more as he kissed her forehead and looked deeply into her eyes. "I'm sorry I wasn't there to stop him."

"Don't. He didn't do anything."

"He assaulted you," Brett growled. "Again! I swear, Sunflower, if he'd have—"

She didn't let him finish as she leaned up on her tiptoes and took his lips again. When she pulled back, he groaned as if in pain. "Don't do that to yourself. He didn't rape me. I'm fine. You rescued your damsel and, trust me, you're gonna get the girl." She winked, but Brett's scowl didn't lighten. She rested her head on his chest and waited until his heartbeat calmed before they moved into the kitchen, where Val and Sky looked up at her, horrified expressions on their faces.

They doted over her and made sure she was ok as Travis and TJ talked to Brett.

The cops came not long after, and Brett was present as they took Madi's and Paxton's statements. All the while, Madi was pretty sure Brett was gonna go Hulk on Langley in the next room over. Much to her surprise, he was able to hold his rage in.

The cops arrested Lang, and they saw everyone out. Madi apologized to Trav and Sky, feeling bad about their engagement being ruined by the incident. They were simply grateful she was alright. Madi hugged Pax tightly, thanking him for all he did and for rescuing her.

"Damsels in distress are my specialty, Mad," he smarted and got a giggle out of her.

TJ, Linc, Val and the boys, Quil and Quinn all left after that, following gratitude and hugs, leaving Brett and Madi to the giant house alone.

Her flip-flops echoed in the marble foyer, and she looked around, as if she were seeing the grand entrance for the first time even though she'd lived in this house for five years. She looked from the staircases to the ceiling and down, to Brett who'd walked up to her.

He ran a big palm from her back up to the tips of her hair then moved his fingers through the unruly curls. "Are you ok, baby?"

Having him call her baby made her feel so many incredible things. Hunt had always called her babe, which annoyed the shit out of her for some reason. Madi just nodded and looked up at him. God, he was so handsome. His square jaw set and slightly scruffy from the day, his broad frame filling out the muscle tank he wore, his emerald green eyes sparkling, his own hair unruly.

Madi turned into him, letting her chest rest against his. Brett sighed, a man at peace in the presence of the woman he loved. She grinned up at him and moved her hands up his big arms to his shoulders. Her fingertips glided through his brown hair.

"Brett, do you remember your first time?" she asked randomly, wondering who and how many women he'd had in his past. She only knew of a few he'd dated for longer than six months and never more than a year.

His jaw clenched. "I'd rather forget it...because it wasn't with you."

Madi's eyes darted away for a moment before answering his frown with her own. "How did you do it?"

"It wasn't easy, Madison. Truthfully, most of my sexual conquests weren't done when I was sober."

She remembered his last steady girlfriend and the words she'd said, the sadness on her face, when she'd come to Madi's office and told her how "lucky" she was. Madi had no idea what Hailey had meant then; security had come to escort her out after she'd laughed maniacally back into Madi's shocked face.

"How long have you loved me?" she asked randomly.

"A long time, my Sunflower." His stern face softened some as he cupped her cheek.

"When did you know?"

"I guess we were in high school before I really knew I was help-lessly lost for you. You remember that game where my shoulder got dislocated?"

"Are you kidding? Of course I remember that game! I thought I was going to have to kill someone to get to you."

"I remember seeing you rushing to that stretcher. Your long ponytail swaying as you pushed those players to get out of your way." He laughed, the deep rumble vibrating his barrel chest.

"I tore my cheer uniform that night, and Momma had to sew it that weekend. But I was so scared. I was screaming at them to get out of my way."

"I remember you coming up to me and taking my hand. The fear in your eyes was what did it. I was so happy, despite the pain, because I knew you loved me then even if you'd never said it, even if I hadn't told you. I knew we were going to be together, and that made everything ok."

"I cried so hard before Momma got me to the ER."

"Why? You saw that I was fine." Brett gave her an amused look. "Hell, the trainer was hell-bent on setting it before the EMTs even put me in the ambulance."

Even now, Madi was tearing up, remembering that horrible tackle and his roar of pain as he fell. "I was so scared that you weren't going to be able to play football anymore. It was what you loved more than anything—your passion, your gift—I was so fright-ened you wouldn't be able to do what you loved."

Brett grinned at her and leaned his head down to kiss her fore-head. "I would've given it all up to have been honest with you from the very beginning about how I felt and have you for my own, the way it should've always been."

Madi gaped as she looked up at him. Jesus, he was telling the truth. She swallowed hard and held his gaze, for it pierced her soul as it never had before. "You can still have me for your own, starting right now."

He knew what she was saying and they stood unmoving for a

moment, his eyes searching hers for any sign of hesitation, but there was none, not anymore. His Adam's apple bobbed then suddenly his head moved as did his hands. One moved to the back of her head, the other gripped her bottom as he lifted her. Their lips connected, hard and possessive, and Madi moaned at the contact. She would never stop loving those perfect lips of his!

Her legs wrapped around Brett's middle as he began to move from the base of the stairs and up the steps. Madi's grip was tight around his big neck and her focus was on his mouth, his beautiful mouth that was kissing her like he was a man on fire; her lips the only thing that could extinguish it.

He had them through the door of the bedroom, pulling at the sorry excuse for a bathing suit cover-up, before he stopped dead in his tracks, looking around. He frowned, realizing this was the room she'd shared with another man, the man who'd taken her first, the man she'd been married to, the man who wasn't him.

"It's ok, Brett." She reassured him, but she could see that he wasn't ok with that, he'd never been ok with it. She started to say it wouldn't matter where, for she and Hunter had made love all over this house, except for one room and Brett knew exactly which one, as if reading her mind.

He moved them to the opposite wing of the house, practically running at this point, and if his mouth hadn't been back on hers, she would've laughed at his rush to get to her. But soon, he was bolting through the guest room door and her back was hitting the mattress as the mountain of a man covered her body with his own.

Her string bikini top was the first thing to go, and Brett's massive hands squeezed and loved her breasts as her head flew back in passion. "Mmm," she purred as his mouth loved one breast then the other. His hands began to undo the strings on her bottoms, and he ripped them off, a man crazed. Madi's entire body literally hummed, ready for him, ready for the big member that was hiding behind those black swim trunks he was pushing down his hips.

When she saw it she moaned again, she wanted to feel his girth filling her like nothing she'd ever wanted before. She reached for him before he'd even gotten the trunks past his knees and squeezed the thick shaft with her fist, getting a growl out of him that made her sex tingle.

"Oh, Brett, I want you inside me. Now. Please?" she begged even as he moved atop her and aligned their bodies.

He brought an elbow next to her head, looking deeply into her eyes. One hand moved into her hair, his other hand cupped her face then descended her torso achingly slowly. His calloused palm covered her belly then hovered over the apex of her thighs. She felt his fingers separate her wet folds as she opened her legs wider and gasped when he dipped a finger inside her, preparing her further.

"I was so scared tonight, Madi, my beautiful Hera. The thoughts of another man..."

"Don't do that to yourself, my love. He didn't—"

"Even still. I've never wanted to kill someone as much as I did tonight. And I could've. I *wanted* to."

"Shh, it's over now." Her hand caressed his square jaw. "I'm yours. I've always been yours. Now *make* me yours, Zeus."

His brows drew and he gulped. Unspoken words passed between them. Years of pent-up emotions, desires, longing. Finally, Brett's face relaxed into a subtle grin. "I've wanted you for so long, Madi. Just like this. I imagined this, dreamed it, yearned for it. For so long, so *very* long."

The fingers in her hair stroked, just as his digits inside her did, and she whimpered and arched her hips, needing more.

And now you're gonna get me, so take me, she wanted to plead but moaned again as he plunged deeper, two fingers this time. He withdrew and brought them to his lips, licking the nectar from them and making her desire skyrocket.

"Mmm, I love your taste, sweet baby." Brett moved his wet fingers to her parted lips, letting her taste the combination of him and herself before switching them out for his tongue. Madi whimpered as he kissed her, her walls clenching as his fingers returned within her.

A growl came from the back of his throat then he said, "I wasn't the first man to be inside you Madison Hope, but I *will* be the last."

Madi didn't protest as his big palm moved to grip her hip, his own hips arching. He let her hand guide his sex to hers. She felt the head of his shaft pierce her opening, gasping as her body hummed with vibrating energy. "Oh God," she moaned as she felt him sliding inside her. Her hands moved up his back to his shoulders gripping him tightly as slow, incredible increments of time passed while he filled her womanhood with his steely member, in all the way to the hilt. When he settled over her, he kissed her mouth, letting her body accommodate to his size before he moved, withdrawing and plunging again. "Mmm."

"Oh, Madi, baby. You're even sweeter than I ever dreamed you could be." He drove in deep as she wrapped her legs around him and pulled his body ever closer.

"Brett," she whimpered, realizing what this moment meant. How in love with him she was and how incredible the union between them. How amazing his sex felt buried within her own, two contrasting pieces aligning together in perfect sync.

"Madison, my love, my queen, my heart." He cupped her cheek as he made love to her tenderly, with both his erection and his eyes. His hands moved to her breasts, worshipping her flesh, then his mouth took her nipple and he suckled ever gently. He moved to the other breast before his head came back up and he gazed into her eyes as he claimed her.

She gasped as her head began to fall back in ecstasy. She was close to the edge, the head of his shaft making spirals of pleasure ripple through her. She gripped his biceps and absorbed his momentum, moving her hips each time he lunged, ever so leisurely—as if he had all the time in the world to hit that incredible spot over and over and over again.

Madi's entire body began to quake with each plunge, and Brett chuckled in pleasure, basking in her responses. His hips angled, stroking her with his sex, loving her like she'd never been loved before. Zeus was skillfully and exquisitely coaxing her body to yield to him—a submission of unbelievable bliss.

And Hera was helpless, splayed wide, his to control, to command, to dominate as he saw fit. Her breaths were ragged as were his while his speed began to increase, the need for release taking hold of him.

"Oh, Brett. I..." She could feel the tingling beginning somewhere deep inside her.

"Mmm...yes, my love. I know."

"Oh, oh, oh."

They came together. In a harmony of moans, gasps, and shudders. Her body squeezed and milked him as he continued to rock inside her long after their climaxes had subsided.

"Oh, my sexy goddess..." His body shook as her walls squeezed around him again. "God, that felt amazing. I almost came the minute I was seated inside you."

Madi just blushed in response, feeling unabashedly sexy in that moment.

He grinned down at her and kissed her again, his hand languidly caressing her breast and bringing her desire full throttle once more. He suckled her and had her bucking against him before he shifted and moved her atop him in one smooth motion.

Brett's hands guided her hips as she began to ride him, her god of the gods, and love him with her body this time. His hands cupped her breasts as he watched her with pride, happiness, and domination. She was his. She'd always been his. Now their bodies were finally harmonizing, culminating, the way their hearts always had prior to now. It was beautiful, it was exquisite, it was love. Truly. Completely. Irrevocably.

"Mmm, my mighty Zeus," she cried as she felt another mind-blowing orgasm coming on. "I love you. I love you so much."

He groaned in pleasure, the larger-than-life, sexy god king beneath her. "I love you, my queen. Always and forever."

CHAPTER FOURTEEN

"What the hell is wrong with you?" Brooke asked as Madi heaved into the toilet again. "Mexican was a bad idea last night, huh?" She handed Madi a paper towel to wipe her mouth.

"Jeez, I guess. Crap." Madi held her belly as she came up off her knees to stand, flushing the commode as she did so. It could be the Mexican that hadn't set well with her or the fact that she was stressed about today's preseason game; either way, she was annoyed with the stomach that always gave out at the first sign of stress. She'd always known it was her weakest organ. "No more Texas margaritas for me." Madi scoffed and moved to the sink to wash her hands.

They were already at the stadium; the guys were suited up, although most wouldn't run more than a few plays before heading back to the sidelines to watch. They were playing the Jaguars today, and Madi knew she shouldn't be worried; preseason was always iffy, but she was still stressed. Preseason games marked the beginning of the season—but not as far as she was concerned. There would still be players cut, trades made, and losses that didn't much count before the regular season's start. So, why was she so amped up? Amped up enough to lose her breakfast?

She couldn't answer the question as Val and Sky came into the luxury box and hugged her. Val always made home games, even in preseason, occasionally away games if she got a babysitter. This was her time, she said, to be an adult, get out of the house, and praise her husband for all his amazing feats. To think almost two years ago, he'd almost died at his own hand.

Sky was radiant today with her flashy new ring atop her finger. Madi still felt a little jealous and couldn't shake why. She was uber happy for Travis and Skyla and knew they made a great couple, complementing each other so well.

"Madi, you look pale. You ok?" Sky asked, and Val frowned up at her.

"What's the matter?" Val asked.

"Guys, she's fine. She ate Mexican last night, and she's just stressed," Brooke answered and waved it off as she moved to get herself a drink—not minding that it was only eleven in the morning.

"I'm really not that stressed, it's just my stomach."

"You don't have that bug going around, do you?" Sky asked warily and took a step back, getting a laugh out of Val.

"Bloody hell, the way you and Zeus have been going at it, you might be up the duff," Val scoffed and patted her arm. She tilted her head questioningly at Madi who frowned. She only knew what the phrase meant because Val had told her about a friend of hers who'd gotten pregnant recently, and she'd said the same thing—up the duff.

At first, it offended Madi. Val knew how hard she'd tried to get pregnant but then the little voice in the back of her head reminded her of something… She turned from her girls and moved to look out onto the field. *Holy shit!* She wasn't on birth control! And she and Brett hadn't used protection…not once. How in God's name had that happened? How had she forgotten to take that precaution! Was she insane? Oh God, what would Brett say? Madi looked down at her belly and cupped her lower abdomen, wondering if she might be pregnant.

"Well, shit. Looks like I'm running to the drug store." Brooke set her glass down and headed out the door.

Madi fell into the chair in front of her, her eyes bouncing around the room. Could it be possible?

"Are you late?" Sky ran up and grabbed Madi's arm.

Her periods hadn't been regular for some time now, but her mind couldn't remember the last time she'd had a period, or needed to use sanitary napkins. It was a blank slate...other than flashing back to the numerous times she and Brett had sex over the last five weeks. In the weight room, the bed, the couch, the wall, the stairs, oh God... every damn where. There wasn't a square inch of his house, or his vehicles, they hadn't christened. They'd been like two damn rabbits. And yet she was surprised that she might be pregnant?

Her heart fluttered at the prospect but burned with fear; she couldn't get her hopes up. What if she wasn't? She was going to be so disappointed.

Madi realized Sky was still waiting on an answer and she nodded.

"Ohhhh," Val squealed, delighted. "I'm so excited."

"Don't jump the gun so quick, Valeria. We don't know yet. I—"

"Girl, you're late and you puked for no reason. You're as pregnant as pregnant can be."

"Shh..." Madi scolded as she saw the GM, Josh O'Connell, and her father coming through the door. "Keep your voices down. Sky, text Brooke and tell her to meet us in the hall bathroom when she gets here."

Sky did as she asked and Madi popped up, planting a smile on her face as her father and Josh greeted her. They talked briefly before Sky was pulling Madi away. She excused herself and walked numbly down the hall to the bathroom where Brooke had three pregnancy tests set up.

"Do all three at once, no doubting, no retaking. The moment has come, sis."

Madi rolled her eyes at her overdramatic sister and took all three tests into a stall with her.

She did the deed, brought the tests out, and washed her hands. All the while, she prayed that they were positive, although she couldn't say why. Brett was going to freak on her, she just knew it. They'd only been together a short time, they weren't married, and they hadn't even talked about their future, yet here Madi was painting a bright little nursery in her head.

When the timer on Brooke's phone beeped, Madi didn't look down, she simply said, "What's the verdict?"

"Well," Sky began, "I hope you've prepared a speech for Zeus cause, honey, you're pregnant."

"What? Really?" Madi finally looked down at the strips showing the evidence. "Oh, my God. I'm pregnant? I'm pregnant." Madi looked up into the overjoyed faces of her best girlfriends in shock. She couldn't believe it, but three positive tests didn't lie. Thank God Brooke had been smart enough to have her do them all three at once instead of one back to back which would have drawn the suspense out even more.

Val was the first to pull her in for a hug. "Welcome to motherhood, Mama." She placed her hand on Madi's lower belly. "Hi there, little one! Aunt Valley is so excited to meet you."

Madi teared up and pulled Val in for another hug. This was all she'd ever wanted, and it was happening. *Holy crap!*

Brooke came next with tears in her eyes. "Oh, big sis. I'm so happy for you. This is amazing. I can't believe I'll have a niece or nephew in eight months."

Holy crap!

Sky came next. "So, I uh, I might have something to share too." Her plump lips pulled in, in apprehension.

Madi's mouth dropped even as Sky nodded and tears fell down her cheeks.

"We're due in March. Travis is over the moon. He can't wait. Oh, Mad, we should do double baby showers."

Madi nodded vigorously and pulled Sky into her arms for a hug. This was surreal. More than she'd ever dreamed of. *Holy crap!*

But the nagging at the back of her heart was becoming a pounding ache in her chest. What the hell was Brett going to say, what would he think, and would he be excited? She didn't want to tell him before the game, but she wasn't sure she could wait for hours on end either.

She felt like she might puke again.

"THERE'S MY GORGEOUS GODDESS," Brett said and pulled Madi into his arms. She held him for a long time, and he soaked up the peace she always made him feel—the serenity, the feeling that he was home, complete when he was with her. He pulled back finally because he sensed something wasn't right. Her cheeks were red, as if she'd been crying, but she also looked a little green around the gills. "Baby, what's the matter?"

Madi blew it off with a fake smile and shook her head. "Nothing. I guess Mexican and tequila didn't sit well last night."

Brett's brows drew. He'd known Madison Thomas way too long to not know when she was fibbing, but she quickly started talking with the other guys, throwing him off.

"Listen," Madi fumbled when the others were distracted, "um, I don't know what you had planned for after the game, but..."

"Well, I had *you* planned, Hera. Post-victory sex, right?" He whispered and winked. They'd been joking about it all week, trying to decide which place got defiled next—like they hadn't tore the sheets up just this morning.

"Umm, right. But I, uh, I want you to myself just for a little while. We...uh...we need to talk."

And just like that, Brett's heart raced. That wasn't good; he knew what that meant. When women said, "We need to talk," it usually meant something bad. Was she breaking up with him?

He gulped down the fear and nodded, trying to rationalize what could possibly have her looking like she was going to cry. Had someone upset her? He felt angry all of a sudden but tried to hold it in; he had a pre-season game to get through.

Madison reached up on her tip-toes, and Brett pulled her back into his arms as he kissed her with all his might, forcing her to feel how much he cared for her, forcing away whatever this was that was upsetting her. He pulled back slowly and looked into her seafoam green-blue eyes. "I love you Madison Hope Thomas. You know that, right?"

Madi's lips curled in; she was holding back tears. What the hell wasn't she saying? "I love you too, Cap—so, so much."

When Coach Cavanaugh started calling for them to warm up, Brett was reluctant to let her go, even though they would both be taking the podium at half-time to say some inspiring words regarding Hunter and this year's team.

Brett kissed her forehead as he released her and gave her a big smile; a smile that he hoped conveyed whatever she needed in that moment.

"HUNTER THOMAS WAS MY BEST FRIEND," Brett said and looked over at the woman beside him, the woman he loved with every centimeter of his being, the one now beaming brightly up at him on this sunny early August day. "Practicing without him, and being on this field without him has been difficult—not only for me, but the other players who loved him as much as I did. This organization took a huge hit when Hunt passed away." Brett stepped back and cleared his throat before moving back to the mic in front of him. "As the team captain and the quarterback, I'm pledging my year to Hunter. May his spirit, the spirit of Hermes, flow through each and every one of us as we strive to achieve the same goals we had last season. This team has heart, this team has ambition, and we aim to give it our all, for not only us but also for our fans. Here's to Hunter Thomas."

The crowd roared in response and chanted "Hermes" as Madi and Brett raised their arms together. He pulled her to him and hugged her, although not as familiarly as he wanted to. After all, they were in front of eighty thousand people in the stands and millions live. He kissed her cheek and smiled into her face, getting one in return. She took his arm as they walked back toward the sidelines, getting cheers from the team as they filed into the tunnel.

The first half had been pretty uneventful where Brett was concerned, he'd only ran three plays—two runs and a pass—before he'd been called back to the safety of the sidelines. Then he'd spent the next hour waiting for time to hurry up while he watched his second string, Hayes Bentley, do what Brett wanted to be doing, playing QB. He knew his coach was just protecting his asset, but Brett was pumped, ready for the season, and eager to find out what Madi wanted to talk to him about.

Obviously, it wasn't too bad or she wouldn't still be smiling at him like she was now.

"I'm gonna head back up. I'll see you after the game."

"I'll be there, sexy lady. Be naked!" His brow rose in challenge, and she blushed appearing to be contemplating it, which got a chuckle out of him.

"Meet me in the box." She leaned in to kiss his cheek, and he savored the feel of her lips on his skin. He grabbed her hand and kissed it, making a big production of not letting her go and getting another smile out of her as she reluctantly pulled away.

He turned then and listened to his coach talk about their angle in the next half and telling Bentley what he wanted out of him. Brett propped himself against the wall and pretended to listen, all the while he was thinking about Madi and when he could have her wrapped around him again.

The last five weeks had been everything he'd ever imagined they would be. He and Madison had loved each other, as he'd always dreamed they would—undeniably, completely, and with raw abandon. They'd lost themselves to one another in the throes of passion on practically a daily basis. He'd never loved anything more in his life than he did Madi, and he couldn't wait to ask her to be his for all eternity. He was the next one planning an elaborate proposal and understood why Travis had wanted his to be big. Brett could've shouted it from the rooftops, but knew he and Madi had to be slow with their announcement, giving the organization and the fans time to see that their relationship had "slowly" progressed into something more than friendship since Hunter's death.

They already had the blessing of their families and even Frank and Rita Thomas who loved their daughter-in-law and still spoke to her regularly. They were glad Madi had found love again and wished them the best. Brett wasn't feeling guilty anymore, except for the fact that he hadn't discussed everything he needed to with Madi.

Brett hadn't told her that Hunter had lived long enough to talk to him, to say his goodbyes. It wasn't that Brett had wanted to keep it from her, it was simply that the conversation had never come up, the timing had never been right. He knew he just needed to come out and tell her, say it and be done. She wouldn't be mad—would she?

Had someone told her that Hunter had lived after he'd been pulled from the car? Had someone confessed that he'd died in the ambulance—twice—and the EMTs had brought him back? Had someone from the hospital informed her that Brett had had about five minutes to talk to Hunt before he'd finally succumbed to death? Was that why they'd "needed to talk"? Brett couldn't shake the fear even as his team huddled, chanted their new chant this year, "Gods of the Gridiron," and ambled back to their lockers to get their gear.

Travis gathered him, Linc, Quil, TJ, and Pax over, while grinning like a shit-eating possum.

"Bring it in, guys. There's something I gotta tell ya."

"What'd you do? Knock up your fiancé?" Pax smarted with a snort—something Hunt would have said—and it made them all chuckle.

"BINGO!" Travis shouted and clapped, laughing excitedly.

"Holy shit, dude. Really?" Linc was the first to clap Travis's back in congrats.

Quil was next, grinning and pointing at him as if to say, "Way to go."

Brett was in shock—and a little jealous, if he were being honest with himself—but he tried not to let his friend see it as he gave him a fist bump and a smile.

Pax shoved him, playfully. "Damn, dude, you're so impatient. You couldn't have waited 'til the honeymoon?"

"Hey, Ares is a greedy god, what can I say? That redhead of mine says, 'Take me, Daddy,'" Travis stated in a high-pitched voice, imitating Skyla, "and I'm there." Travis smirked, gaining an eye roll from the rest of them.

"Oh, Sky calls you Daddy? That's what Val calls me," Linc teased, although Brett wasn't so sure.

"Yeah, we know. Uggh," Quil stated, wrinkling his nose in disgust. When Linc frowned at him, confused, he added, "You forget weekend before last while we were camping? We all heard your performance, '*Big Daddy*.'"

The five of them laughed heartily at a blushing Linc, and TJ patted Brett's bicep. "This one will be next, mark my words."

"Me?"

"Yup. Madi's next. I guarantee it."

Brett scoffed but, even as he attempted to guard his girl's good name, he understood his friends knew what was up. His and Madi's chemistry was indisputable; he simply shrugged.

He'd love to see Madi pregnant with his baby. The thought of it made his heart flutter, and he grinned big.

"Well, I'm gonna sit this one out fellas," Pax muttered, hands up in surrender.

"You don't want kids, Pax?" TJ asked as if Paxton were insane.

"Nah, it isn't that. This here surfer boy's still got some wind left in his sails. I'm not ready to settle down yet."

"He's still a young sprout," Brett muttered and ruffled Pax's long unkempt hair. "He'll ease into the idea." Pax was the youngest of them; a couple years younger than their "newbie" Quillan, who happened to be twenty-seven years old.

"Single and ready to mingle, I get it. Just give it time, *Junior*." Travis smirked. "Find you a girl that you can't think straight around but also one you can't possibly live a day without. That's the money shot, Poseidon."

"Amen to that," Linc and Brett added, pointing to one another.

They all laughed again before Linc said, "Hey, wait a sec. We still haven't named our newcomer here. It's time. It's our first pre-season game. We have to get him titled so we can sell it."

They all regarded Quil who looked around at them, seemingly eager and anxious to know what they'd come up with.

Brett began to think. Quillan was fast, he was smooth, seamless in the way he caught the ball and ran it into the end zone. He was their only acting TE now that Lang was gone. He was powerful. But Brett sucked at picking these god names, maybe Google would help. He was about to turn to his locker to retrieve his phone only to stop as Travis said, "He's tall, dark, and solemn. Fast and volatile." Ok, now he was just spouting random shit off. "We've got Zeus and Poseidon... I think it's time Hades joined the team."

Quil gave him a crooked grin and a shrug. "I mean it fits pretty good, I guess."

"He *does* disappear in a black cloud of smoke when Zeus throws him one of those thunderbolts of his," TJ winked, getting a laugh out of the rest of them.

"Hades. I like it. Welcome, King of the Underworld." Brett reached out his hand and Hades took it, shaking his head in amusement. "We're glad to have you, brother."

MADI'S KNEES were knocking before Brett ever made it up to the box, long after the game was over. She had been watching them practice following the game and saw it would be a while. She decided to read a book from the Kindle app on her phone; it was an interesting read, but the nervousness began to take over. She gave it up after reading the same paragraph three times without comprehending the words and just looked out over the field, trying to calm her breathing.

She tried to reason with the fact that Brett loved her and would be happy about this baby, though she couldn't, for the life of her, settle her pounding heart. She rubbed her belly where their baby nestled—probably smaller than the tiniest fish she'd ever seen—but the fact that he was there made her heart soar with love, awe, and happiness.

She heard her *God of the Gridiron's* heavy footfalls before his deep voice called in a huff, "Damn, sorry, Sunflower. Coach was wanting to run drills and talk and all kinds of shit. I got out of there as fast as I could."

He stopped when she didn't turn to look at him; tears were flooding her eyes at the thoughts of confessing this secret to him.

"Madi, baby—please talk to me. This has been the longest four hours of my entire life, love." He knelt down in front of her, resting a hand on her knee.

"It has been for me, too." She never kept secrets from him; not telling him when she and Hunter were trying to get pregnant was one of the hardest things she'd ever done.

"Ok, I'm here. Let's talk. Tell me everything. I want to know. Did I do something?"

She held back a laugh and nodded.

"Oh, crap. What did I do, baby? Did I hurt you?" The anguish in his eyes tore through her, and she shook her head, not wanting him to think he'd hurt her; no, he'd given her the best gift of all. "Did I upset you?" Again, Madi shook her head. "Oookkkayy. Ummm..." He frowned. "Perhaps, I should go first."

Madi was the one frowning this time.

"You said we should talk and you're right. I haven't been completely honest about something. It's been weighing on me, and the only reason I haven't told you is because there just hasn't been... well, the right time never..."

Madi gulped, anxiety filling her heart. What was he about to say?

"It's about Hunter."

Madi shook her head. No, right now wasn't the right time to talk about Hunter. She wanted to talk about her and Brett, their future, their baby. Hunt was gone. He'd died six months ago.

"Madi, I spoke with him on his death bed."

And suddenly Madi's mind was whirling, her memory reaching painfully back to that awful day. The day that blurred between a veil of nightmare and reality. There was so much about that day that she didn't know, hadn't asked because she didn't need or want the gory details. All she'd known was her husband had passed away as a result of a deadly car crash, and her life had turned completely upside down. She flashed back to running into the hospital, where she'd met Brett in the ER and fallen to her knees as he told her Hunt was gone. Of course the only way he could've known that was if he...

"I'm gonna be sick," Madi whispered even as she pushed Brett's hand away and moved to stand.

She ran to the ladies' room just feet away and barely made it to the toilet as her stomach emptied its remnants for the third time that day. Her head pounded along with her heart as her head hung there in the commode for several minutes. She hadn't heard Brett enter behind her but took the paper towel he offered, placing it against her forehead.

"Baby, I'm so sorry. I—"

"What did he say?" she whispered again, tears clouding her vision.

"That he was sorry, that he loved you..." Brett bowed his head then squatted down, taking her hand. "He made me promise to take care of you. Although that was something I didn't even need to promise. I would've done so, no matter what. You *know* that!"

Madi gulped. She needed to know more and waited for him to continue.

"He begged me to keep you from finding out about the affair—as if I had any damn control about that... He regretted it, said it was the biggest regret of his life, that you were the perfect wife." Brett paused, overcome with emotion as tears fell down his cheeks. "He said, 'This is your second chance.'" Brett covered his face with his hands. "Like I even *deserve* a damn second chance. It only took losing my best friend for that to happen." He sobbed, and it broke Madi's heart in two as she turned and pulled him to her frame, cradling his head to her shoulder. "I don't know how he knew about my love for you, but he did. I never told him, I never told a soul. He said it was supposed to be me with you. Is that supposed to make it all better? Because it doesn't. It doesn't matter. If I would've done what I was supposed to do to begin with, it *would* have been me. Don't you see how bittersweet this victory is for me?"

"Shhh," she murmured even as the sting of his words sizzled her heart. "I know, Brett. I know. It's ok though. You have to let it go now. It's the past. We only have the future."

He pulled his head from her shoulder and wiped his eyes, giving her a weak grin. "You always were the strongest one of us."

Madi shrugged, getting a laugh out of Brett. "Hera, right?" She arched her brows.

Brett bowed his head again. There was more. "He told me to give you children." He looked up at her, his green eyes full of regret, sorrow, and hope all at once. "He said you wanted a boy."

Madi felt her heart rip in to pieces. She'd never told anyone but Hunter that tidbit of knowledge. She wept then, herself. She cried for Hunter, for the life lost, the good soul he'd been despite his many flaws, a past that had damaged yet renewed her, for the pain that six months hadn't fully healed. She cried until her tears were spent, wetting Brett's shirt as she had so many times before. But finally, she pulled back as her lover stroked her hair and back and cupped her cheek, wiping her tears away. He was so good at that, after all.

"You're always wiping away my tears, Brett."

"And I always will, Madison. You're the love of my life, my sweet Sunflower. I'll never miss another chance to tell you so. I want to be with you always."

Madi gave him a bright smile, her heart overflowing with joy.

"Well, you've fulfilled all of Hunter's requests, it would seem," she stated and a grin teased at the corner of her mouth.

Brett stared dumbfounded back into her eyes, brows furrowed, truly perplexed. Then realization hit him hard, and he looked down at her abdomen, his fist coming to his mouth in shock. "Madi, you— you're…" he was speechless, and she giggled and nodded.

"Yes, my love. You and I are going to have a baby."

CHAPTER FIFTEEN

Brett smiled as he looked down at the gravestone. He took the vase of flowers he'd brought today, a dozen sunflowers, and set it on the base of the headstone, alongside the others there. It had taken months for him to be able to look at the name chiseled into the stone and not feel his heart tear into pieces. Today, was different, it felt different because it was the next chapter in the book of Brett's life. He'd been coming every morning on his way to the complex for the last several weeks, simply to talk to his best friend, fill him in on the goings-on of his life, give him the latest news. Not like Hunt probably couldn't *see* it for himself, but it made Brett feel more at peace so there he was.

"Tonight's the night, Hermes," he said and sat down atop the grave, leaning in to rub the headstone, his usual spot that made him feel more connected to Hunter. "I'm hoping she'll say yes, but I'm not certain. Maybe you could sprinkle some magic, kinda like Cupid. Wasn't he a son of Hermes or something? I can't remember. God, I'm nervous, can you tell?"

Brett laughed and imagined Hunt was getting a kick out of it, himself.

"Yeah, I still can't believe she's gonna have my baby, man. It seems so surreal. We've already picked which room will be the nursery, and she's got me tryin' to come up with a good solid name for this little tyke. You know he's gonna be a looker for sure with how gorgeous his momma is."

Brett had begun to call the baby a boy for some reason unknown to him, he couldn't stop himself. "I figure he'll be either a QB or receiver, either works for me. If he comes out looking like Pax, I'm gonna worry." Brett laughed and felt his emotions rising. "Look, I know you've already given me some signs but tonight, I could really use one again to know you're ok with all this. I know what you said, but…" Brett trailed off, he knew he was being silly, but it still made him feel unworthy to have all this joy while a once healthy, lively man like Hunt lay six feet under him.

"Hunter, son, you gotta stop runnin' off," Brett heard a gruff voice say behind him and turned.

His heart hammered in his chest, and he couldn't fight the smile that came to his lips at the cute little boy standing there, his curly brown hair ruffled by the wind. Once again, he was clad in a Gladiators jersey.

"Mr. McFadden, I sincerely apologize. He tends to wander." The man Brett assumed to be the boy's father strode up and gripped the little guy's shoulder even as the kid gaped at Brett, his big brown eyes staring into his.

"It's no problem at all," Brett stated with a laugh and pointed to his jersey. "You watchin' the game tonight, kiddo?"

"Oh, he doesn't miss a Gladiators game for anything in the world. Isn't that right, buddy?" The father stated; he favored the boy, save his hair was thin and straight.

"Did you keep him?" the boy asked, and Brett frowned, not understanding what he was asking him. "The tortoise, did you keep him?"

Brett grinned and looked down for a moment before looking back up at the boy. "I did. He's enjoying his new home on my farm. I named him Hermes." Brett patted Hunt's gravestone as he replied, thinking the boy probably looked a lot like Hunter would've as a kid.

"We're real sorry for your loss, Mr. McFadden."

Brett gulped and thanked him for his kind words.

"We're rooting for y'all tonight." The man looked down to his son then. "Tell him, say, 'Go Gladiators.'"

The boy mimicked his father, and the man took the boy's hand, turning to give Brett the privacy they'd interrupted.

"Hey, what's your name, kiddo?" Brett asked, even though he'd heard the kid's father say it already.

The little boy turned and grinned big. "Hunter Xavier Martinez."

"Thanks, Hunter." This kid had done more for Brett than he'd ever know. "Say, you wouldn't happen to want an autograph by any chance, would ya?"

The boy's eyes got as big as saucers; he nodded vigorously as he smiled back at Brett.

Alright, Hunt—I hear ya, buddy. I'm going for the green, man. I promise I'll make you proud.

BRETT WAS PUMPED but nervous as he took the field that night listening to the crowd chant, "Gods of the Gridiron," and grinned knowingly. He waved over to Madi on the sidelines, who smiled. She looked radiant in a crimson dress that accentuated her perfect curves; pregnancy became her.

This was the night he and his team had prepared for, their season opener against New Orleans, the first home game. The strong start to an epic season, and he was ready to own his title as Zeus, the King of the Gods, as his thunderbolt-throwing skills had been on point all week. Hades was bringing Hell with him, along with Ares, their ram of a running back. On their defense, LB Poseidon, who seemed fully ready to "release the Kraken" and corner, Lazarus, who'd been brought back to life for the sole purpose of tackling receivers, it would appear.

He huddled the eleven offensive players together, gave them a little pep talk, and told them the play before their arms went into the pile. They all yelled, "G.O.G" and moved to their respective positions.

The first play Brett called was a running play. He dropped back, faked a throw, and tossed the ball to Travis, who ran for thirty yards. It was that strong start he'd wanted, and they went right into the no-huddle offense they'd been practicing. His next play was also a run but a hand-off going in the opposite direction, where Brett blocked, for yet another big run, twenty-yards. The next play, Zeus was feeling good about—until he eyed the change in the defense. He could read the blitz coming and called a different play, shouting over to his receivers, "Draco 80. Hut. Draco 80. Hut hut."

He could see the furious eyes burning into his own through the masks of the defense as they came at him, shoving at his offensive line, but he knew they'd hold 'em back. His center, Robicheaux, was named Cyclops as much for his keen vision as for his strong stature.

Brett turned and faked the ball to Travis. He dropped back as Ares passed by, taking his time in the pocket and looking for Hades. The fast bastard was already in line as Zeus threw up his thunderbolt. He saw the white and gold jersey coming at him and braced himself for the impact as he went down. Brett then shuffled away from the defender to see if his target had met its intended mark. He hopped up off the turf, watching as Hades centered his body and jumped for the ball. Quil caught it and came down, teetering. *C'mon, stay up, stay up!* Sure enough, Quillan was still on his feet and running… past the ten, the five…into the end zone.

"TOUCHDOWN!" Brett cried and turned to TJ, who embraced him. He slammed his hand down on TJ's helmet in glee as big OT TJ lifted his QB.

In three plays, they were already on the board! It was an awesome feeling.

Their streak continued through the first half and into the second where they led by three scores. The Gods of the Gridiron were on fire; no one could stop them from scoring and their defense was holding the opposing team's offense to field goals. It was a record for the Gladiators against the Saints. But as the time wound down closer to halftime, Brett grew anxious, for this was the big moment he'd planned. Madi might hate it, but he didn't care—it was time for the world to know how he felt about Madison Hope Taylor Thomas.

He'd asked Jerry's permission for her hand just last week, and Jerry had teared up and said, "It's about damn time, son."

That was all the encouragement he'd needed. He'd had the ring for two weeks now and it was perfect—a sparkling 2.5 karat yellow diamond, symbolizing his sweet Sunflower.

As he came to the podium where Jerry and Madi stood, he looked into her eyes. God, he was so in love with her. Her honey-gold locks framed her oval face, her Caribbean blue-green eyes sparkled beneath smoky eyeshadow, and her lips were a perfect coral color. He gave her a smile and stood stoic, puffing his chest out, the proud god that he was.

"I come to you tonight—fans, Atlanta, America—as a humble servant. Six months ago, we lost a family member. Most of you who know me, know that me and this beautiful lady here," Brett motioned to Madi, "go way back in time. We met as children not far from this stadium, on the very practice field I work on most days of the week. She was a girl that could actually throw a football." His brow went up, showing his pride. "I know, right? What's not to love about *that?*" The crowd laughed along with him, and he waited for them to quiet down before he continued. "We obviously became great friends after that. Our fathers worked together for an entire decade and a half before my father retired early. Madi and I went to UGA together, where we met Hunter and the rest is history...or is it?" He looked back at Madi and grinned. "I never dreamed I'd fall in love with my best friend." Ok, he was overdramatizing the truth a little for the crowd, but he had Madi's reputation on the line here.

"But as I live and breathe—and stand before you here today—that's exactly what happened." He saw Madi's face blush as she looked around as if to say, "Brett, what the hell are you doing?"

He continued, "Madison Hope Thomas, I've never been happier than when I'm with you. You make me feel at peace, at home, like life can't get any sweeter. And we both know how short it can really be. I love everything about you. Your laugh, your smile, the way you care for other people, the way you sing in the car, even the fact that you're technically my boss." Another laugh came through the crowd. And Brett grinned and shrugged. "But baby, I *love* that you're my best friend, and I want so much for you to be mine forever. So, I'll ask you in front of all these people: fans, players, our families and friends." He moved away from the podium then, took the ring from his soon-to-be father in law, and dropped to one knee. He looked up at Madi, who'd covered her mouth with her hands, tears running from her gorgeous eyes. "Will you make all my dreams come true? Will you marry me?"

Madi nodded and uncovered her face. "Yes. Yes, I'll marry you."

He bolted upright and pulled her against his padded frame. He kissed her like it was fourth and goal and the kiss would be the final way to score, like his damn life depended on it. Her arms wrapped around his neck and she kissed him back, cupping his face in her hands and beaming from ear to ear.

"I love you, my Sunflower. I love you forever and always."

"Always and forever, Cap." She kissed him again before pulling back as he took the ring from its box to place on her ring finger; she'd long ago put her wedding band on a chain around her neck. She looked down at the sparkling diamond and smiled.

"You're my Sunflower, baby—my hope, my happiness, my joy. Never forget that."

She pulled him back to her for another scorching kiss, then teased as she said. "Alright, fiancé—now go and win this ball game. That's an order, from your boss." She planted her hands on her hips with a smirk.

"Yes, ma'am." He saluted her and got one more kiss before he turned and left the podium.

"THAT'S GORGEOUS, MADI," Sky murmured and eyed the ring on her finger as Madi returned to the luxury box. "But I'm so glad it was you who got the public service announcement instead of me." Sky held her chest in relief. "I threatened to snip Trav's balls off if he did that."

So, that was why Trav had proposed at her house instead of on the field as he'd originally planned to do.

"How does it feel, Mrs. Soon-to-be-McFadden?" Val asked with a giggle and plopped down behind them with a plate of food.

"Good but a little scary," Madi admitted. "I mean, baby on the way, engaged. It's kind of intimidating, seeing as Hunter's only been gone six months now." She looked down, feeling bad.

"Don't you dare!" Sky took her face in her hands. "You deserve to be happy. Hunt wouldn't take that away from you, not ever."

"You guys don't think Brett and I are moving a little fast?"

"Fast? Hell, he only took twenty years to tell you how he felt. How is that *fast*?" Brooke smirked and took Madi's hand, examining the ring there. "He did good, but listen to me." When Madi turned, Brooke continued, "You and Hunt weren't so great together. He didn't always bring out the best in you. I miss the asshole but, let's be honest, he wasn't the one for you. Brett is. You're going to have his baby. It's only fitting that you two should be married. And ya know, the sooner the better 'cause when you tell Momma that you're pregnant, your ass had better have had your honeymoon."

Madi gritted her teeth. It was true; their mom was gonna have a shit-fit.

"So, I'm thinking Vegas—tick-tock, tick-tock—the sooner y'all tie the knot, the sooner you rip that Band-Aid off. Your only saving grace is that it's Brett and they love him, plus this will be their first grand-baby, so there *is* that."

"You'd sugar coat a giant dump, Brooke," Madi scolded, feeling sick to her stomach now. Brooke just shrugged in return.

"Well, I'm up for Vegas. How's week after next sound? They have a bye then." Val stated and shrugged, leaving Sky gaping and Brooke laughing.

LATER THAT NIGHT, Brett carried Madi into their bedroom. The room was farmhouse style, like everything else inside the home. Shiplap covered the wall behind the large poster bed, a blue quilt comforter lay atop it. The furniture was a dark mahogany that blended well with the original wood floors. Taupe rugs designed with pastoral scenes covered the floor, and the ceiling had large wooden beams, similar to the kitchen and living room.

Brett's big body covered Madi's as he hiked the dress up to her hips, kissing her belly and hovering there, talking to his baby like he tended to do as of late. "How's Daddy's little champ doing tonight, huh?"

"He's good. Finally letting Mommy keep her food down for a change."

Brett grinned up at her. "I love you, fiancée."

"I love *you*, soon-to-be husband."

He gazed into her eyes for a moment before peeling her dress up and over her head, removing his own shirt, and tossing it aside. Damn, she'd never get sick of that view. His big, broad frame, those chiseled muscles, as if he'd been sculpted just for her body. She moved her hands over him as he laid her back, admiring his strength, the work it took for him to be as hard and muscular as he was; she felt her immediate desire began to coat her panties. Jeez, it just took a look nowadays it seemed. Perhaps that was the pregnancy hormones she'd been told about.

Brett's mouth moved from her lips to her neck, and he began to nibble there, making her arch up into his palm when his hand slid into her panties. "Oh, baby," she whimpered, feeling her womanhood clench.

"Mmm… Someone's ready for her god tonight, huh?"

His head tilted and he looked into her eyes, those fiery green specks flaming. She pulled her lips in, stifling her response. He withdrew his hand from her underwear slowly and moved off the bed.

Before Madi could protest, he remedied with, "Let's play a game tonight, my queen."

Oh goodness! The dominant Zeus wanted to play? How could she say no?

He moved to his drawer of enigmas and pulled out what looked to be something to tie her down with, but instead of tying her hands, he pulled it across her eyes to blindfold her.

"I can't see you?" Madi pouted as Brett pulled it taut behind her head and tied it off.

"It's only for your ultimate pleasure, my love. At any time, you can simply peel it down and see me loving your beautiful body with my cock." At the word "cock," he licked her earlobe with his tongue and she shivered—Oh God, as if his words alone weren't enough to make her lose herself.

Brett pulled her hands over her head and started by kissing her lips hungrily. He stroked his tongue across hers and licked her lips erotically. He sucked her bottom lip then moved his mouth to her cheek. His tongue ran over to her jawline then down her neck, torturing slowly. He had her whimpering and writhing even before his hands came to her lace-covered breasts. The front clasp of her bra came undone easily, exposing them for his taking. He used his hands to knead and squeeze while his fingers brought her nipples to hard peaks. He tortured one, then the other before letting his mouth have a turn.

By then, Madi was a quivering bundle of nerves, begging for the release only her god-king could give her.

Brett began licking a ravenous trail down to the hem of her

underwear, then nuzzled her through the thin cloth forcing her to beg as he chuckled. He spread her legs wide while he assaulted her sex with his tongue through the thin lace of her panties. His hands returned to her breasts, pinching her nipples with his thumbs and index fingers while his teeth, lips, and tongue brought her closer to oblivion.

Just as she was about to climax, Brett jerked her panties aside and his rapacious lips connected with her aching flesh. That's when she fell over the edge. His mouth ravaged her as the orgasm gripped her in a vicious grasp.

Brett was chuckling as he flipped her over, following her return. "My wanton sex goddess is always putty in my hands," he stated in triumph.

"AKA your *boss*," she hissed out an empty threat, even as her mind still swam over the mountain of bliss he'd thrust her upon.

He chuckled again, and she felt his lips on her bottom. "Mmm, yes, but don't call me a kiss ass because God knows, I simply can't resist this plump ass of yours."

Madi was the one laughing this time, then she moaned when he bit into it. "Oh my…"

His fingers moved between her legs, and he spread her cheeks wider as his fingers entered her. Brett thrust once, twice, three times before she felt him withdraw and his sex penetrated her. She felt his chest against her back as he filled her. He kissed her shoulder blade and pulled her hair from her neck, twisting it into a pony tail. He then lifted her with his other arm onto all fours and pulled her hair taut, making her moan as his cock plunged deep within her and his thighs hit hers over and over again.

"Oh Brett, oh God. Yes! Ride me, baby," she whined as the hand beneath her gripped her breast. This was so hot and erotic and made her feel like such a bad girl being taken from behind, blindfolded, and having her hair pulled.

He pounded into her relentlessly, owning her body with each

thrust of his hard shaft as her orgasm built and built. "Mmm, whose queen are you?"

"Oh, baby. I'm yours. Zeus. My almighty Zeus."

"Do you submit to your king?" His lips hovered at her throat and she whimpered.

"Yes, yes, oh God, yes," she cried, her climax coming in tandem with his, his roar rumbling them both as his hips violently hit hers.

Soon, they were returning to earth as Brett began to soften his thrusts and their breathing returned. His grip lightened on her hair and he pulled her upright, her back hitting his chest. He kissed her shoulder and rested his chin there, his nose tickling her earlobe.

"Mmm, I wonder if this gets better when we're married."

"Let's find out, shall we?" she smirked.

She peeled the blindfold down her face and turned to look at him. "Let's go to Vegas."

"What? Really?" When she nodded, he said, "I dunno, Sunflower. It seems so impersonal."

"Did you have a better idea, *Zeus*?"

"Well, Zeus always has fairly good ideas," he quipped, lifting his brows. "I think Hera and her multiple orgasms would tend to agree."

Madi laughed then rolled her eyes. "We should do it during bye week."

"Weekend after next?"

Madi shrugged. "We *are* pregnant. And we still have to tell our parents."

Brett pulled his lips to one side thoughtfully. "Good point. I'm sure we can find a wedding planner who can figure something out that quickly."

Madi smiled deviously. "Leave that up to Hera, the goddess of marriage." Madi turned in his arms and took the blindfold, flicking it with her wrist. "Now, I think it's her turn to have a little fun, what do ya say?"

"You know Zeus likes to dominate, my love. He's a controlling god after all," he teased.

"Trust me," she whispered and leaned into her king's ear, licking his ear lobe and pulling it into her mouth, lightly biting with her teeth. Zeus trembled, and Hera jumped for joy. "Zeus, *and* his cock, will enjoy this greatly. I assure you."

"Damn, naughty girl! You keep talking like that and I'll have to spank you again."

"I'd have it no other way, my king," Madi smirked and pulled her fiancé down to the bed to torture him with her goddess-like sexual prowess.

"Why's he mad at you?" Madi pouted at a red-faced Skyla.

"Because I want to keep working and not stay home like a spoiled little princess."

"Hey!" Val interceded. "I'm not a spoiled little princess."

Skyla looked to Val with a sneer. "I wasn't talking about you, Aussie Gold. Can it!" The feisty redhead spoke, and everyone paused, looking at her like she might be the next volcanic eruption.

"Sorry, Val, damn these pregnancy hormones. I'm horny one minute, ready to tear somebody's head off the next." Skyla huffed and sat down at the breakfast nook table, rubbing her "baby bump." Val gave her an understanding smile and Sky continued. "I just mean I'm not cut out for that. I was aiming to be the next DA when this happened, and I'm not ungrateful by *any* means. It's just...it's not what I planned, you know?"

Madi took her hand and smiled. "You don't have to give it up. We're women warriors. We can have both motherhood and careers."

"Right? With public ridicule and scorn from our soon-to-be husbands," Red smarted off.

"What did Trav say?" Madi asked.

"Just that he expected I would stay home." She grumbled. "I mean he *knows* how much my career means to me, how could he even say that?"

"'Cause he's a man. He doesn't get it," Brooke piped in, chewing on a bagel. "Look, sooner or later—not to burst your bubble, sis—but Brett's gonna ask the same thing of you." Her brows rose matter-of-factly. "It's in their DNA, you know? I was watching this documentary about it the other day. They all have this caveman mentality. It's stronger in some than others. They marry women like their mothers, subconsciously, so that they can become like their second mothers to take care of them. It's like this innate thing; they work, we nurture, like something out of a damn fifty's sitcom. Besides, your men have money to last you ten lifetimes. If you don't work, it's not a big deal."

"Ok, you," Madi pointed at her baby sister, frowning, "lay off the Hulu documentaries, first off. And second, stop raining on the parade, April showers. Jeez, some of us are *excited* about marriage and husbands and babies and we don't need your single sass."

"Yeah, well single-sass isn't dealing with no man telling *her* what to do."

"What's your beef with men anyway, Brooke?" It was Valeria who asked as Brooke threw daggers into Madi's eyes.

"I was raped."

All eyes went to Madi's beautiful brown-haired sister. Madi couldn't believe she was talking about it, confessing her secrets—but she dared not intercede with the look on Brooke's face.

Brooke continued, "He was my boyfriend, and I thought he 'loved' me. Yeah, so much for that. No didn't mean anything in the 'throes of passion' and, because I loved him, I was expected to put out at fourteen. Don't get me wrong, I'd been curious like most young teens are, but when it came right down to the deed, I wasn't ready... but he didn't care."

Madi expected her to tell them the rest. How she'd withdrawn for a time before absorbing her life in ballet, until her injury. Now, she was reckless with love, her life, and her body and nothing Madi had done or said ever seemed to make a difference. She feared for her sister, but hoped that Brooke would find herself in time.

Val was the first to speak, "Wow, Brooke, I'm so sorry that happened to you."

"It went on for a time before I finally got the guts to break up with him. By then the damage had already been done. Brooke Taylor had put out and other guys wanted a taste. I'd been labeled, so what did I do? I lived up to that label." Brooke sneered sarcastically, but the pain of her plight ripped into Madi so hard she teared up.

She rested her hand on Brooke's knee and gave her a weak smile.

"Ha, the nun and the slut, that was Madi and me. Hard to believe we're really sisters, right?"

"Broo—"

"I'm gonna go grab the flowers for tomorrow...and some ice cream. Y'all want some pickles too, right?" Brooke moved swiftly and bounced up, throwing her bagel in the trash before heading out the door.

"Wow! That was heavy," Sky whispered.

They didn't even know the half of it. The sordid life of Brooke Taylor would make for a docu-drama on A&E and a best-selling book series.

"So, back to what I was saying—don't feel bad about having your career and your baby too. It can be done and it's what you want; Travis knew this before he knocked you up."

"True. He's just guilt-tripping me about having a nanny raise our child."

"Any man would. I volunteered to stay with the twins, but I know it's what Linc really wanted." Val shrugged.

"How long before you stopped working, Val?" Sky asked.

"Right away, but they're twins. It's double the work and then some."

"Well, I don't plan to quit working, and I *dare* Brett to ask me to."

Brett, Travis, and Pax all walked in at that time and stopped dead in their tracks at the looks on the women's faces—sassy, hormonal, and ready to pounce on any man that defied them at that moment.

"Poor timing, guys… Back up slowly—very, *very* slowly," Pax said and began to do so, getting a laugh out of Madi.

"Did I do something wrong last night, *Hera?*" Brett asked confidently, a self-assured member of the bomb squad ready to defuse the situation.

"Hera, huh?" Trav grinned like the cat that ate the canary. "Why don't you tell 'em my nickname for you, Fireball."

"Travis Redmond, if you ever wish to visit your 'favorite place' again, I suggest you zip it." Skyla's blue eyes pierced Travis's, but he didn't flinch. He looked ready to tangle with her, and it was rather sexy if Madi had any say in the matter. *Jeez, these damn hormones.*

"She's Aphrodite." Travis shrugged, undeterred that he'd poked the bear—and that she-bear was about to eat him alive.

Sky's jaw dropped in audacity, and Madi gritted her teeth, waiting for the shit to hit the fan.

"Well, I see we aren't the only ones to take advantage of our god names," Brett mumbled with a shrug.

Sky's cheeks reddened, matching her hair, then her eyes narrowed at Travis who appeared unaffected, his confidence unshaken.

Pax broke the silence first. "You guys have all the fun." He stuck his lip out and crossed his arms over his chest.

"Hey, nobody said you couldn't have your own goddess, *Poseidon.*"

Pax seemed to mull that over for a minute, and Madi laughed at him.

"It definitely has its perks," Brett confirmed and walked over to Madi, pulling her up off the chair and into his embrace for a searing kiss as his hand fell to her lower abdomen. "Just be prepared to further your legacy." Brett's beautiful smile greeted her as she opened her eyes. He was so excited about this baby.

"The Kraken ain't the only thing you'll be releasing." Trav winked and moved toward Skyla, whose scowl deepened. Uh oh, he was in for it. He side-stepped, closer to Brett and Madi, and whisper-yelled,

"Hey, mind if I borrow your guest room for like twenty minutes? I need to go pray at the altar of my goddess."

Brett laughed and shook his head. Just as Sky began to protest, Travis was scooping her up and carrying her off down the hallway. Madi stifled a giggle, and Val's face widened in shock. "Damn," she said. "I think Lazarus needs a new nickname."

They all burst out laughing, and Pax nodded. "I definitely need to start taking advantage of my own, it would seem."

"Just for the record, Sunflower, I never intended for you to stop working." The love showing back in his face made her tear up. "You do whatever your heart desires, and I'll stand behind you one hundred percent."

She swooned hard.

"Besides," he leaned in to whisper in her ear, "I *love* having you for my boss."

Madi giggled at that.

Tomorrow, she was marrying the most wonderful man in the world, and she couldn't be happier.

THE SUN SHONE brightly on that September day. The temperature was perfect at a crisp sixty-seven degrees, and Brett's heart swelled to bursting as he watched his bride, his perfect Madi, walking down a crimson red runner toward him.

They'd had everything set up on the back pasture of his land. Reverend Young had been thrilled and the wedding planner Madi had found was on her game. In less than two weeks, the whole thing had been pulled off with an altar, guests, drinks, food, flowers, decorations, a DJ—the works. No expense spared. No detail overlooked. It was perfect.

Their guests stared in awe at the gorgeous goddess before them—clad in a figure-flattering, lacy, off-white halter gown—the one who only had eyes for Brett. She was holding in tears, he knew; they were leaking down his own face, and he didn't care. He'd waited his whole life for this moment, for her to promise herself to him, for her to become his in every sense of the word. It felt unreal—too good to be true. It felt amazing.

Brett had gone to talk to Hunt this morning, intending to thank him and apologize. But when he got there, he simply sat and cried, telling him how much he loved Madison, how excited he was about their marriage and their baby, and how much he missed his best friend. Brett always felt better when he stopped to talk to the gray granite stone. The verse written there held him for a moment. "I came that they may have life and have it abundantly. John 10:10"

He'd never really noticed it, or had he and just not really took the words in? Today, he did though. He knew Madi had chosen the biblical quote. Hunter Thomas had lived abundantly if he'd done nothing else.

"I love you, brother," Brett had told him. "I love our girl and dammit, man, she's even more gorgeous being so happy. I've never seen her smile so much. I hope you're looking down on us today and seeing that I made good on my promises."

Now, Madi, along with her father who was escorting her, stopped before him. His eyes beheld the most beautiful thing he'd ever seen in all his life: his bride about to pledge herself—her love —to him.

When Jerry handed Madi over, he clapped Brett's shoulder and smiled. He moved to sit next to Amelia, who wiped her tears on a handkerchief, Brooke was next to her. Brett's mom and dad were on the opposite side with his brothers. Also in attendance were their closest friends: Linc and Val, Trav and Sky, TJ, Quil and Quinn, Pax, Coach Cavanaugh, their GM, and even Coach Haskins made it out. Brett hadn't expected to see Frank and Rita Thomas, but they too came to wish their daughter-in-law well.

Brett and Madi had decided to keep the wedding small. They planned to let the media in on it soon enough but didn't want helicopters flying over the farm during their ceremony or the sneaky assholes trespassing to get clandestine shots of their nuptials.

It was just them and the people they cared for most in the world.

As Reverend Young spoke of love, commitment, and reverence, Brett watched his bride with calm devotion and desire. And when the vows came, he spoke from his heart and pledged to love, honor, and cherish her until his last day. It was emotional, it was beautiful—it had hard-ass Zeus crying like a baby.

When Reverend Young pronounced them as man and wife, Brett embraced Madison; as they shared their first kiss as man and wife, he'd never been happier. It was as if time stood still, as if every prayer he'd ever had had come true, as if his life had been fully and completely fulfilled. And it would be even fuller come April when she gave birth to their child.

They reveled in the applause and cheers that greeted them as they moved down the runner, arm-in-arm.

They had several moments to themselves as their photographer swooped in and began posing them in various positions: some loving, some sexy, some sweet, some funny.

Brett's face began to hurt from smiling so much, but he didn't mind. He was truly overjoyed on this incredible day God had blessed them with.

He pulled his bride into his arms when they danced their first dance, sharing his thoughts. She grinned back up at him, the same joy he felt reflecting in her deep, sea-green eyes.

"Have we gotten any closer to a name for this baby boy?" she asked.

Brett grinned big. They'd literally just found out the sex of their baby yesterday and Brett had been over the moon. He couldn't wait to have a healthy, bouncing baby boy. And Hunt had told him that's what Madi had wanted, too. It was as if their dreams had become realities overnight.

"Well, my sexy queen, it would only be fitting to name him Hercules, as you *well* know," Brett stated with fake conviction, getting a giggle from his bride. "But seriously... I really like the name Xavier. Xavier Lawrence McFadden."

"Xavier, huh? It's different."

"That it is and symbolic too." He winked. He hadn't told Madi about the little boy he'd seen twice now at the cemetery.

After all, there were a few things that needed to stay just between him and Hunt... and this would be one of them.

EPILOGUE

"Step into my office, Mr. Layton," Madi suggested as Quil scowled down at her in front of the team.

Her husband didn't say a word, but she could see he was impressed—and probably a little turned on—by her assertiveness with his teammate. She was sure he'd use it erotically against her later, which she would thoroughly enjoy; but, for now, she had to really *be* boss lady.

She took the elevator back up to her office and sat, typing out an email before hearing a knock and Quil entered.

"Madi, I don't wanna do it," he practically whined and folded his tall, handsome frame into the seat across from her desk.

"Stop being such a baby, Quil. It's good publicity for you and the organization. And it's for a damn good cause, as you *well* know."

"C'mon, Madi, please don't make me?" Was he begging? How silly!

"Oh, grow up. It's just a short two-hour date!"

"I'm not ready. You of all people can understand why." Dammit, of course he would guilt-trip her about this. "How was your *honeymoon*, Mrs. McFadden?"

Madi couldn't help but be swept back to Cancun for the three days she and her Greek god husband spent there. It had been amazing. Adventurous snorkeling, incredible sex, and all the fresh seafood she could hold. It had been Heaven, truly, and her husband had never been more wonderful...and sexy...and dominating.

Madi shivered at the memory, then drew her brows at Quillan. "It was perfect. Now stop changing the subject."

He huffed and crossed his arms over his chest.

"Quil, you're the most eligible bachelor on the team."

"Am not," he grumbled and looked down.

"Look..." she softened her tone.

"Just—please? Send someone else. I'm not the *only* bachelor on the team. I'm a closet introvert, and I'll make a big mess of this. Send someone who loves being the center of attention."

"Well, Travis is engaged so *that* won't work," she teased.

"What about Paxton?"

"What about him?"

"Duh, he's freakin' Thor in a football uniform. Studly, smooth-talking, always smiling. I'm too broody. Thus, why I'm called Hades. Not exactly charity raffle date material. Poseidon on the other hand..." He had a good argument there.

Madi held her hand up, stopping him and mulled his words over carefully before pressing her intercom.

"Yes, Mrs. Thom—I mean, Mrs. McFadden."

"Kathryn," Madi scolded, "just Madi works. Can you send Paxton up here, on the double?"

Kathryn stuttered but did so, and after several minutes of Quil scowling and Madi feeling no sympathy for him, Pax came in all sweaty and out of breath.

"You rang, *Hera*."

Madi's brow rose and she pointed the pen in her hand at the leather chair next to Quil.

"Ok, you two can duke this out, play Rock-Paper-Scissors—I don't care—but either way, *one* of the two of you is going to represent this team for the charity date at ACH next Friday night. So, pick which one. You have sixty seconds."

Pax looked at Quil as if to say, "What the hell did you just sign me up for?"

Quil was quick on the draw. "He'll do it." He moved to stand, and Madi pointed her pen back down to the chair. "Oh, c'mon, he would *love* to do it. Wouldn't you, Pax?" Quil gritted his teeth at him.

Pax shrugged happily, loving the intrigue, the young and naïve man clueless to what he was volunteering for. "Sure. Why not? What do I gotta do?"

"Yeah, tell him, Mrs. McFadden." Quil scoffed, and Madi narrowed her eyes, shutting him up.

"It's simply a date." When Pax's brows rose, she elaborated, "The single ladies across the state will donate money to the hospital to be entered to win a date with you."

"That's it?" Pax snorted in surprise. "Dude, you're *such* a pussy." He shoved at Quil.

"Fuck off, *Poseidon*." Quil shot him a bird before rolling his eyes.

"Pax, this is important. No sexual relations. No kissing. Just a good old-fashioned date. Remember, you represent the organization. You'll be a perfect gentleman and *graciously* take the winner out. Make it enjoyable, make her feel appreciated. I'm assured it will be females only."

"Oh good...I mean, I *am* from California, which automatically makes me more open-minded than you conservative southern folks, but I draw the line taking a man out on a date." He shook his head and crossed his arms over his broad chest.

Madi's brow arched. "Are you done?" she sassed, and Pax blushed dejectedly. "*As* I was saying: you represent the organization, so I'll expect your best behavior—otherwise you'll be running laps until you pass out and I'll fine the shit out of you."

Pax stifled a laugh at her serious tone. "Aye aye, boss. You've been hanging out with Zeus too much, I see. He's rubbing off on you."

Quil looked at Pax fearfully, baring his teeth, as if waiting for

Pax's head to get blown off by the hollow-tipped bullets Madi was suddenly shooting from her eyes.

"I can't keep food down. I'm exhausted no matter how much sleep I get. I'm not allowed enough caffeine, and I constantly balance between the desire to screw my husband and wanting to kill him. Tell me, how would you feel?"

Pax bowed his head; a puppy being scolded for peeing on the rug. "Sorry I said anything," he mumbled. "Sooo…back to the date. I guess most these broads will be old and rich, so I shouldn't have an issue about wanting to fu—er—screw any of them, huh?"

Madi just grinned deviously. She wouldn't elaborate that this charity event wasn't just for the rich and famous of Atlanta but a community-wide collaboration between the team and the hospital. It would raise money for the children's hospital while garnering more interest in the football team and players. People could donate anything from pennies to thousands and each time they did, their names were put into a raffle pot where one would be drawn out randomly as the lucky winner. She'd just let him believe what he wanted to. After all, all he had to do was show up, go on the date, then go home afterwards. No strings. No catches.

How hard could that be?

SNEAK PEAK AT PASS INTERFERENCE
PROLOGUE

Paxton "Poseidon" Guthrie laughed and patted his teammate's shoulder as they entered the doors of the exclusive gentlemen's club, *RISE*.

It was one of the classiest, most luxurious strip clubs he'd ever been in, and he'd frequented many in his twenty-five years on the planet. Brilliant Chandeliers cascaded from the ceiling and the curtains were gold and black; even the poles were shimmering, along with the masked dancers. Damn, so this was what $5,000 a year membership bought a man, huh?

Quillan Layton seemed to be just as impressed as he smirked over at Pax, his thick brows rising.

It was Monday night, practically their "Friday." They'd been watching game film all day and got out of meetings by four. It had been Pax's idea for a night on the town and who could pass up an opportunity to come to one of the most infamous gentlemen's clubs in Atlanta? Especially when Quil had an invite he'd never cashed in. Plus, he owed Pax big time for the charity event he was doing come Friday night, all because Quil had pussied out on Madi.

They were escorted by one of the hostesses to a table closest to the center stage where a woman in a deep purple and silver wig and matching mask danced on the pole. She had a great body from what he could see. It was covered in thin lace that matched the rest of her "costume." She winked at Quil, and Pax rolled his eyes.

Quil had that broody, broken hero look—the one the ladies just swooned over. Tall, dark, and handsome—or so they'd said. Pax was a sandy blond, blue-eyed California boy with a gold tan and a build as solid as a Ford F-150. He could lift tires as big as Quil without straining. He was a linebacker who crushed quarterbacks for a living. Pax was...*totally* getting passed up by the hot stripper for Quil.

"Dude, what the fuck!" Paxton mumbled under his breath. "Every damn time."

Funny thing was, Quil wasn't even interested...or so it always seemed. And Pax could understand. Quillan's wife died last year and he was now raising a seven-year-old little girl alone thanks to her drug addiction.

"Uh, no thank you," Quil answered as the stripper whispered into his ear, running her hand along his jaw then down his chest to his ink-sleeved forearm.

Pax was close enough to hear her say, "Don't worry, stud. I'm clean."

It wouldn't have mattered if she was clean and housed a platinum-coated pussy, Quil wasn't gonna touch a stripper. He hadn't thus far anyway. What made this one any different?

Pax noted her body was covered in tattoos: various flowers, hearts, a pirate, a skull. Her porcelain skin was a paradox of seamless designs running from the wrist of her left arm, diagonally across her back and down her entire right leg. Her nose was pierced with a sexy little diamond that emphasized her button nose and her eyes were big and doe-like, lashes thick.

"C'mon over here and sit on Poseidon's lap, angel. I'll let you release the Kraken if you're a good girl."

She smirked at the challenge before her, turning her attention back to Quil. She moved into his lap, much to his dismay it would seem. She tilted her head quizzically and studied him as if he had a hidden road map in his eyes.

"If he's Poseidon then who are you?" she asked Quillan.

"Oh, he's Hades," Pax answered for him, knowing Quil was a man of few words.

"*Hades*, huh?" That seemed to excite her even more. *Well, damn,* Pax thought.

Pax looked over at Quillan as the stripper began to rock her body against him and checked his watch. He'd give the girl another three minutes before Quil told her to am-scray in typical Hades fashion. The TE didn't mind watching, but he didn't want to participate—not usually, anyway.

As Pax waited, a shot girl came by and took his drink order. Quil ordered a tonic on ice. Just a tonic.

Damn, looks like I'm drinking by myself too, Pax scowled to himself. Pax didn't drink often, but he was craving hard liquor tonight. He was anxious, dreading the shit-show to come—a shit-show his CEO had got him into. He was certain his date on Friday night wouldn't be quite as sexy as the chick seated on his buddy's lap.

"You don't like me, do you, god of darkness?" The exotic—in more ways than one—dancer asked Quil.

She didn't know that Quil wasn't one for small talk. Until one got to know him, he didn't have much to say. Quil was philosophical after all; he got that from both his Spanish and Native American roots.

"Perhaps a kiss will change your mind." She arched a brow.

Before Quillan could protest, the stripper was grabbing his shirt collar and had her tongue down his throat. Pax harrumphed. Damn, what the hell kinda club was this and where was *his* stripper—or was only one assigned per table?

He looked around and motioned to the approaching shooter girl; he thanked her for the drinks and asked for a dance too. She gave him a nod and set their drinks down. Meanwhile, Quil suddenly seemed interested in the stripper now that she'd overpowered him; not that Pax could blame him, she was licking Quil's lips like he was made of chocolate or something. Shit! The lucky S.O.B. And fuck, she had a tongue ring too.

Pax shook his head. *No damn fair.* He was the one who'd wanted to come out tonight and have a good time, but it looked like Quil was the one having the good time.

Quil appeared to come to then, the wicked enchantresses' curse breaking, if only momentarily. He gripped her shoulders and pulled her back some, gaping at her strangely.

"Oh, you suddenly remember you two aren't *alone?* Hi! Yeah, remember me?" Pax smarted, and Quil glanced over at him, looking dazed and confused.

Damn! Again, Pax was blown away. When was the last time he'd been kissed stupid like that? It'd been a long time.

"Yeah, you're buying the drinks too, asshole. I can't believe I'm stuck doing your dirty work Friday night because you aren't man enough to take some stuck-up Atlanta socialite out to dinner. Meanwhile, I'll just sit here and watch you make out with the hot stripper too. Yeah, suck all the fun out of my week, why don't you? Rub it in my face a little more. You're a real dick, you know that?" Pax whined and crossed his arms over his chest.

"Would you excuse us, *señorita?*" Quil gave purple-silver stripper a sweet grin. She leaned into him, sucking his earlobe for a moment before finally hopping off his lap and throwing a business card in her place.

"The name's Obsidian. Give me a call when you're not babysitting 'Whiny' over here, dark god, and I'll give you a *real* show." She blew a kiss to Quil and cocked her head sassily at Pax before turning on her heel and sashaying off.

"Welcome back, earthling," Paxton scoffed as Quil glanced his way, mouth wide in a grin.

"Pax, you're a total buzzkill."

"Me? This was supposed to be *my* night, not yours, damn you!"

"God, you're always only thinking of yourself, *mocoso.*" Quil shook his head incredulously.

"*Brat?* Seriously? You wanna go there?"

"Oh, shut up. I got rid of her. Now let's find one for you since you can't have fun without a woman around."

Pax knew he was pouting, but dammit, it wasn't fair. The thoughts of having to go out to dinner with some overstuffed, ugly, rich broad he didn't know just for show was about as appealing as getting a root canal. He realized he'd volunteered and hadn't made a big deal out of it at the time, but Quil had been giving him that puppy dog look and Madi had been so damn persistent; he'd been put into a catch-22.

"I still can't believe I'm doing this for you."

"Oh come off it! You're doing this for the *team*, not just for me."

"Last I remember, *pal*, it was your neck in the noose, not mine."

"Stop acting like you're doing us both a favor here, *amigo.* You don't wanna do it, say the fucking word and I'll—"

"No, I already agreed, and Madi—"

"Then shut the fuck up about it. Go on the damn date, go home, and get over it... *pendejo.*"

They sipped their drinks before Quil nudged him and they watched the next masked dancer on stage as she performed in a sexy and gifted way, moving over the pole and floor like she was part of both. These girls weren't just typical strippers; there was advanced choreography to all this. Even the way they walked was different, the songs were different. This club was...well, just different. And in a good way, too.

"I would say 'Gracias,' but you haven't done anything yet," Quil teased him.

"Yeah, yeah! You're just upset that I scared off tongue-ring girl."

"You would be too if she'd kissed *you* like that," Quillan scoffed.

"Is that black heart of yours softening, Hades?" Pax feigned shock.

"You know, Pax, as surprised as you'd be with my answer, there are things about married life that I *do* miss... and not just the sex." Quil leaned back in his chair and looked over at him.

"Yeah, well, you go right ahead, man. I don't want nothing to do with it. Brett and Trav are whipped, like totally and completely, and just wait til those babies get here. It'll be even worse."

Quil snorted. "Oh? You think so, huh? Let me tell you a little secret, *playboy*. When you hold the *niño* that you created in your arms for the first time, there's *nothing* in the world that even comes close. Not even a hot stripper with a tongue ring French-kissing you." Quil sighed heavily. "Remember I told you that!"

The man had to be crazy. As a scantily clad stripper in a red mask walked by and winked, Pax admired her tight body; he knew Quil'd just been too long without a woman.

Nothing beat the single life, nothing beat the quiet, nothing beat the freedom of being "unchained."

And *nothing* would ever lead him to think otherwise!

***

And *nothing* will sweep him **right** off his feet come October 23rd in *PASS INTERFERENCE*.

PRE-ORDER IT HERE.

AFTERWORD

Thank you *so* much for reading *FALSE START*.
I hope you enjoyed this heartbreakingly lovable second book of the
series. If so, please be sure to leave a review.

This book hurt a little to write. Killing off a character is never fun
nor easy—unless of course it's Troy Cameron ;-)

Even still, I was glad Brett and Madi got their happily ever after.

The next book up is *PASS INTERFERENCE* featuring Paxton's story,
a modern football twist on the classic *Cinderella*. It's set for an
October 23rd release date.

Pre-order your copy now.

BLURB:

The god of the seas, ***Poseidon***, is known for unleashing the Kraken...

Paxton Guthrie, aka Poseidon, is in the prime of his young life. He's one of the best linebackers in the league and has a carefree attitude that rivals his chosen profession.

When a charity date takes place and *he's* the raffle prize for the lovely, diehard #52 fan and local historian, **Rebecca Ryan**, a promising night on the town ensues. But these two unsuspecting souls are in for the surprise of their lives after the media catches them red-handed in a compromising position!

All bets are off as they must fake an impromptu engagement, deal with their angry friends and families, and "play house" while the Gladiators' reputation hangs in the balance... along with the real possibility of a Super Bowl.

But Poseidon never imagined he would find his Amphitrite before he was ready! And neither the sweet-spoken Irish lass nor the jealous god himself anticipated falling in love.

Their characters aren't the only things at stake here. Family ties are perhaps sturdier than anything the Greek gods can invoke. ***PASS INTERFERENCE*** must be run in this instance—even if it's from the defense.

Will Pax and Becca's love be strong enough to withstand a raging ocean of mistrust or is the arrogance of the sea god enough to knock him off his pedestal on Mt. Olympus?

ACKNOWLEDGMENTS

Many, many, **many** thanks go to my alphas, betas, and ARC readers.

To Jamie for being my first round, Jen for the endless edits (I know you combed the pages as thoroughly as I did) and all my supporters—Nicole, Rachel, Crystal, Sarah, Cat, and Emina to name a few.

Without your encouragement and love for these godly football players, I couldn't have done it. So, thank you!

Thank you *God* for the gift of writing, I love it so much. No story is without its ah-ha moments and I'm still amazed when I go back through and find myself in awe that: "Yes, I wrote that!" It truly is a talent and a pleasure doing it.

To my husband—you are amazing, and don't ever forget it! You keep me grounded and happy...and the house clean in my absence. (You also keep me fed. Otherwise, I would go hungry while writing LOL!) I love you, always and forever.

ALSO BY SHANNA SWENSON

~THE SIN AND SECRETS COLLECTION~

RISE: A Sin and Secrets Novella

(Coming November 2020)

~Aurora Rose Reynold's HEA WORLD~

Until Kingston

(Coming 2021)

LEARN MORE AT WWW.SHANNASWENSON.COM

ABOUT SHANNA SWENSON

Shanna Swenson is a cardiac sonographer by day and a weaver of various fictional tales by night.

She's been an avid reader all her life and began writing at the age of fourteen. She finally published her first novel, *Abundance*, after it sat patiently on her laptop for well over fifteen years and she hasn't stopped writing since.

Shanna fits her zodiac sign of Cancer with a capital C and enjoys life's simplest things—sunsets, rain, and coffee—to name a few.

When Shanna's not supporting her fellow indies with her face buried in a book or writing her next novel/novella, she enjoys action and horror movies, pro football, hiking, working out, and traveling with her own "knight in shining armor".

You can find her on the following social media platforms.

Her website is www.shannaswenson.com

facebook.com/shannaswen
twitter.com/shanna_swenson
instagram.com/shannaswen_author
goodreads.com/Shannaswen
amazon.com/author/shannaswenson
pinterest.com/shannaswen
bookbub.com/profile/shanna-swenson

www.ingramcontent.com/pod-product-compliance
Lightning Source LLC
Chambersburg PA
CBHW031320170626
46807CB00002B/492

*9 7 8 1 7 3 2 9 6 2 6 6 8 *